I0737099

SINISTER SANCTUARY

WICKS HOLLOW

COLLEEN GLEASON

AVID PRESS

The characters and basic set-up of *Sinister Sanctuary* previously appeared in the short story "Hot Springs Magic."

I've taken the idea and developed it into a full-length novel here in this book.

Thank you for giving it a read!

— Colleen Gleason
August 2018

ONE

*Stony Cape Lighthouse
on beautiful Lake Michigan…
A relaxing sanctuary from the rest of the world.
Only four miles from quaint
Wicks Hollow, the
vintage Keeper's House is a unique
getaway for the guest who enjoys solitude and quiet.
Find Your Paradise at Stony Cape Lighthouse!*

———

MY PARADISE? We'll see about that. Teddy Mack grimaced as she read the energetic sales pitch.

My paradise is to figure out the bloody ending to my damn book.

She shoved the pamphlet into her large leather tote and grimaced.

"I'll finish it by the end of July," she'd promised her agent Harriet—who'd gone on to guarantee to Teddy's editor that, yes, the next T.J. Mack book would be turned in on time.

Or nearly on time.

Well, six months late wasn't really on time. But publishing was a slow business at best, and it wasn't as if Teddy hadn't turned in her other five manuscripts—all of which went on to be bestselling thrillers—when they were due.

"This book is kicking my ass," she'd told Harriet two weeks ago. Though she kept her voice calm, inside it was nearly a wail. "I don't know why."

"You need to get away. Somewhere where no one will bother you. Where you won't be tempted to post pictures of your office on Facebook instead of writing, or go out to lunch every day instead of writing, or watch Netflix instead of wri—"

"That's research. Netflix is," Teddy said. "I have to stay up on pop culture, or how will I know what to write about? And Facebook is social media, and I have to have a presence there, and on Instagram and Twitter, and—"

"You have to write a good book. That's what you have to do. Forget Facebook and Twitter, and watching a whole season of *Friday Night Lights* in one week—"

"Five seasons. Kyle Chandler is impossible to resist. Not to mention Taylor Kitsch—"

"*Five seasons? In one week?* No wonder your book isn't done!" Harriet's voice rose, then tapered off into a more modulated tone. "You need to go somewhere without Internet or Wi-Fi. Somewhere where you won't be distracted."

And that was how, thanks to her cousin Declan, Teddy had come to be settling in at the smallest, most remote rental property in the vicinity of touristy Wicks Hollow, Michigan.

The Stony Cape Lighthouse might only be four miles from Wicks Hollow, but for all intents and purposes, it was in the middle of nowhere. On a tiny island connected to the mainland by a single-lane bridge, the lighthouse was hardly visible from ground level on the mainland due to the rolling hills and thick forestation of the bluffs overlooking Lake Michigan.

And because of this figurative remoteness, the place didn't have Wi-Fi.

That meant no email, no Facebook, no Wikipedia. No Netflix or Hulu.

Teddy had even left her smartphone in Harriet's care—all the way back in New York City—so she wouldn't be tempted to try out the 3G connectivity in Wicks Hollow. She'd even temporarily transferred her number to a cheap "burner" cell phone.

(That part had been rather fun, for although Teddy had often written about people—usually villains—using burner phones, she, of course, had never had reason to use one. Doing so made her feel very edgy and incognito.)

However, she'd nearly gotten motion sickness sitting in the back of the car that had picked her up from the airport as she was driven to Stony Cape—for once they turned off Highway 31 and onto the road leading to the lighthouse's bridge, it was all bumps, snakelike curves, and jounces. And the driver took the road like he was a Daytona racer—making the ride feel like a mini rollercoaster.

Teddy might write about wild car chases and acrobatic plane maneuvers, but in real life, she avoided thrill rides for a reason.

The trees were so thick that they grew like a permanent tunnel over the road, casting it in shadow even in the middle of the day. She could smell the fresh splash of water from Lake Michigan, and when the car finally crossed the bridge then emerged, minutes later, from the wooded road into a small clearing, she caught her breath.

Wow.

If this place doesn't inspire me, I don't know what will.

The car had barely stopped when Teddy slipped out of the vehicle, and she turned in a slow semicircle, taking in the place that was to be her writing sanctuary for the next month. The place was adorable and charming and stately all at once.

The entire property was a small island about a mile from shore. A little bridge connected the tiny peninsula that extended from the mainland in a finger parallel to shore to the acre-sized island on which the lighthouse and its attached keeper's cottage sat. The island was little more than a small, rocky outcropping with some reedy grass surrounded by Lake Michigan.

Stony Cape Lighthouse was painted white, and its cap, where the now-defunct light was enclosed, was red. Teddy could see the small walkway around the large gallery, some thirty feet in the air. There were random windows in the whitewashed brick column, and the keeper's residence was a compact cottage attached to the base of the lighthouse on the southwest side. The cottage was covered by white Shaker shingles, and each window—including the round window over the door—had a pair of shutters in cobalt blue. A wild vine of green ivy grew up one side of the cottage, clinging to the stone chimney that appeared to belong to a real fireplace.

On the side facing the lake was a long, covered porch enclosed by a yellow railing. A riot of flowers that desperately needed weeding spilled from beds on three sides of the cottage (the fourth being attached to the lighthouse). Teddy recognized zinnias, daisies, cosmos, verbena, and hydrangea. Hmm. The combination of perennials and annuals indicated someone —the caretaker?—had been around to plant the gardens. The boxwoods and spirea needed pruning, but they weren't completely untended. And the minuscule square of grass, a small patch between the cottage and the thickly wooded two-track road, had probably been mowed in the last week.

A little stone path crossed from the small parking area to the side door of the cottage, and another one made from shallow stone steps led over to and down the incline that presumably ended at the beach.

"Looks like a nice place," said the driver as he began to pull her bags from the trunk. "Kinda remote, though."

She glanced at him, assessing whether he was taking her measure so he could come back and rob or attack her later. You just never knew.

Being a writer, Teddy had a very active imagination when it came to possibilities and tactics. She was always thinking of other options, of what-ifs, of how murderous or villainous activities could be accomplished.

"Oh, my boyfriend and his sister and her husband will be here in a few hours," she lied airily. "I'll have just enough time to settle in before they get here."

"Small place for four people," he commented—though he didn't seem to be disappointed that she'd ruined his nefarious plan. If indeed he'd had one. Not that she had any real reason to believe he did, but…again…you never knew. "But the view makes up for it."

"Oh, let me get the door open," she said, realizing he was waiting for her to do that so he could bring in her luggage—which wasn't all that much, of course, since the *only* thing she was going to be doing here was writing.

The *only* thing.

Looking out over the glistening blue of Lake Michigan as it rushed onto the shore below, Teddy stifled a sigh as she dug in her large tote for the FedEx envelope with the key she'd been mailed.

No swimming. No boating. No hiking. No shopping. No sightseeing. No relaxing. No restauranting.

Just writing.

She had brought a swimsuit, though. She could at least put her toes in the water.

The door opened with reluctance; the lock was obviously not used very often, and it stuck. But at last she muscled it open and stepped back so the driver could bring in her bags.

"You gonna run the light?" asked the driver as, still standing on the porch, she dug out her credit card to pay for the ride. "The one up there?" He jerked an eyebrow in the direction of the top of the lighthouse.

"No," Teddy told him with sincere regret. "This lighthouse has been dark—ha, ha—for over forty years. They don't really need it because there are two other ones up along the coast, one south and one north of here, and there aren't any ships or boats that come along this way. Though there have been plenty of shipwrecks on the lake—including the famous one where the *Catherine Teal,* which was owned by the Astors—you know, of New York City? during the Gilded Age?—went down in a storm somewhere in Lake Michigan between Traverse City and Chicago. They were sending a large wedding gift to some friends in Chicago—"

"Thank you, ma'am," the driver said, taking the computer tablet from her as soon as she'd finger-signed (and given him a decent tip, even though he'd driven like a maniac). "Hope you enjoy your stay out here."

All by yourself.

He didn't say the words, but he didn't have to.

Teddy heard them loud and clear, and as he climbed into the shiny black Town Car and drove off down the gritty, dirty road, she gave a long, deep sigh.

Yes. *All by myself.*

A little trickle of panic threatened, but she pushed it away as she stepped inside the vestibule of Stony Cape Keeper's House.

Vestibule was an optimistic word, to be sure. In Teddy's mind, vestibules were large and airy with a ceiling at least two floors high. In this case, the vestibule was hardly more than a small entranceway, dark and dim—as it was currently in the shadow of the lighthouse—painted some standard cream color with, of course, a lighthouse painting on the wall. The mat on the floor appeared to have been there since Woodstock, and the lamp and matching chandelier were hideous mangles of metal, wood, and mirrors.

To the left of the vestibule was the lighthouse itself, accessed through a small door with a curved top. Through the door was access to the small bedroom suite in which she'd be staying, and, she assumed, the stairs that led to the top of the non-working light.

Because of course she was going to stay on the *lighthouse* side of the cottage.

To her right was the "common area"—a kitchen and living room space decorated with more of the hideous mangled metal lamps that someone clearly thought were artwork, for the rest of the place was furnished in what she thought of as 1980s "blue goose" decor. Beyond the common area, to the right, was a short hallway down which she suspected was another bedroom suite. No one else was staying here, nor *would* anyone else be here.

She'd told the booking agent she didn't even need the daily housekeeping.

Because Teddy didn't need any distractions. She needed to be alone. She needed to be a monk, locked in her tower—in this case, represented quite saccurately by the lighthouse accommodations—like a prisoner in her cell so she could figure out *and write* the rest of her damned book.

"Well," she said aloud to herself—as she had a habit of doing. "Guess I'll check things out inside, get the lay of the land, unpack. I can take some time to unpack," Teddy said, as if Harriet might be lurking about, judging her for hanging up her sundresses and finding a place for her underthings, three pairs of sandals, two swimsuits, and all the rest.

Of course she'd overpacked. That had been part of the procrastination, and the indecision that paralyzed her for the last nine months. It wasn't as if she'd be wearing anything besides sundresses, shorts, or yoga pants and a tank top for the next month.

She felt sick to her stomach. Weeks. *I've only got four weeks. I* have *to finish this.*

She'd just rolled her suitcase through the curve-topped door and was opening the door into the bedroom, which had a view of the lake and butted up to the covered porch, when her burner phone rang. She was half surprised she even got service out here, to be honest.

She fumbled with the phone—it was smaller and lighter and not at all familiar, compared to the larger smartphone she had back home—and managed to answer it by the fourth ring. "Hi, Harriet."

"Are you there? Are you settled?" Her agent's nasally New York tone was businesslike, yet Teddy detected a hint of concern. "Is it nice? Do you have everything you need?"

"I literally just walked in the door, but so far it seems nice. It's not really new," Teddy said, looking around at the eighties Berber carpeting and the plain white walls decorated with framed photographs of more lighthouses. "But other than these really awful metal lamps that look like mutant spiders with mirrored eyes, it's kind of cute."

A queen-sized bed was made up with a neat quilt and four pillows (two in shams)—all in a pretty blue and yellow floral theme. There was a desk against the wall near a large window overlooking the lake. Bonus.

"Best of all, it's clean. My cousin told me no one has lived here for several years, though obviously someone keeps it up. Or, at least, they did a good job cleaning it for me," Teddy said. "The lighthouse is pretty much abandoned; it doesn't illuminate anymore. No one runs it."

"That's nice," Harriet said briskly, clearly not caring in the least. "Well, I'm glad you're there and settled. I'll tell Erin. She'll be pleased to know."

Erin was Teddy's editor, nervous about the book coming in —and rightly so.

"What did you say?" Teddy asked, as Harriet's voice disappeared into a crackle of static. "Hello?" She moved closer to the window, hoping to improve the reception.

"I said, there's no Wi-Fi there, right? Can you hear me now?"

"Yes, you're back. And no Wi-Fi to my knowledge. Like I said, no one has lived here for years, according to Declan. But it just occurred to me—what if I need to do some research?" Teddy realized she sounded a smidge whiny, but after all, she was going cold turkey here. No Internet was pretty significant.

"You'll go to the library." Harriet's voice crackled again, but was still discernible. "Are you there?"

Teddy walked back to the window as she replied, "Yes, I'm here. And I don't have a car here, remember?"

"Have your cousin drive you. And hey—isn't he the blacksmith who does all that restoration work? The hot ginger who visited you in New York?"

"I guess you could call him hot," Teddy said, gripping the windowsill so she wouldn't forget and wander again, putting their connection in jeopardy. "I mean, most women think he's hot. Dec's just my cousin, so, you know, meh. I remember him when he was scrawny and his hair was a lot brighter. Now it's more of a mahogany than a Weasley-like ginger. Besides, he's too young for you, Harriet—and he's got a serious girlfriend."

"Didn't you write a book about a sexy blacksmith?" her agent asked. "A long time ago?"

"What? Can't hear you…I'd better unpack and get to work," Teddy said breezily. "And since you asked, no, I won't starve, stuck out here in the middle of nowhere without a car or Wi-Fi or anything. And I've got food deliveries arranged for every other day." Plus, Declan was picking her up to have dinner tonight in Wicks Hollow. But she wasn't going to tell Harriet that.

"Good. You'll need to keep your strength up. All right, I'll check in with you in a couple of days. Cheers!"

Teddy unpacked quickly then left her room to explore the remainder of the cottage. The whole place was small and efficient, with a kitchen area that merged into the living room, the two tiny bedrooms down a short hallway, and a smaller bathroom. No television either, so she couldn't even try to watch a DVD.

Her phone rang. "Hey, Dec."

"You here? All settled?"

"Yes. Thanks. Are you still able to pick me up for dinner?"

"Of course. That's why I'm calling. Leslie and I will be coming back from Grand Rapids. We can swing by and pick you up around six. That's about an hour."

"I was going to go for a walk. Didn't you tell me there's a natural hot tub—like a pond—out here somewhere?"

"Yes. If you can find it. It's a bit of a hike—about two miles from where you are." He gave her general directions—which included having to walk from the small island across the short bridge to the mainland. "Not many people know where it is, and no one really goes there because we have Lake Michigan and Wicks Lake."

"Well I'm in the mood for a walk. I really need to clear my head before I can get to work. Why don't you just pick me up down there by the hot tub—hot spring, I mean—instead of having to make a detour and come all the way up here to the island."

"Sure. That makes it even easier. I'll text when we're close."

Teddy disconnected and looked thoughtfully at her bathing suit. Something about churning, warm water in a natural habitat seemed like it would be a good way to clear her mind, get her creative juices flowing. If she could find the hot spring, maybe she could sit in it and veg for a while. Just let things flow. Relax. Get rid of the stress so the story could come to her.

With a satisfied smile, she dragged on her bluebell-colored one-piece suit. *I really have to start working out*, she thought. Having a sedentary job didn't do a thing to help the size of her butt.

Then, after tossing a towel, a comb, and dry underthings into her large leather tote, she pulled on a loose but pretty sundress, stuck on her sunglasses, slid into sturdy sandals… and left the house. Feeling only slightly guilty.

Harriet would never have to know.

And an evening out in the fresh air, then with friends, would surely get things moving.

"What do you mean, there's been a mistake?" Oscar London swiped a forearm across his forehead to catch the trickle of sweat, and the heavy bag of equipment he was holding clunked into his shoulder.

The college kid who'd obviously been sent as sacrificial lamb stammered, "Uh…well, Dr. London, I'm so sorry, but there was a last-minute booking that came in, and someone *else* approved it, not realizing you'd already leased Stony Cape Cottage for the month—I mean, no one's stayed here for years, and then all of a sudden two people wanted—and... so...well, there's someone else staying here already." He glanced at the door as if expecting said rival boarder to make an appearance.

Oscar looked at the three man-sized equipment bags he'd just lugged onto the porch of the keeper's house, then back at the Jeep where a fourth one, as well as his backpack, sat, and shook his head firmly. "I'm not leaving. You people made the mistake, I paid for the rental, so you can just move your other client to another location."

"Uhm...but, like, there's...not any other location available. You see, it's the beginning of July—that means high season in Wicks Hollow, and everything's been booked for—"

"Look." Oscar squinted out at the rippling blue of Lake Michigan. "I'm not trying to be unreasonable, but I need to stay here. I rented this place because of its location near a water ecosystem I'm going to be studying, and because I won't be disturbed. Plus it has the space I need to set up my lab. So I'm not giving it up."

"Well. Uh. You brought your own *refrigerator*?" The kid looked at the compact unit next to the rest of the equipment, then at Oscar, who just nodded wearily. "Well, uh... there *are* two bedroom suites. The other—er—tenant is staying in the bottom of the lighthouse. You could, like... both of you could stay." He rushed out this suggestion. "I mean, the place is set up, like, for that. You each have your own suite."

"Fine. I don't care. As long as they don't get in my way. Wait. How many of them are there?" With his luck, Oscar would end up sharing the damned place with a couple on their honeymoon. *No fecking way.* He thrust away visions of Marcie and Trevor.

"Just one person. A, uh, writer named Teddy Mack."

"Right. He can leave if he wants, but I'm not going anywhere. Now let me finish unloading my stuff so I can get to work." Oscar looked toward the narrow promontory from the mainland that was connected to this tiny island by a wood and metal bridge. The hot spring—the only known one in Michigan, and deliciously close to the Great Lake—was supposedly located just to the southeast of the finger-like peninsula.

"Do you…uh…want me to tell Teddy?" asked the kid.

"Huh?" Oscar turned from scanning the horizon. The sacrificial lamb was already edging off the porch, clearly ready to bleat and flee, so Oscar took pity on him. "No. I'll take care of it. But if there are any problems, I'm sending him to you."

"Yes. Of course. Oh, and the agency is offering a thirty percent discount on your stay for the inconvenience, or you can apply it to a future booking." The kid was already at his car, preparing to climb in.

"Thirty percent? With a double booking, it should be at least a fifty percent discount," Oscar grumbled under his breath. But the reality of solitude dangled in front of him, so he decided to hold off arguing about that in favor of being left alone.

Happily, for both of them, the young man drove off in his car as Oscar lugged the rest of his supplies inside.

Thirty minutes to set up the basics, then I'm off to find the only natural hot spring in Michigan.

It was a ridiculous way for a well-published PhD from Princeton to spend his summer, analyzing a tiny pool of water in Michigan when he had four other research projects he was managing with his grad students. And Oscar was fully aware that his plan would be little more than busywork. But it beat staying in New Jersey.

He just didn't want to be anywhere near the city when Marcie married Trevor next weekend—because with his luck, he'd run into them, or her parents, or their mutual colleagues who'd been invited and had come to town. Including his sister, who was one of Marcie's bridesmaids. So, since he wasn't teaching any summer classes at the U, he got the hell out of Dodge.

So he was here. In a small, white, blue-shuttered cottage attached to a non-working lighthouse. It consisted of a one-room kitchen/dining/living space that didn't appear to have air conditioning, but was equipped with very large ceiling fans. A space he was going to have to share with a writer. Oscar mumbled a curse.

At least writers were supposed to be antisocial. Maybe the guy would be locked up in his bedroom in the lighthouse all day, working on whatever he was working on.

One thing was sure: the bloody writer wasn't going to be using the living room or kitchen, because that was where Oscar was setting up his lab.

Forty minutes later, he had the basics in place: the mini fridge for samples, a small centrifuge, a pressure cooker, a shaker, an incubator, and two microscopes. He had all his flasks, tubes, plates, and pipettes arranged. All of the chemicals he'd need—resin, alcohol, and more—were lined up alphabetically on the long coffee table. Good thing he'd brought his own power strips, because the bungalow—which was probably built or at least updated in the fifties—was severely lacking in outlets. It'd be a miracle if he didn't blow a fuse when he had everything up and running.

Oscar pulled on his work vest and tucked gloves and syringes into their slots. The rest of his equipment

(Cubitainers, glass bottles, and biohazard bags) he packed in a small cooler. Then, slinging it over his shoulder like a messenger bag, he set off on foot with a bottle of water in hand.

Might as well get started.

It was a pleasant hike on a defined path, but one that clearly didn't see a lot of foot traffic.

Though he'd been to every continent except Antarctica, and visited the West Coast and Southern U.S. often, Oscar hadn't ever been to Michigan. What he'd seen so far since driving across the border from Ohio was a sort of natural melting pot.

The Great Lakes State had everything from flat farmland to rolling hills to small ski mountains; thick, lush forests, to tall, scrawny, piney ones, and broad meadows of farmland where alfalfa and rows of corn flourished. Pretty much every time you turned around, there was a lake or pond or river or creek in view; and yet, here at the shoreline of the vast and powerful Lake Michigan, there were desertlike sand dunes studded with scrubby clumps of grass. And adjacent to this smidge of desert shore was a thick, dark forest that reminded him of Grimm's fairy tales.

Though heavy with humidity today, the air was clean and smelled loamy and fresh. Oscar spotted several species of wildflowers he could name thanks to his Scouting days—Indian paintbrush, Queen Anne's lace, daisies—and others he'd never seen before. Moss grew everywhere in a variety of textures: short, bright green that reminded him of a miniature putting green; another patch in a hue closer to the color of grass that had slightly taller stems, which reminded him of the close-cropped fur of Marcie's terrier; and still others in shades of olive, reddish-bronze, yellow.

After a good twenty minutes of hiking—along the bridge back to the mainland, then south from the promontory—he heard the faint rumble of rushing water. At last. Now he just had to follow his ears through the forest.

Climbing over fallen logs, avoiding eye-level pine branches and wild raspberry bushes, Oscar picked up the pace, his knapsack thunking companionably against his side. The forest was dead silent but for the rumbling and an occasional rustle of leaves, or the call of a bird. Once in a while, the distant purr of a vehicle buzzed by in the far distance.

He saw a doe and her fawn, which shocked him when they merely stared at the intruder before bounding off into the forest, flipping up their tails to show the white that gave them their name. The slender, dark whip of a snake slithered into the underbrush when he disturbed its place in a sunny patch on the rough path. Meanwhile, the water's rumbling was growing louder, and Oscar was aware of a little spike of enthusiasm.

A natural hot spring was, after all, a unique ecosystem. In this case, it was the only known one in the region. Maybe there'd even be something interesting there—some new bacterium or alga that could be useful. Or at least something he could mess around with to keep his mind off home.

At last, he could make out the stony outcropping that appeared to make up the backdrop of the pool. Then he saw the steam rising into the air.

At last the pool came into view: a gently roiling mass of steaming water.

And, sitting in the water, messing up his plan and contaminating it all to hell, was a *woman*.

Oscar stifled a groan, but went on.

She looked over at him as Oscar approached.

"Nice day for a swim," she said.

Though her hair was dry, her face was rosy and moist from the steam. It was a pretty face, no denying it, with large eyes, arching brows, and full lips. And from what he could see above the surging water, the rest of her wasn't too bad either. She had brown hair pulled back in a clip or something, and even from here, he could see that her eyes were filled with humor.

Oscar looked around. She seemed to be by herself. "Yep."

"Though on a hot day like today, I'm not sure a steam bath is the best idea. Still. Here I am." She shifted, and he caught sight of more cleavage than was healthy for a guy who was currently avoiding women like the plague.

"You here by yourself?"

"Yes." She lifted her chin and gave him a mild look. "Is there something wrong with a woman being in a hot spring by herself instead of with some guy—or another woman, for that matter?"

"No. Just wondered." He unslung his tool bag, considering whether there was a polite way to ask her to get the hell out of his ecosystem.

Probably not.

"If I were a nervous sort of woman—which I'm not—with a great imagination—which I do, in fact, have—I'd be wondering what's in that bag. And why you want to make sure I'm here all alone." She narrowed her eyes at his things. "For all I know, you could have rope in there. Or duct tape. Maybe a gun or a knife, even. A camera, to take pictures of the scene?"

"Or syringes and plastic baggies and gloves." He produced them with a flourish. "You do have an imagination."

"Yeah. Sometimes." She slumped down in the water so it

bubbled up around her shoulders, suddenly looking miserable. "*Only* sometimes." She tipped her head up, closing her eyes as she rested her head against the stone rim behind her.

Oscar ignored her as he pulled on a pair of gloves. He could still take a sample, but he'd much rather have one not freshly contaminated with sunblock, perfume, deodorant, and whatever else she might have clinging to her body. Shampoo. Body lotion.

"Gloves? Hm. Maybe I *should* be worried." She was sitting up again, watching him with interest.

If you don't stop talking to me, you might need to be.

He dug out a Cubitainer and syringe, closing the top of the cooler to keep it cold.

"What are you doing?" She sat back up and was watching with bright, interested eyes. "What's all that for?"

"I'm sampling for E. coli in the water," he said, slanting a sideways look at her. Maybe that would get her out. "Among other nasty things."

"Really." She didn't sound concerned. Nor did she seem ready to leap out of the possibly infested water.

"How much longer are you going to be in there?"

"Why? Are you thinking about skinny-dipping? I promise to close my eyes till you get in." She grinned, and he almost grinned back.

But she was in the middle of his private ecosystem, contaminating it with God knew what—and worst of all, she was far too friendly and chatty.

"I just told you I'm testing for E. coli and you ask if I'm planning to take off my clothes and get in?" he replied.

"Well, since most E. coli isn't harmful, I figured you were either exaggerating or teasing me." She shrugged.

He gritted his teeth. Smarty-pants.

"As for how long I'm going to be in here—skinny-dipping

partner and potentially deadly bacteria notwithstanding," she continued, slanting him a look that could only be described as sassy, "I don't know."

Her expression dimmed suddenly, as if a bad memory had come to mind. She slid back down into the roiling pool, a wash of desperation and misery erasing her smile. "Until my brain starts working again. Which might be forever. But they say water actually helps the mind work better, so..." She grimaced as the water splashed and roiled against her jaw. "I'll soak away. Like a human teabag."

Oscar moved over to the edge of the pool. The heat rose in waves, dampening his skin. Droplets of water splashed up from the churning water, spraying him in the face.

"So are you really testing the water? Is there really a chance there might be the nasty kind of E. coli in it?" She did look a little concerned now.

"I don't know what's in it. A natural hot spring is a unique ecosystem unto itself—and this is the only one in Michigan. So who knows what I'll find. That's why I'm testing it."

He hesitated, scoping out the situation. To get a good sample, he should be in the center of the pool, not near the edge, where it was shallow. The water was so enthusiastic that there was no danger of his sample being stagnant. Still, the sample needed to come from the center, where the grit and dirt from the floor wouldn't be mixed in.

"What's wrong?" The woman was still watching him from her deep-in-the-water position.

"Nothing. Just trying to figure out the best way to reach the center."

He was close enough now to see locks of dark brown hair clinging to her cheek and the damp skin of her neck. A few other strands had curled up in the humidity near her temples and the fronts of her ears. A trio of small gold hoops hung from each lobe, and a delicate chain glinted against the damp skin of her throat. She had light skin flushed red from the heat and blue eyes that sparkled with enthusiasm. He put her age at around thirty or so.

"If you don't want to get in, I can do it for you," she offered. "But if you were planning to strip, don't let me stop you." That glint of ready humor was back in her gaze.

Oscar looked at her, ready to refuse—then decided letting her help wasn't a bad idea after all. That way he wouldn't have to zip off his switchbacks and remove his shoes and socks—which would entail taking off the sterile gloves he'd just donned. Which he'd have been thinking about previously if he hadn't been distracted by her. "You'd have to wear gloves."

"I think I can handle that." She sat up and scooted across the pool toward him. He gave her a pair that would be too big for her, but at least would cover her hands.

"Don't touch the inside of the container," he instructed her when she was ready. "And put it below the surface about six to eight inches, like so." He demonstrated by turning the Cubitainer upside down and bringing it straight down. "Fill it all the way up, then empty it out. Do that three times, and the last time, keep it filled. I'll give you the cap when you're finished."

"Why do I have to fill it—and empty it—three times?"

"To make sure every area of the surface is touched by the sample before you actually fill it up."

"Are you sure you trust me to do this?" She held out her gloved hand for the container. The ends of the fingers flopped loosely.

"I'm beginning to wonder," he muttered, but let his mouth soften into a little smile. Other than being far too chatty and a definite contaminant, she seemed harmless—relatively intelligent and able to follow directions.

"Well, you could climb in yourself."

"I'm sure you'll do a fine job," he replied, handing her the container a little more abruptly than he intended. But she didn't drop it. As she turned to swim to the center, he caught a glimpse of a spectacular rear end, nice and curvy, covered in a bright blue swimsuit.

He couldn't *wait* to get out of here.

TWO

IF TEDDY HAD a pang of guilt that she'd blown off most of her first day by splashing around in a natural hot spring, she squashed it like a bug.

What Harriet didn't know wouldn't hurt her—or Teddy.

Plus…it really was too late in the day to actually set up her computer and start working. And there wasn't anything to eat at the cottage, anyway. The food deliveries didn't start until tomorrow. So she figured a good night's sleep, acclimating her to her new, quiet, Wi-Fi-less surroundings, would put her in the right frame of mind to get to work first thing in the morning.

She had to duck behind a thick clump of bushes to strip off her swimsuit from beneath her sundress and shimmy into her panties and bra, expertly preserving her modesty all the while.

As she waited for her ride, standing on the road at the juncture of the lighthouse island's bridge and the mainland, she wondered if she'd run into the microbiologist again. At least, she assumed he was a microbiologist, though she'd never gotten around to asking.

Despite the fact that the guy didn't say much and was bordering on *Big Bang Theory* nerdiness, he was pretty cute. His white button-down shirt had looked crisp and cool, contrasting with his freckled forearms and their rich, gold tan. And talk about a ginger—a real ginger! He had a head of close-cropped, fiery golden-red hair that curled up damply where it was longer on top, and large hands that should have been clumsy, but had handled his tools and accoutrements with ease. He'd been wearing zip-off cargo pants with lots of pockets, so she hadn't been able to see his legs, but the bag he carried with ease appeared damn heavy. She suspected some decent musculature beneath the Dr. Science clothes.

Maybe she'd see him in town tonight. Maybe Declan knew who he was.

As she waited for her ride, Teddy realized she was in a good mood—feeling social and also very hungry. *Tonight'll be my last hurrah before it's nose to grindstone, so I'm going to enjoy every minute of it.*

A few minutes later, she climbed into Leslie's Mercedes—which was a blessing, because she remembered that Dec drove a pickup, and the three of them would have been squished into the front seat—and it would probably have been none too clean.

She also smiled in private approval, too, that Leslie was driving her own car instead of letting her boyfriend take over the wheel. That had always been a sticking point with Teddy and Arthur—just one of those many subtle little things that had made it easy for her to break things off. Eventually.

Not that Teddy was a procrastinator.

"So, how's the cottage up there? I've always been curious about Stony Cape," Leslie asked, glancing at Teddy in the rearview mirror as she pulled out into the road. She was a petite woman, with the skin tone and straight black hair of her

Japanese heritage. Today, she'd pinned her hair in a loose bun, with long strands falling over her neck. She looked nothing like the hotshot CEO she'd once been back in Philadelphia. "I almost wish we'd picked you up there so I could sneak a peek."

"It's kind of cute—sort of what you'd expect for a lighthouse cottage. Quilts and pillow shams, eighties carpet and vertical blinds, and lots of seagull and lighthouse decor. Everything is clean and neat, though, and the bed looks very comfortable." *Maybe too comfortable.*

"You know I would have loved to have you at Shenstone House, Teddy." Leslie had just opened a bed and breakfast in Wicks Hollow—right on a small hill just outside of town. She'd met Declan when he came to renovate some wrought iron stair railing, and there'd been some big episode involving a murder. Teddy didn't know all the details, but she definitely was going to find out.

"Thank you, Les, I really appreciate it. But I know it's high season for you, and Declan said you're completely booked anyway. Me coming to Wicks Hollow was a last-minute thing, and I let my agent handle the reservation after Declan gave me the suggestion. Besides, I need to be cloistered away so I can get my book done." A waver of guilt threatened to ruin Teddy's mood, but she firmly thrust it away.

Tomorrow.

Tomorrow, I'll type my fingers off.

"But once the book is turned in, I'll come back when I can relax and enjoy—and I'll stay in your best room."

"Are you sure you can spare the time for dinner tonight?" Declan asked, turning around from the passenger seat in the front and unwittingly piling on the guilt. "We understand if you need to work—we can just get a carry-out."

"Oh, no, don't worry about me. I start bright and early tomorrow morning. So," she said, quickly changing the subject, "where are we going for dinner? I haven't been to Wicks Hollow in about twenty years, so I have no idea what to expect."

"We're going to a place usually only the locals go because it's high season and we can't get a seat at Trib's—the best place in town—without a reservation this late in the day," he replied. "The Lakeside Grille is off the beaten path, and Reggie makes the best fried grouper sandwich you've ever had. Plus, there's a good selection of beer from our local guy."

"Sounds perfect."

The Lakeside was as promised: filled with locals—obvious because many of them greeted Declan, Leslie, and even Teddy as they came in—and the delicious smells made Teddy's mouth water.

A very busty woman in her late forties worked behind the long, diner-like counter. She wore a tight yellow dress splashed with plate-sized violets and more makeup than a high school freshman at her first dance. Her hair was done up in a B-52s beehive, and was an icy platinum with a lavender streak from the side-part to the twist. She was a mistress of the multitask, snatching up the cordless phone to take down a to-go order, snapping commands through the food window to the kitchen, filling draft beers from an array of seven levers, and slapping plates down on the counter in front of their owners.

"Declan—there's a table in the back," she called. "I saved it for you so your cousin could be incognito. Can't have a best-selling writer waiting for a table." Her voice was loud, heedless of the fact that everyone in the restaurant could hear and there was no chance of Teddy remaining "incognito"—even if that had been necessary.

Which it wasn't, because authors—with the possible exception of J.K. Rowling and Stephen King—just weren't recognized by the average person. And Teddy was in no way in the same league as either of them.

"Thanks, Bella," replied Dec, taking Leslie by the hand and navigating through a path of crowded tables. "Hey, Bax!" He paused to shake hands with a very good-looking black man who was sitting at the end of the counter.

He slid off his stool and gave Leslie a hug, then turned to offer his hand to Teddy. "I'm Baxter James. It's a pleasure to meet you, Ms. Mack—I'm a *huge* fan of your books. I was so surprised to hear that you're related to *this* guy." He grinned, and Dec rolled his eyes.

"Thank you," Teddy replied, trying not to feel self-conscious as she felt more and more people looking in her direction. "And call me Teddy."

"Baxter's a writer too," Declan said, unaware that he was setting off tiny little alarm bells in Teddy's head, "but more importantly, he's the creator and brewmaster of B-Cubed Beer."

"B-Cubed?" Teddy replied politely.

"Baxter's Beatnik Brews," replied Baxter. "And don't worry, I'm a freelance journalist and have absolutely no desire to write a novel. So I'm not going to ask you to read my work or pitch it to your agent—nor am I going to offer to give you an idea to write." His smile was fast and wicked, and Teddy immediately liked him.

"Then in that case, why don't you join us for dinner? I'd love to hear all about your beer. You never know when I'm going to write a craft brewer." She loved getting to talk to someone with an interesting profession. Plus, then she could justify her dinner as "research"—therefore she was actually working.

Baxter's eyes lit up, and he said, "I'd like that. I'm just dying to know what's going to happen to Sargent Blue in the next book. Maybe if I ply you with a few samples of my beer, you'll give me a hint. Mirabella, darling, how about a round on me? I'm moving to their table."

Teddy thoroughly enjoyed herself, chatting with Baxter (who had several ideas for delicious *and* malicious ways to kill someone in a brewery) and sampling a flight of B-Cubed beer.

"So you're staying up at Stony Cape Lighthouse?" asked Baxter as Bella put their food in front of them. "That's kind of far away from civilization."

"Yes," Teddy replied. "It's a cozy little place, but with no Wi-Fi. Which is important. I've got it for a month."

"Wasn't there something about someone dying out there a while back?" Declan asked, looking at his friend. He'd moved back to town only a year ago, but Baxter had been living there for much longer. "Is that why it's been vacant for so long?"

"Someone fell from the lighthouse," Baxter replied.

"Fell or jumped?" Teddy forked up a piece of rainbow trout that had probably been caught that day. "Or was *pushed?*"

"Well…the official word is that he fell." Baxter rubbed his trim goatee. "But who knows?"

"How long has the lighthouse been non-operational?" Teddy said. "Did it close down because of the death?"

Baxter shook his head. "No, though I do think that kept people from wanting to stay there for a while. The lighthouse hasn't been used since the nineties, and Stuart Millore—that's the guy who fell—died only about three years ago. Maybe four. I don't really remember…" His attention strayed from the table. It seemed to settle somewhere across the room. And stay.

Teddy glanced at Declan, who was fighting a grin. He elbowed Leslie, then jerked his head toward the other side of the room. She grinned too, and by then, Teddy had to turn around in her chair to see what was going on.

But there was nothing obvious, and she couldn't tell if Baxter was looking at the cute thirty-year-old mother and her teenage daughter who sat at a booth along the wall, or a group of three couples about the same age, toasting some exciting accomplishment. Or something else.

"You were saying…?" Declan teased as Baxter dragged his attention back to their table. "Maybe it's time for a haircut, hmm, Bax?" He looked at Teddy, still grinning. "Baxter likes to go to the expensive salon on the north side of town to get his 'fro trimmed because the owner is hot, single, and has a great ra—"

"That's enough." Baxter quickly held up a hand. It was difficult to tell with his dark skin, but Teddy was certain he was blushing. "I was just…uh…" He lifted his beer to drink.

Leslie leaned toward Teddy. "Bax's got a thing for Emily Delton—that perky blond over there, with the teenage daughter. *She* used to have a thing for Declan, but, well…fortunately for both Baxter and Declan, the feeling wasn't reciprocated." Her eyes danced with laughter. "Steph and Emily's daughter are friends."

Stephanie was Declan's sixteen-year-old daughter. He'd moved back to Wicks Hollow so he could do some single parenting when Steph's mother and stepfather moved out of state.

"Don't worry—Emily doesn't have a date. And I haven't heard anything about her seeing anyone, Bax. I'm sure I'd know if she was. Why don't you just bite the bullet and ask her out?" Leslie said gently.

"Maybe." Bax turned his attention to the golden-brown beer he was sampling. "So, anyway, Teddy—or should I say

T.J.?—can you give me *anything* about what's going to happen in the next Sargent Blue book?"

With that, Teddy's easy mood deflated just a little. Because she didn't bloody well *know* what was going to happen. "Well…" she said, drawing out the word and trying to look mysterious, "if I tell you, I'll have to kill you."

"It'd be worth it." Baxter seemed more at ease now that he wasn't the subject of their teasing.

"Tell you what, Bax," Declan said, hooking his finger in the air to call Bella over, "I'll get Leslie to whisk Teddy up to Grand Rapids someday soon, and while they're gone, we can break in—er, I mean, we can go check out Stony Cape Keeper's Cottage and see if we happen to stumble on any manuscript pages lying around." He lifted an eyebrow at Teddy.

"Nice try," she said, folding her arms over her chest. "But I write on my laptop, and it goes everywhere with me."

Baxter made a show of looking at her very large leather tote. "You mean, the next Sargent Blue book is *in that bag*?"

Teddy laughed and shook her head as Declan ordered another round of beer from Mirabella. "Well, not tonight. But you know, Baxter, I might just try your idea of having someone drown in a huge barrel of hops."

"Speaking of which, have you ever smelled the smoke that comes from the wort?" Declan asked. "It's *rank*. That alone could kill a guy."

"It's just yeasty— Oh *crap*. Look who all just walked in." Baxter sighed.

Declan turned, then spun back right away in an obvious effort to hide from being noticed. "I thought Maxine turned into a pumpkin at nine o'clock? What's she doing here?"

"Well, scout, it's only eight thirty," Leslie told him with a smile. "Gird your loins—Cherry's bringing her on over."

"Who's Maxine?" asked Teddy, once again craning in her seat.

"Oh, you'll find out," Declan said grimly. "Thank God you got here after her birthday party last week."

Teddy looked at Leslie. "Did you just say 'gird your loins'? That sounds so…old-fashioned. Like it belongs in a medieval novel."

Leslie grinned and spread her hands wide. "Yes, well, I happen to read a lot of historical romance."

"Yeah, particularly ones about *sexy blacksmiths*," Declan said, then gave her a loud smooch on the lips. "Which is why you didn't have a chance when you met me. You were already half in love with the *idea* of me."

Leslie rolled her eyes, but her cheeks were a little pink. "I like romance novels. They're a great escape and are wonderfully entertaining." She sounded mildly defensive, and Teddy thought she understood why—particularly since she currently wrote thrillers. Romance novels were big moneymakers, but they were also often denigrated as lesser forms of literature next to other genres like thrillers, mysteries, and women's fiction.

"I love all books," Teddy replied. "Including romance. With this age of everyone streaming everything on any device imaginable, I'm just happy people still read. And I—"

"Is this the writer?" screeched a voice just behind Teddy.

Teddy turned to discover that a cluster of elderly ladies had basically ambushed her, forming a circle around her from behind.

There were four of them, and the one who'd spoken appeared to be the oldest of the bunch. She had to be at least eighty, and she had very dark skin that was as smooth as ebony despite her age. Her hair was a thick mop of iron gray that was almost perfect enough to be a wig, and she brandished a walking stick that Teddy immediately decided was lethal—especially in the hands of a demanding elderly woman.

"You must be Maxine," Teddy said with a smile. "I've heard all about you from Declan."

"You *have*, have you?" replied the old lady. "Well, I don't—"

"Yes, this is loudmouth Maxine Took," said a plump woman with perfectly manicured purple fingernails. Her hair was an improbable bronzy-reddish henna, clearly covering some major gray, because Teddy suspected she was about the same age as Maxine. "I'm Juanita Acerita, and if you're really T.J. Mack, I have to say it's a pleasure to meet you!"

When Teddy reached to shake Juanita's hand, however, Juanita reared back a little, moving her large leather bag out of reach. "Sorry—Brucie gets a little testy at sudden movements," Juanita said with a smile, maneuvering so she could shake Teddy's hand but keep the tote at a distance.

That was when Teddy saw the small canine with bright eyes peeking out from inside. It was the cutest dog she'd ever seen. He had huge ears—they were each the size of its head—and mostly white fur, but with splotches of black and brown over his nose. His butterflylike ears were jet black, and had long, silky hair hanging from them.

"That's Bruce Banner," Maxine informed Teddy, shoving her hand in for her own greeting. "He's named after the Hunk."

"Move over, Maxine," said another of the four women, who seemed to ignore Maxine's confusion about who Bruce Banner was. "I want to meet her too." This one sounded more professional, yet there was an air of excitement in her tone. She was tall—probably at least six foot—and sturdy, with lots of thick blue-white hair combed into a simple style of short in the back, but bouffant-like on top.

She looked several years younger than Maxine and Juanita —maybe seventy—and as if she could take down a Secret Service agent without breaking a sweat. "I'm Orbra van Hest, Ms. Mack, and I am a *huge* fan. I buy all of your books in hardcover the minute they come out, and I also buy the e-books so I can make the font bigger and read them better. And I listen to the audiobooks too, when I'm cleaning up—I own the tea shop in town, and anytime you want to come in, I'll serve you the best scones you've ever had." She said all of this in a nervous rush of words that indicated to Teddy that she truly was a *big* fan.

"That's right," Maxine said, clearly intent on keeping control of the conversation. "Orbra's cinnamon scones are a national treasure. Can't say the same about them lavender-blueberry ones you tried on us, though, Orbry—"

"I'm Cherry Wilder," said a slender, very fit woman in her mid-sixties who obviously knew the necessity of not waiting for Maxine to stop talking. "I'm a big fan too, Ms. Mack, and I was hoping you might sign a few of these books for me."

"I've got mine too," said Orbra, amid a chorus of other "me toos," which came not only from the semicircle of elderly women, but also some other customers—including the busty blond that Baxter had a thing for.

"I'd love to sign your books," Teddy said with a broad smile and genuine pleasure. "All of them," she added, looking around at everyone else. To her surprise, suddenly, there was quite a crowd. It appeared that Maxine Took and her friends had been the catalyst for several, shyer Wicks Hollow residents to come forward.

And apparently, somehow, they'd all known Teddy would be eating at the Grille tonight. She glanced at Declan, who lifted his hands with a "sorry, what can I do?" look and smiled.

Teddy wasn't lying when she said she'd be happy to sign

their books—there was nothing she liked better than to meet readers. Thus, the impromptu book signing turned into an energetic chat with the diners. Between Baxter and Mirabella, the beers kept coming, and the sense of joviality swelled. People pulled up chairs, Teddy answered questions and asked a few of her own, and got some feedback on her books (mostly welcome, some confusing, and some completely off the wall—but it was all in good fun, and very entertaining).

By the time Teddy was ready to leave and the bar/diner was closing, she was shocked to discover it was after eleven thirty.

Fifteen minutes later, exhausted, and pretty tipsy from several rounds of B-Cubed beer, Teddy climbed out of Leslie's car. "Thanks for the ride," she said, waving a little unsteadily as her cousin and his girlfriend drove off.

Yawning, Teddy let herself in the front door of the cottage. She fumbled around for a light switch, didn't immediately find one, and gave up looking, choosing to use the moonlight to find the door to the lighthouse suite.

But she wasn't so out of it that she didn't notice the boxes on the kitchen and living room tables.

Well, I guess the food's been delivered. Jeepers. That looks like enough to feed an army. I'll check it out in the morning. Hope they put the perishable stuff away because I'm not doing it now.

Five minutes later, she was tucked beneath her covers and slipping into sleep.

A loud noise had Teddy bolting upright in bed.

Sun blazed through the window, and a squinty look at the bedside clock (her cell phone was too far away to reach) told her it was just after seven. Groggy and shocked out of a sound sleep, she stumbled out of bed.

Whatever had awakened her sounded like a heavy thud—very nearby.

Like, in the living room.

She of the very active imagination looked around for a weapon—although why someone would break in in the morning rather than in the dead of night was beyond her—and her eyes lit on a pair of water skis propped in the corner. She didn't even have the wherewithal to wonder what they were doing there.

Another loud noise from beyond, followed by a muffled human exclamation, had Teddy grabbing one of the skis (it was either that, the hairdryer, or her laptop). Hefting the unwieldy weapon, she sneaked to the curve-topped door connecting the lighthouse to the main part of the cottage and opened it a crack.

There was a man in her living room.

Teddy ducked back. Her heart pounding, her palms slick, she drew in a deep breath, trying to calm herself. *What the hell?*

Fortunately, he was facing the other way and hadn't appeared to notice her.

She peered back out and took a better look. All she could see was an arm and a broad, solid shoulder, plus the hint of a leg and hip as he moved around. Whoever he was, he had stuff —equipment—all over the place. All the boxes and things she'd seen last night and had assumed was food seemed to belong to him.

"Who the hell are you?" She stalked out, ski clutched awkwardly in both hands.

Unfortunately, the damn thing was too long, and she misjudged. The pointy end of the ski snagged in the bumpy

Berber carpet, causing it to catch and her to stumble, slamming her head against the waxed wood. *Nice going, Mack.*

The man whirled around, and they both froze, gaping at each other. "It's you?" he said.

"*You!* What the hell are you doing here? Did you *follow* me?" Teddy couldn't have written a better story herself: the man who'd set up some sort of scientific lab *in her summer rental* was the nerdy scientist from the hot spring.

But maybe he wasn't a nerdy scientist after all.

Maybe he *was* a serial killer. He had enough of a lab set up to torture her if he pleased. And they were too far from civilization for anyone to hear her scream… (Great tagline for her next book.)

"*You're* the writer?" he said, snapping off a plastic glove. And he didn't sound at all pleased about it. "You didn't mention that yesterday."

"*I'm* the writer," she snarled, and realized her head was pounding, right above her nose. Maybe she shouldn't have had that last beer Baxter ordered for her after all. "And I didn't realize a chance meeting required me to tell you my occupa— Anyway, this is my cottage—where I'm supposed to have privacy and solitude so I can finish my damn book—and what in the hell is all *this*?"

"Carl— Did you meet Carl?"

"Who? Hell, it doesn't matter. I'm calling the rental agent. No, I'm calling Harriet, for pity's sake. *She's* going to be having words with them about—"

But he shook his head, talking above her rant. "It won't help. They screwed up and rented the place to both of us, and there aren't any other rooms available in Wicks Hollow. So we're stuck sharing the place." He looked at her, his eyes tracing the ski and then skimming over her tank top—under which she was braless, of course—then down her legs (bared by a pair of boxer shorts). "When he said there was a writer, I didn't know it was you—I mean, that you were a woman. He said your name was Teddy. And come to think of it, he conveniently didn't assign a pronoun."

"The name's Teddy Mack. Wish I could say it was a pleasure to meet you, but I can't." She set the ski to lean against the wall and crossed her arms over her breasts as reality sank in. "Are you serious—there's *nowhere* else you can go? I have to finish a book! I'm already late, and I *can't write* with all this going on! With you here."

Panic clutched her chest. She'd planned to wake up this morning, bright and early, have a cup of tea on the wraparound porch, and absorb the fresh air and sunshine as she looked out at Lake Michigan…and then pull out her laptop and dive right in to the story.

But now everything was off. Mucked up. And her thoughts couldn't be further from the edgy, cliff-hanging thrillers about sexy, sarcastic Sargent Blue, who saved the world at least once in every single book.

What the hell am I going to do? Teddy felt the sting of tears gathering at the corners of her eyes. *I'm so damn behind, so uninspired, so freaking burned out and scared…I just don't think I can do this.*

And now this.

My career is over.

She realized with a start that the man—whose name she still didn't know—had said something. "What? Sorry…I…was thinking." She blinked and refocused. *Get it together, Mack. You're not giving up yet.*

"I guess that's natural for a writer—uh, to be daydreaming. I offered you some coffee."

"No thanks. I have some tea. But it sure would be great to know your name." *So when I call Harriet to chew her butt over this, I have a name for my problem. No,* her *problem. She booked the place. She can fix it.*

"Oscar London."

"Seriously?"

He grimaced and opened a small fridge (he'd brought his own fridge?). "My parents had no idea."

"No, I mean—it's a *great* name. Really. I know names, believe me. It took me three weeks to come up with my main character's name—he's a sort of spy-slash-adventurer who's also a librarian, but once I did, I knew it was perfect. And Oscar London…well, it's great." She took in his bright, golden-red hair, neatly buttoned white shirt, and British-like formality. No accent, other than a bit of East Coast. "It suits you."

"I'm delighted you approve." There was a little more snarkiness in his voice than she'd expected.

Hmm. Interesting. And compelling.

"I have work to do, and so, apparently, do you. So…" He made a little waving gesture, as if to say, *Off with you, you pesky creature.*

"I can't write with you making all sorts of racket out here. And I can't concentrate with you *in my space.*" The panic escaped and clawed at her chest again, its talons sharper than ever. "This isn't going to work. One of us is going to have to leave. And it isn't going to be me." Teddy knew her voice had gone high and thready, and she despised herself for it. But her career was on the line.

And Oscar London was ignoring her, the rat.

He'd turned back to his project—whatever it was—and was putting a glass container in a device that looked like a small top-loading washer.

"What's that machine? And what are you doing, anyway? Are you really testing for E. coli?" Teddy realized she was desperate to do anything but sit in front of her laptop and stare at a blank white screen.

"It's a centrifuge." He closed the door and pushed a button, then adjusted a dial. As the machine began to rumble quietly, he pivoted to a desktop computer, complete with monitor.

Sheesh. What kind of geek traveled with all of this stuff?

Still ignoring her, Oscar began tapping on the keyboard, using the hunt-and-peck method. Just watching him pick at the keys with two fingers—*thunk, thunk, thunk-thunk, thunk*—made her twitchy.

"You never learned to type properly?" She edged closer, looking at the screen, and conveniently ignoring how much she hated it when someone looked over *her* shoulder while she was working.

"No."

The screen was filled with a form he was completing: numbers, date, time, location, etc. Nothing worth being distracted over. "So the centrifuge spins the, what, the samples around?"

He turned. "You sure are talkative for someone who has a book to write."

Teddy exhaled a long breath. "Yeah. Well, I've been having a little writer's block." She watched as he measured out a sample of water from a container like the one she'd filled yesterday—maybe the same one—using a pipette to transfer it carefully into a test tube. She sighed wistfully and slumped against the wall, arms crossed over her middle. "Microbiologists don't get writer's block. You just know what you have to do, and you do it. You follow the procedures and *voila*! Done."

"Yep. It's that easy. So if you're going to stand there instead of work, how about getting me another cup of coffee? Black, please."

"Might as well." When she came back from the tiny kitchen, which—she had to give him credit for—was neat as a pin, with his clean breakfast dishes lined up in the drainer, he'd stripped off the gloves. His fiery hair was standing nearly on end, obviously rumpled from a hand jamming through it, presumably post-glove-removal.

"So you've got writer's block." He took the cup and sipped. His eyes, a rich mix of green and brown, settled on her. "What kind of story are you working on?"

Teddy wandered over, looking in the boxes of equipment. Tubes, small bottles, larger bottles, petri dishes, labels, and syringes of all sizes. "You brought your own refrigerator with you?"

"Yes." He sounded *extremely* patient. "I have to make sure the samples are kept at a precise temperature, and the only way to do that is to use my own equipment—equipment that I know is accurate. I check the temp first thing in the morning, and several times through the day."

"Have fridge, will travel. Huh. That's one dangerous-looking microscope you have there." She walked over to the complicated instrument branded Horix and peered through the eyepieces. She saw nothing but black.

"It's a digital microscope. The image appears on that computer monitor. But, of course, the light has to be turned on, and there has to be something on a slide." He snapped on another pair of gloves. "And it's worth over two K, so please be careful."

"Fascinating." He gave her a jaundiced look, and she said, "No, seriously. This is the kind of thing I find utterly interesting. You never know when I'll learn something that will show up in a book— Hey. *Wait.*" A spike of excitement rushed through her. "Maybe you can help me!"

He muttered something that sounded like "Oh, brilliant,"

but she wasn't certain. Either way, Teddy didn't care. If there was one thing she'd learned about being a writer, it was that ideas—and plot solutions—could come from anyone at any time. She just had to be open to them.

"So I have my character in a real fix. I need to have him—"

"Let me guess. Save the world." Even though he was facing the other direction, smearing something on a glass slide, she swore he rolled his eyes.

"Hey. It *sells*."

"So does sex. Or so they say. Why doesn't someone ever write a book about the world *not* getting saved? Just to see what happens—you know, the aftermath and all? What would it be like fifty years after the earth was destroyed, you know? Say if California fell into the ocean, and half the Vegas Strip ended up under the Pacific?"

"Wow. You sure are an optimistic kind of guy." Teddy edged closer. "Are you always like this?"

"My former fiancée is getting married in ten days. Sorry I'm not in a great mood."

"Oh, wow. That's a bummer. I'm really sorry. Is she getting married here in Wicks Hollow?"

"No. Hell no. Do you think I'd stick around if she were? I left Princeton yesterday morning—I teach there—and came directly here. It was a *long* drive."

Princeton, huh? She was more than mildly impressed. "So you came here, equipment and all, to test the water from a hot spring in Michigan?" He grunted an ambiguous reply, and she said, "So, can I help?"

"I thought you were supposed to be writing." But he gestured to a box of latex gloves. "I suppose I could use an assistant. Just don't touch anything with your bare skin, and don't sneeze or cough or otherwise spread germs."

"Got it," Teddy said with enthusiasm, then realized she was still wearing her sleep clothes. She'd better change before the poor guy noticed she wasn't wearing a bra and put the wrong chemical into the wrong tube and blew up the place.

Oscar didn't really need an assistant, but it was obvious the writer wasn't going to leave him alone. And at least her incessant questions and poking around kept him distracted from what was happening back in Princeton.

Whenever Teddy pressed him about why he was testing the hot-springs water (did he really think the bad E. coli lived there?), he launched into a long-winded explanation about major cations and anions, and how the turbidity could be problematic if it was too high, and whether the total iron level complied with the expected presence of tardigrades and phages in the body of water, among other things, until her eyes glazed over.

He figured inflicting boredom was one way to rid himself of a pest.

And thank goodness she'd excused herself for a minute and changed into something less…distracting. He was a scientist, of course, but he was also a man, and, well, she had a lot of curves. In all the right places.

"I get the impression you don't read very many action-adventure novels," she said, handing him a petri dish he'd requested. "Oh, *there's* an idea." Her blue eyes suddenly went wide, sparkling with interest. "The villains could be growing some random bad stuff—"

"Random bad stuff?" He lifted a brow. She was entertaining, he had to give her that, with a conversation that bounced from topic to topic. He found himself admitting her presence was less intrusive than he'd expected—though not the least bit welcome. And she smelled good too—minty (she must have taken the opportunity to brush her teeth during her change of clothes) and also something soft and floral.

"Well, we'll have to figure out what it exactly *is*," she said.

"We?"

"But it's something bad…and the bad guys have been growing it in a slew of petri dishes. They're going to release it into the New York City water system—no, wait, they're going to put it in the water pitchers at the United Nations! You know how they always have water for all the attendees at a meeting like that—you see those pitchers at their seats?"

"Right. Someone's going to grow some… What did you call it? Oh, right, 'random bad stuff' in a bunch of petri dishes…and poison the water at the United Nations…and why are they doing this, exactly?"

She drew in a long, deep breath, then expelled it forcefully. "I don't know. I haven't the foggiest idea. That's why I'm stuck. I've got my hero in New York City, and he's got to save a bunch of people—"

"Besides, I hate to tell you this—even if they grew a variety of specimens of the RBS—"

"RBS? Oh, I get it." She grinned, and her eyes lit up again. But this time, her whole face changed as she gave a low, husky laugh—and right then she went from being irritatingly entertaining and mildly attractive to a woman who totally pushed his hormone buttons. *Crap.*

"RBS. Random bad stuff." She was still chuckling.

He found his voice. "Right. So. Even if they were growing a variety of these specimens, first of all, there's no way to transport them safely—"

"Sure there is. We'd figure it out."

He couldn't quite get with the "we" stuff, but Oscar let her continue. It was kind of fun and stimulating to have a brain-storming session with someone who wasn't restricted by science, but only by her own creativity. Which seemed pretty damned bountiful, if not practical.

"They could transport the petri dishes in a cooler, for example," she said. "And bring it in with the caterers for the UN. It'll be a big meeting, with all the important world leaders there."

"That could work, if it could get past security—which is a big if—but the bigger problem is the minute the RBS is released from the petri dishes, it'll be exposed and most likely die. You can't grow microbes in a carefully controlled environment like petri dishes and then release it to the wild, so to speak. The chances of it surviving are extremely low."

Teddy grumbled, and her lower lip protruded in a definite pout. "Well, there is a *chance*, isn't there?" she asked, as if science could be bent to her wishes.

"A very slim one. Can you grab me that pencil?"

She reached for it too quickly, bumping a beaker, which knocked the pencil into rolling off the table. She, of course, had to bend over and pick it up…which gave him an uninterrupted view directly down the front of her tank top. Low-cut bra, a hint of pink nipples, and a deep valley.

Oscar dragged his eyes away before she came up, and made sure his attention was focused on the plate he held.

"So it must be tough being a scientist and watching action-adventure movies or reading those kinds of books," she said, seeming to have no idea of the sight she'd just displayed. "You know too much, and the suspension of disbelief is even more difficult for someone like you."

"I can only get through the ones where the author has actually done research," he said, taking the pencil then turning away before he found himself knocking over something else for her to pick up. "And when the story makes sense, even from a scientific point of view."

She looked as if she were about to say something when a song began to play from beyond the door that connected to the lighthouse.

"Is that the 'James Bond Theme'?" he asked. "Did you leave the TV on or something?"

But Teddy's entire demeanor had changed. "Oh, crap," she wailed. "Oh no. That's my agent—her ringtone. Oh, God. I haven't even opened my laptop this morning." She looked a little green around the gills, but she squared her shoulders, stripped off her gloves and tossed them on the table, then hurried off into the base of the lighthouse, presumably to answer her phone.

Oscar expelled a sigh of relief when the door slammed behind her. Good riddance. Assistant or not, he really didn't need any distractions—especially the female type.

Especially the chatty female type who was somehow interesting and entertaining even though she was bothering the hell out of him. And harshing his lab-brain mellow. And displaying all sorts of interesting sights and giving off pleasant scents.

Not that he was in any way attracted to Teddy Mack, with her masculine name and the feminine curves that had been a little too apparent both times he'd interacted with her. Between her swimsuit and the loose tank and shorts she'd been wearing, there wasn't much left to the imagination. Good thing he preferred a sleeker, more understated, less *bountiful* look—and personality—when it came to women.

Marcie, with a smooth blond haircut that skimmed her chin, and a neat, compact body dressed in crisp button-down blouses and slim, flowery skirts or demure slacks, was and had always been the type that attracted him.

So even if he was sharing a rental property with the audacious writer (who was far more talkative than he'd expected a writer to be), there was no real danger of him being distracted by her.

Then there was the strange thing that had happened last night…the thing he hadn't wanted to mention.

And the thing he'd been hoping *she'd* mention first.

For, in the middle of the darkest part of night, a horrible, agonizing sound had had him jolting bolt upright up in bed, shocked from a restful sleep.

The mere memory of that eerie, wailing shriek still raised the hairs on his arms and the back of his neck. It sounded like someone was dying. Right outside his window…or maybe it was in the living room. He couldn't tell—the terrifying sound seemed to fill his ears, fill the entire *world* with its horror.

Oscar had stumbled from bed, dazed and disoriented in an unfamiliar place, and still drowning in the last vestiges of deep sleep.

All he knew was someone was hurt…dying…being tortured—

In his haste, he'd bumped into a few things—he had telltale bruises on an elbow and a shin, and some porcelain thing had been in shards on the floor this morning—before fumbling out the door and into the living room.

By then, the night was still. The shriek had subsided. He scrubbed at his head, then rubbed his eyes, and gave himself a little shake.

It was so silent. Surely he hadn't imagined the noise.

Or dreamt it.

He stepped outside, looking around for anything out of place. His truck, parked way off to the side, was the only vehicle around, leaving him to wonder whether the writer had found another place to stay after all.

So he was here alone at—he looked at his digital watch—one thirty in the morning.

The only sound was the rhythmic rush and retreat of waves on the stony, sandy shore only a few yards away, and a light rustle of leaves from a breeze. The night air was pleasantly cool, and it held the fresh scent of summer and lake. Serene and calm.

He heard the hoot of an owl in the distance. It sounded mournful and lonely.

There was no indication of anyone or anything that might have caused such a horrible sound, and if the writer was there and hadn't been awakened, Oscar could only conclude he must have been dreaming.

Maybe it had been the sound of his soul grieving over Marcie—distant, disconnected, disengaged.

Though he finally convinced himself that the unearthly shriek had been a product of his dreams (or nightmares, depending on how you looked at it), Oscar found himself unable to fall back asleep easily. At last, just after dawn, he dragged himself from the surprisingly comfortable bed and got to work.

Thus, he'd specifically *not* mentioned the horrifying scream he'd heard last night. And since Teddy Mack hadn't said anything about it—and she didn't seem the type to hold back on mentioning *anything*—he was relieved he'd not brought it up himself. It had either been a dream or some wild animal in heat.

Now, once more left alone to his devices with Teddy off talking to her agent, Oscar was determined to lose himself in his work. With a glance at the clock—it was just pushing nine; so *early*—he turned his attention back to the distraction of work.

He had to focus on something, or he'd be pulling out his

phone and manufacturing a reason to text his sister. Dina (short for Engadine) was one of Marcie's best friends—and, unfortunately, had been before Oscar even met her, and somehow continued to be a BFF. Dina was far too sharp to be fooled by any bland excuse her brother might use to "just say hi" to see how things were going.

But, foolish or not, he figured it wasn't over until the fat lady sang—and that aria wouldn't happen until the rings were exchanged at the altar, and the bride and groom were announced as the new Mr. and Mrs. Trevor Baker. That gave Oscar ten whole days for something to go wrong and the wedding to get called off.

Which was pathetic.

Which was why he absolutely wouldn't be texting Dina for any reason.

If he happened to be scrolling through Facebook over the weekend and saw her page instead, well, that would be an accident. But he wasn't certain whether he'd want to actually see if there were pictures of the bachelorette party—or not.

In deference to his unwanted housemate—who was likely going to be tied up doing her own work now, if her expression of fear had been any indication—Oscar dug out his earbuds and shuffled a playlist of The Cure, The Sex Pistols, and The Kinks as he navigated carefully through the process of preparing, recording, and examining the samples. It was a form of mindfulness—something Marcie had talked a lot about after she came home from her yoga classes. He blocked everything out except his work—the routine and the shift from sample to plate to microscope to computer and around and around became a soothing rhythm—and even the pounding music became a mere backdrop to the process.

He didn't expect to find anything earth-shattering—not like the Japanese team that had recently discovered a bacterium that *eats plastic*—despite the fact that his natural hot tub was a unique area to explore. Maybe he'd find an unusual alga or make some interesting observations about a hot spring seeded from a Great Lake. Still. It was a plausible way to spend the month, working on a project just for fun.

When his playlist turned up "Lovesong" (which he'd forgotten was on there and, of course, reminded him of Marcie), Oscar was jolted out of his lab-brain mellow and came up for air. He was shocked to discover it was well past noon.

And he hadn't seen nor heard from the writer since she disappeared to take her phone call.

Good. The less he saw of her, the less likely he'd be tempted to mention last night's disruption.

But after he'd had lunch (tuna salad on wheat, an apple, and some fresh tomatoes), and went back to work for several more hours, Oscar began to feel a little…well, *concerned* was the word, when he realized he hadn't seen nor heard from Teddy since before nine o'clock. And it was nearly five.

The woman had to eat, didn't she? And he knew she hadn't had anything for breakfast or lunch, because he'd have seen her.

Not that it was his concern.

She was probably pounding away on her keyboard like a good writer on deadline and, like Oscar, had lost track of time.

Still.

He forced himself back to his project, making notes and fussing with the lab work, checking his email and studiously avoiding Facebook and his cell phone for potential texts, until he realized the sunlight had shifted and he would need to turn on some lamps if he wanted to keep working.

Blinking owlishly, he looked at the clock and realized it was nearly seven thirty.

A quick glance toward the kitchen told him it was undisturbed from when he'd been in there making lunch a while ago. The door to the lighthouse was still closed and he was certain he'd have noticed it open, even if he was blasting "God Save the Queen" while engrossed in the microscope.

A niggling sensation prickled at him, and Oscar removed his gloves, followed by his lab coat.

I should probably just check on her—maybe see if she wants to share dinner.

He washed his hands at the kitchen sink and dried them while considering the best approach—after all, if she was in the throes of her novel, like she should be, she might not want to be bothered. Really, he shouldn't be looking such a gift horse in the mouth.

Hadn't he wanted to be left alone?

He dried his hands, re-tucked his shirt neatly, and squared his shoulders.

Then, certain he would live to regret it, Oscar knocked on the connecting door.

THREE

THERE WAS NO ANSWER.

Oscar glared at the door. Now what?

He knocked again, a little louder this time, and even opened it a crack to peek inside. "Hello? Teddy?"

Again, no answer.

Maybe she'd gone somewhere. But he hadn't seen a car, either parked or coming or going.

She could have gone for a walk, he supposed. But…he'd better check.

"Teddy?" He stepped through the door and found himself in a small vestibule with two more doors. One, he guessed, would open to the bedroom she was using—that one was ajar —and the other possibly to the outside. Or maybe to the core of the lighthouse, to the presumptive spiral staircase that would lead to the top. "Helloooo? Teddy? It's Oscar."

He was just about to ease back through to the living room when he heard a sound like a low, agonized moan.

"Teddy?" he called louder, starting toward the door that was slightly open. "Are you all right?"

He didn't wait for another response; he pushed open the

door. He had a split second of seeing her hunched over a table or desk, headphones covering her ears, before she jolted, turned, and screamed.

"Ohmigod," she shrieked in a slightly lower volume, clapping a hand to her chest. "You scared the *hell* out of me!" She pulled off her headphones and settled them around her neck.

He blinked, collected his thoughts, and managed to say, "I heard— It sounded like you were in pain. I thought— I'm sorry—"

"I *am* in pain," she said, standing so abruptly that her chair fell backward. "Look at that! Just *look*!" She stabbed a finger toward the laptop, which was open on the desk.

He stepped forward cautiously, suddenly acutely aware that he was in her bedroom and that the bed was *right there*. The sheets were rumpled and the pillows were in a lumpy pile. There was a bra and a pair of lacy pink panties—he averted his eyes quickly—slung over a chair, along with a blue dress the same color as her eyes.

"Uh," he said, picking up the chair she'd knocked over and relieved to have that distraction. "What?"

"*Do you see that?*"

"I see…a computer screen."

"And what's on it?" she demanded, hands on her hips, loose headphone cord swinging across her chest.

"Um…it's white. And it says *Chapter Ten.*"

"That's right." Her voice had dropped to a dangerous whisper. "Chapter Ten. Do you know how long I've been working on Chapter Ten, Oscar?"

"How long?" He was already regretting his act of gallantry to check on her.

"Two months, Oscar. *Two bloody months* I've been working on Chapter Mother-Fracking-Ten."

"You—uh—don't have much written," he said, feeling his way. "That I can—uh—see."

"No," she replied in that alarmingly quiet voice. "No, I don't."

"Okay, well, then," he said, backing out of the room. "I'll let you get back to it."

"Right."

Oscar made his escape and was just opening the connecting door when he stopped and turned back. She'd sounded so…miserable. So defeated.

"And she's got to eat," he said. In his own defense.

He walked back to her bedroom door. Just before he knocked, he heard another pained moan from within. That removed his last bit of hesitation. "Teddy?"

He pushed the door open a little and saw her hunched over the desk, head in her hands. She groaned again, low enough that he knew she didn't think he'd hear her. Since the headphones weren't back in place, he hoped he wouldn't startle her this time. "Teddy?"

She whipped around, but not as wildly as last time. "You're back." Her eyes looked suspiciously red, but she straightened in her chair.

"Hey, I—uh—thought maybe you might want some dinner. I was going to—uh—make something on the—There's a grill. Since we share a kitchen…" He shrugged, then waited. Either there would be an explosion, or…he wasn't certain what.

"What time is it?" she asked, looking around. "I'm probably hungry."

"It's after seven thirty."

"Seriously?" Her eyes widened, and they began to glisten with tears—and they weren't happy ones. "I've wasted a whole day? And written—what—a couple hundred words? *And then deleted them all?"*

Oscar braced himself for a flood of something—tears, expletives, stomping—but she still had that unsettling calm that he knew, just *knew*, wasn't real. Or was a portent of something far worse. "Why don't you come out and—and get some fresh air."

"Sure. Thanks." She looked around with that vacant expression again, and reached for the blue sundress draped over the chair. "I'll just put this on really quickly, and—"

"Great, see you in a few," he said, bolting back out of the door when it appeared she was going to yank off her tank top and change right then.

By the time she joined him in the kitchen, Oscar had managed to wipe away all thoughts of the rumpled bed, lacy underwear, and what Teddy might have put on under the bright blue dress she was wearing. He was prepping some chicken breasts for the grill he'd noticed outside—gas, thank goodness, for the one thing he hadn't brought was charcoal— when she joined him in the kitchen.

To his surprise, she looked nothing like the dull-eyed, straggly-haired desperado he'd just seen. She'd pulled her cocoa-brown hair up into a loose knot at the top of her head. He noticed hints of gold and honey shining among the dark tresses. Her eyes showed no evidence of tears. The sundress she wore had skinny straps, but was fairly loose around the rest of her body, though it dipped a little low in the front. Her legs were bare from above the knee and her toenails were painted pink, and he admitted both were more than nice to look at.

"I could use a glass of wine," Teddy said, rummaging in one of the cupboards. "I was supposed to get some food delivery, which Harriet helped me set up so I could concentrate on writing—hah!—and I told her she'd better include some wine or I was coming back to Manhattan to wring her neck," she added cheerfully. "Looks like she complied—and that whoever delivered the food even put it away. White or red? Unless this is all yours?" She spun and gave him a startled, questioning look.

"No, you're right. It's not mine. Must've been put away, maybe yesterday while we—I—you—were at the hot spring. I didn't notice. Uh…white?"

"Good choice. Ah," she said with a soft purr as she examined a bottle. "Harriet has good taste in wine. I'll give her that. Let me chill this a bit first. I like my whites ice-cold in the summer." She shoved the bottle into the freezer.

"So, this Harriet. She sounds like a real hard-ass," Oscar said. He surprised himself by making conversation; he'd figured they'd slap the chicken on the grill, have a salad, and then be off to their own devices—and with as little engagement as possible. But apparently, his brain had other ideas. "A slave driver at best."

"No, no, she's the best." Teddy sighed as she pulled two wine glasses from the cupboard. "Really. She's my literary agent, if you didn't get that. And she's just trying to help me get over this…hump."

"Right." Oscar didn't mention how white-faced terrified of the agent Teddy had seemed earlier. "Well, that's good." He sounded dubious to his own ears, but she didn't seem to notice and began to dig around in the fridge for salad makings.

"I told her about this whole mess," she said as she backed out of the open door of the appliance with an armload of colorful vegetables. "Laid into her a little, in fact, because, really—the whole point of me coming here was not to be bothered. Not to have anyone around. I mean, hell, I don't even have a *car*."

She thunked the salad makings onto the counter and

began to yank open drawers in search of, he assumed, utensils and bowls. "She said she'd do what she could to find another place for me to go, and apologized for the mistake. Not that I think it was totally her fault—but someone did screw up."

"Speaking of not having a car," he said when she paused for breath, "what time did you get back here last night? Did someone drive you?"

"It was around midnight, I think." She gave him a rueful look. "Yes, my cousin Declan dropped me off. I'd gone out to dinner with him and his girlfriend, and I had a few too many samples of the wares of the local craft brewer. By the time I got back, I was more than ready to hit the hay—and a little more than tipsy."

Oscar stopped short of asking her if she'd heard anything strange in the night, but he did probe a little further. "So you went right to bed? Didn't stub your toe or walk into the wall in the dark?"

Didn't make any loud, horrifying screams—or hear one?

To his relief, she didn't seem to think his question was strange. "Nope. Once I hit my mattress, I was out. Until I heard you banging around in there this morning."

"Right." With that, Oscar decided to escape his chatty companion before he said something he'd regret. He went outside to grill the chicken while she worked in the kitchen and chopped veggies for salad. He was surprised a short time later when, just as he was taking the meat off the grill, she brought the salad and wine outside.

"We have to eat out here on the porch," she explained. "I've been cooped up all day, and it's just so beautiful."

He couldn't argue with that. Though it was facing the beach, this side of the covered porch was also partly in shadow from the sprawling forest that filled most of the tiny island. Stony Cape Lighthouse loomed above them, painted white with a jaunty blue band two-thirds up and a matching cap on top, casting a long, broad shadow behind the cottage. The air was lightly humid and filled with the scent of summer flowers—maybe some honeysuckle and wild roses—plus lake. It was warm, but not hot, and the breeze from Lake Michigan was enough to keep the bugs away but not to blow napkins about.

The shoreline was pale sand, and weedy with tall clumps of prickly, hay-like grass growing beyond the farthest reaches of the lake's waves. Larger stones, smooth from rushing water, made a natural barrier between sand and grasses. There was a wooden walkway that led from the cottage down to the lake— a distance of less than twenty yards.

They settled onto two metal chairs, balancing plates on their respective laps. The wine was crisp and light, the chicken (simply marinated in Italian dressing) was grilled till the outside was crispy but the inside still moist and then cut up over the colorful salad, and the view was beautiful. The sun was still several knuckles above the horizon, casting gold and orange rays over the surging waves.

"Thank you for this," Teddy said with a sigh as she looked out over the water. "I might have stayed in there all day."

"I figured you hadn't eaten, and you must be hungry," he said.

She gave a little laugh—throaty and sexy—and said, "Not that I'm about to waste away anytime soon." She gestured at her curves with a shrug. "I do love to eat."

Oscar ignored the little sizzle of awareness from her laugh and focused on his meal instead of on her curves. As soon as he was finished, he could hightail it back to work. Now that he knew she was alive and fed and no longer so angst-ridden.

But Teddy Mack had other plans. She started talking.

"It's just so peaceful here," she said, looking out over the vast array of blues shimmering on the Great Lake. "I'm sure it's different when there's a storm—I can imagine what it's like when a nasty one rolls in over the lake. Lightning bolts shooting from a heavy gray sky—slamming into the churning water. Loud rolls of thunder…pounding waves surging onto the shore.

"There've been quite a few shipwrecks in the Great Lakes, and the coastline of Michigan is longer than any other state—hence the reason it has more lighthouses than any other state. Did you know that?"

"Actually, I did. I think it was mentioned in the rental brochure," Oscar replied.

Teddy studied him. He seemed as if he was ready to bolt from his chair at any moment. Probably to return to his lab work, strewn all over the living room. Easy for him to pick up and get back to work at any time—he didn't have to figure out plots or characters or stop all the time to do research or check obscure facts, to measure his words and tweak them, to think about pacing and foreshadowing and clues and—

"Too bad they don't use this lighthouse anymore," she said, fully aware that she was making conversation in a desperate attempt to keep from being left alone—or to work. Oscar had folded his napkin and laid the flatware over his salad bowl, giving the appearance he was preparing to stand up and go inside. "It would be interesting to see how it works. I wonder why they don't use it anymore."

He shrugged. "Who knows."

"It could have something to do with the guy who jumped off—or fell—a few years back. Probably why no one wanted to stay here for so long."

"A guy jumped off the top of the lighthouse?" Oscar squinted up at the tall column.

"Or was pushed."

"Or was pushed? What makes you think that?" He frowned at her.

Teddy laughed. "Only my writer's imagination. The official word is that the guy jumped, but I'm a suspicious sort—and I write action and crime novels—so, I'm going to suspect the worst. Murder and mayhem whenever possible—that's my motto."

He mumbled something unintelligible. Teddy suspected she didn't want to know what it was, for he was looking at her with a wary expression. "I'm sure there was a complete investigation by the authorities," he said mildly. But he adjusted his gaze to look up at the top of the lighthouse.

"Let's go up there and see what it's like," Teddy said, standing up quickly.

"To jump off?"

He caught her by surprise, and she gave a hearty laugh. "You know what I meant."

He dragged himself to his feet much more slowly than she did. "All right."

His easy agreement, though not particularly enthusiastic, surprised her. She thought she'd have to wheedle him into coming with her. Sure, she could have gone alone, but it was more fun with someone else. Besides, if she was alone, she'd probably start to think about how she should be working instead of exploring.

"So have you really been working on Chapter fracking Ten for two months?" he asked as they brought their dishes into the kitchen. Without discussion, they each tackled different tasks for the cleanup.

"At least," Teddy replied, surprised that he'd asked. A

twinge of guilt and nervousness pinged in her belly, but she pushed it away. After all, she *had* worked all day.

Except when she was pacing around her room, napping, or swearing at the white screen of the laptop. Or napping. Or typing *this sucks this sucks this sucks* just to make sure her keyboard still worked.

"How long does it usually take to write a chapter?"

"It depends on the chapter. The first nine chapters went pretty well. But this one…" She sighed. Being a scientist was so much easier than being a creative person. Everything was so cut and dried, so objective, so organized. You drew the sample, you put in on a slide, you looked at it under a microscope, you made notes, and *voila!* the project was done.

"Where—uh—is it in the book?" he asked, handing her a dripping plate to dry. "The end?"

"Oh, I wish," she said, giving a pained laugh. "The ending chapters are usually the easiest. This one's about halfway through—what we writers call the sagging middle." She'd noticed that for being a nerdy scientist, Oscar had nothing even remotely like a sagging middle. In fact, his button-down shirt (why was he wearing something so formal, anyway?) seemed to fit loosely around his midriff—in other words, no bulge—but was snug over square shoulders and rounded biceps.

"How many chapters are there usually in a book?" he asked.

"It depends on the book."

"Right. Can't you just—I don't know—skip to Chapter Eleven?"

Teddy gave a sad laugh as she slid the last plate into its slot in the cabinet. "I wish. Unfortunately, that's not how I work. I'm a linear writer, meaning I write from beginning to end, pretty much, since I am *not* a plotter—that's plot-*ter* with a T, not a D—although there are times when I feel like a plod-*der* as well, so skipping ahead doesn't help me because I don't know what comes next or where I'm going until I write it."

"That sounds horrible," he said.

"Yeah." Teddy sighed again as she folded up the dishtowel. "Let's go check out the lighthouse—the top of it is called the lantern room."

"And there's a Fresnel lens up there, too, I believe," he said. "Beehive shape with bull's-eye prisms."

She gave him a quick, appreciative smile. "You've been doing your research."

His skin was pretty fair, and it turned a little ruddy in the cheeks as he gave a wry smile. "Well, yes. I mean, I was going to stay in a lighthouse—I figured I should know about it. Even if it isn't operational."

"You probably even know what year the Fresnel lens—a breakthrough in lighthouse lantern design—was invented," she teased as they walked through the arched doorway into the base of the lighthouse. Not that she hadn't done her own research—when she was supposed to be working on her book. For, like Oscar said, if she was going to *stay* in a lighthouse, she should know about the structure and history.

Besides, Teddy never knew when a bit of trivia or seemingly unrelated information could help her with a story.

"Eighteen twenty-two," he replied. "The reason the Fresnel lens became so popular was because it used prisms—called bull's-eyes for obvious reasons—which collected the light from the flame or bulb and reflected it more strongly. That meant that eighty percent of the light given off by the lantern was directed and reflected out, rather than the less than twenty percent before the Fresnel lens."

She'd opened the door to the tall spiral staircase that

wound around the inside of the lighthouse column. It was metal, and their shoes made dull clangs as they climbed.

"And," he said, "when they began to use revolving lanterns —which meant the light went around in a circle, moving from prism to prism—it gave off the appearance of a flashing light. Between that and the colors of the lantern shield—which could be red or blue or yellow or whatever—the beams from each lighthouse could be made to look unique so as to allow them to be distinguished from one another by the navigators…"

His voice trailed off, and Teddy knew it wasn't because he was out of breath from the climb.

She, on the other hand, *was* a bit out of breath from the climb. And they were only about halfway up. Argh. She really should start walking regularly again.

Once she finished the damned book.

"Sorry," Oscar said. "Sometimes I get into lecture mode and forget I'm not in class, giving off information people actually need."

"Nevertheless, I found your—uh—*lecture* very interesting and quite thorough." Teddy grinned at him from two steps up. Since she'd turned, she took the opportunity to pause and look out one of the small, lakeside-facing windows. "Wow. What a view. We should have brought a pair of binoculars."

"Agreed. Next time." Oscar moved in behind her, close enough that she felt his warmth and caught a hint of his scent —shampoo, soap, hair products; whatever it was, it was nice. Masculine without being obnoxious. His foot bumped hers as he adjusted to see out the window. "Oh, sorry," he said, and stepped back as if he'd been burned. "Let's keep going."

This time, Teddy followed him so she could go a little slower, and without feeling self-conscious about the size of her butt—which sat in a desk chair far too often. She also had the benefit of seeing the way the shorts fit to his rear end, and noticed the tight, lean muscles of his calves. They were tanned several shades darker than his face—he must wear a hat outside—and sprinkled with blond hair instead of the rosy-gold color on his head.

Teddy was pleased that she was lagging only a turn of the spiral away when Oscar stepped off the top stair onto a small landing with a door that must lead to the gallery. "The door's locked," he called down to her. "Don't suppose you have a key?"

"There are a bunch on the ring I have. I hope one of them works." Because it would be a real drag to have climbed up a hundred and sixty-eight (yes, she'd counted) stairs and not be able to get to the good part.

She handed him the keychain and paused to catch her breath while he studied the keys on it. Teddy smothered a smile. If she'd been doing it, she'd have just started sticking each key in, one at a time, until she found one that fit. Oscar, on the other hand, examined the lock, looked at the keys one by one, then picked one out, stuck it into the keyhole, and turned.

"Success," he pronounced, then handed the keychain back to her. "Ladies first—especially since it was your idea." He opened the door, and she stepped in.

As she came through, some great, dark entity came to life in a flutter of wings and rush of movement.

"Eeek!" She ducked and automatically covered her head, but the flock of bats—of course it was bats—knew their way out of the encasement in which they'd been making their home for some years.

She reared back, flailing a little, and bumped into Oscar, who caught her before they both went tumbling onto the small landing—and potentially down the spiral stairway.

"I'm sorry," she said, pulling away—totally mortified and feeling ridiculous. "I'm not usually that—uh—squeamish. But they caught me by surprise, and there were so many of them. Sorry for screaming in your ear."

"No problem. And you didn't scream." His hands were still hovering near her hips, as if to catch her if she bolted back again.

"I didn't?" she said. "Well, thank goodness for that. In my head, I screamed."

He chuckled, and as she happened to have turned to face him, she saw how his green-brown eyes lit up and the way handsome laugh lines crinkled at their corners. "You exclaimed, but you didn't scream," he said. "Big difference—as you, a wordsmith, would know."

"*I* think so, but for some people, such subtlety might be lost on them." She smiled, suddenly realizing she *liked* this guy —her unexpected and unwanted housemate.

He was nice. And funny. And pretty laid-back, all things considered.

And he'd come to her suite to make sure she ate.

"Well, I feel a little bad about disturbing the poor things," she said, stepping through a little more gingerly this time. "It's a little early for them to be out and about—still light out for another hour or so." She squinted in the unrelieved sunlight blasting through the glass walls, looking up into the lantern room's cap. "They must have gone out through some hole in the top."

To her relief, nothing else moved in the small space. She stepped aside to make room for Oscar to join her on the narrow walkway around the giant glass lenses that did, in fact, form the shape of a beehive.

The glass-walled lantern room was approximately twenty-five feet in diameter, with the massive set of lenses taking up the center of the space. Each lens was shaped like the interior of a cathedral: straight sides arching to a point at the top. There were six lenses—or sides—each about eight feet tall, attached to each other in the hive shape. Every side was an intricate study in glass: rippling and wavy in texture at the top and bottom, but circular in the center where the bull's-eye was located.

There was just enough room for two people to walk side by side around the lenses between its glass enclosure and the glass hive itself. There were three different windows that opened like doors onto the exterior walkway around the outside of the lantern room. Open to the elements and lake breeze, that walkway had only a slender metal railing around it.

Still inside the protective glass enclosure, Teddy walked around the massive set of lenses. Because of the texture on the glass, it was difficult to clearly see the lighting element inside, but it looked like a very large electric piece. They'd passed by the entrance to the small room beneath the lantern where the lighting element could be accessed for repair, and when she looked down, she could see the opening that led to the space —and the evidence of the bat congregation down in its depths.

"Look what I found," he said, holding up a pair of binoculars. "They were hanging right here."

He offered them to Teddy, and she took them with a smile. "Thanks."

By the time she'd made her way completely around the lens, looking both inward and outside, with and without the field glasses, Oscar had opened one of the glass doors and gone out to the exterior walkway. She hesitated, but the lantern windows hadn't been cleaned for years, and the view was distorted by dirt and bird droppings. She could see, but not as well as she'd like.

So Teddy carefully stepped out the door and paused, standing in the opening well away from the edge as a strong breeze buffeted her. "Wow."

Lake Michigan stretched as far as the eye could see—and from thirty feet up, that was far. From this height, she looked down on the texture of varied treetops: pines, oaks, maples, birches, cottonwoods, and many others she couldn't name. The mainland shore was behind her and curved southward along the left, a broad stripe of pale sand bordered by shrubby grasses, then forestation. Further away, small, rolling hills were turning dark with shadows as twilight approached.

In the west, the sun had moved swiftly toward the horizon over the last thirty minutes, and its bottom was just touching the lake. Fiery pinks, reds, oranges, and golds splashed over the sky like a spilled tray of watercolors onto a blue canvas, then dripped in ripples on the moving waters of the Great Lake.

Seagulls, calling with their annoying shrieks, dove and soared above, and Teddy saw a blue heron take flight from some patch of tall grass near the shore on the mainland. The bats she'd disturbed were nowhere in sight. Two fishing boats were zipping along far from shore, likely heading back to their marinas before dark, and in the distance, Teddy saw the outline of a freighter scooting along the horizon. It looked as if it were heading south-west, toward Chicago. She lifted the binoculars and watched the vessel gliding along the seam between water and sky.

When she lowered the glasses, she stood and watched with her naked eyes. For a moment, she was a sea captain's wife, watching for the safe return of his ship…praying that the horizon would remain clear of rolling clouds that portended evil storms, that the sails of his vessel would appear like white beacons on the water.

Red sky at night, sailor's delight. Red sky in the morning, sailor's warning.

So tonight would be a clear one, and he would get that much closer to home safely.

"Are you afraid of heights or something?" Oscar had walked back to stand next to her, jolting her from her fanciful thoughts.

"No. Not really. But it's a little disconcerting, being up this high with only that tiny railing between me and the ground." Teddy couldn't control a little shiver as she brushed loose wisps of hair from her face. The wind was riffling Oscar's short, bright hair and molding the light cotton shirt to his arms and shoulders like the hands of a lover.

To prove to herself she wasn't nervous, Teddy stepped out from the doorway and approached the railing next to Oscar. It was hardly more than a metal pipe strung around the parapet, just above waist height, fixed every four or five feet with an iron bar.

And the ground was a loooong way down.

"So someone jumped or fell from up here?" Oscar said. "Or was pushed," he added, giving her a sidewise look.

"Would be an easy thing to do," she said, gripping the railing. "One little shove by the villain, and over they go—"

Crash!

Already a little on edge, Teddy pivoted wildly at the loud, violent sound, sending the binoculars around her neck slamming into Oscar's belly. "What the—"

But the wind had simply blown the glass door shut.

She looked at Oscar, ready to apologize for being so jumpy, when she saw his expression. *Arrested* was the only word to describe it.

He muttered something and started to move toward the door. His brow was furrowed and his mouth set.

"What is it?" she said, squishing herself up against the (safe) side of glass wall as he edged past her on the narrow ledge.

"How did that happen?" he said, more intelligibly now.

"The wind," she replied calmly. Wasn't it obvious?

He shook his head as he reached for the door handle. "No. It couldn't have been the wind—it was coming from a different direction. It couldn't have—well— *Bloody hell.*" He froze, his hand on the door handle.

"What's wrong?"

"It's—stuck. Locked. Or something." He shook it hard, rattling the door in its hinges, but the handle didn't turn and the door didn't open.

Teddy's heart was in her throat. "You're teasing me, right?" Forgetting her nervousness about the narrow railing, she pushed her way over to him.

But she didn't even have to try the door handle once she saw the expression on his face.

"We're *locked out,*" she said, her voice high. "We're stuck up here. Ohmigod, Harriet is *never* going to believe this!"

FOUR

DIDN'T IT JUST FIGURE?

This was what happened when you did something nice for someone, Oscar thought with a mental roll of the eyes. *There you have it.*

He should have just left Teddy Mack to her own devices—in her own room, with her bloody laptop and her agonized moans—and then he wouldn't be perched up here like a stranded eaglet.

Those thoughts rushed into his mind, then out again just as quickly. At some point, he'd probably laugh about the situation.

Once they got down.

If they got down.

"Uh, let me check the other doors," Teddy said. Her voice was steady, if not stretched a little thin, and she seemed relatively calm.

"You go that way, I'll go this way," Oscar suggested.

But when they got to the opposite side, each met the other with a grim expression—and neither needed to speak the obvious.

"Okay, now what?" Teddy said. "Do you have your cell phone with you? Maybe we can call someone. My cousin lives in Wicks Hollow—"

"No."

"Damn."

They stood there in silence, and Oscar leaned against the glass enclosure that kept them from escape. If he had something to break the glass with, that could work—but he hadn't seen anything during his walk around the perimeter of the lantern room. The walkway was clear of any debris, tools, or anything useful.

"Any other ideas?" he said.

She rattled the locked door vigorously, but it hardly moved. The glass lantern was extremely well built to stand up to the worst of nature's elements. Nothing was going anywhere.

"What about breaking the glass?" she suggested. "Maybe with a shoe? Mine are too flimsy. What about yours? Or do you have a belt with a heavy buckle that might do it?"

Unfortunately, he was wearing soft canvas slip-ons, and no belt. "I don't have anything that would do it. But the binoculars might work."

"On television it always looks so easy to bust through a glass door or window," she said sadly, giving him the field glasses. "But it's not. I did some research on it for a book. It's pretty impossible, actually."

"I know."

"Of course you do."

He looked at the binoculars. "They're rimmed in rubber, and that glass is about three inches thick." He shook his head. "I doubt they'll work." He gathered up the strap, wrapping it around his wrist, and, pretending he was holding a baseball bat, swung.

Thunk.

"Not even a crack. Not even a *mark* on it," Teddy said, peering closely at the glass.

Oscar was still considering options. "And there's not enough room up here to even get a good running start, or even a strong enough kick—"

"No, that's too dangerous. It'd be so easy to fall right over the rail."

"I suppose we could try and shout—make some noise. Maybe someone out on the lake will hear us." But he knew that was a dubious option at best, considering the closest people were miles away.

"Worst-case scenario, if we can't figure out any other way to get down, we can wait till my cousin shows up."

"Oh," Oscar said, his heart lifting a little. "Is he coming over tonight?"

"No, not tonight. Tomorrow morning sometime. To drop off a few books for me to sign for a friend of his."

"Tomorrow morning." Oscar tried, and failed, to keep the dismay from his voice.

"Yeah. Around nine, he said." With a long, sighing sort of groan, she sank to the floor. Leaning against the glass wall behind her, she faced the sunset. Drawing her feet up near her body, she tucked edges of her sundress modestly over her knees. "Well, at least we have a nice view."

But the sun was going down—more quickly now, for it was halfway below the horizon. Oscar estimated another thirty minutes of light once it was gone, then they'd be stuck up here in the dark—with the temperature dropping. It could get quite cold, up this high and so near the lake. He glanced at Teddy, with her bare arms and the teeny-tiny straps that did nothing to protect her shoulders or upper chest.

Still. The view *was* incredible. The blazing sun had become a ball of orange, shooting out streaks of color as it disappeared.

Oscar walked around the perimeter again, hoping for a tool to magically appear, or an idea to manifest—waiting for *something* to present itself.

And the whole time, he kept telling himself: there was no way the wind had blown that door closed.

Finally, after rapping as hard as he could on the thick glass panes—and giving them a few solid, awkwardly placed kicks—in a last-ditch effort to find a weak or loose one, he sank down next to Teddy. There was only a sliver of sun left, and shadows had begun to arrange themselves on the ground below. His arm brushed hers, and even through his cotton shirt, he could feel the chill of her skin instead of the warmth he'd expected.

"You're already cold," he said, unbuttoning his shirt. "And it's going to get even chillier. The wind is picking up."

Oscar shrugged out of his shirt and pushed it at her, feeling the rush of the cool breeze over his bare skin. It felt good—*now*—but if they didn't get off here soon, it would soon be uncomfortable. But he was glad for the lowering light to hide the faint flush he felt warming his cheeks when Teddy turned to look at him. Her eyes were wide, and, for once, she seemed speechless.

She took the shirt, still gaping at him like she wasn't certain how to respond. Finally, she said, "You obviously don't spend all your time in a lab, Dr. London. It *is* doctor, isn't it?"

"Uh, yes."

She pulled the shirt around her shoulders, then stuck her arms in the sleeves. "Yes to doctor, or yes to not spending all your time in the lab?"

"Yes to the actual question, not the implied one," he replied, a little uncertain how he felt about this—this banter…

and the fact that she'd very obviously noticed that he did, in fact, not spend all of his time in a lab and did, in fact, do the occasional push-up and pull-up before his daily five-mile swim. Not that he was Arnold Schwarzenegger or anything like that…but he sure as hell wasn't flabby.

Teddy nodded, the quirk of a smile on her mouth. It was, Oscar realized suddenly—mainly because it was difficult not to, due to its proximity—a very nice, very kissable mouth. Not that he had any intention or interest in kissing it; he was still in love with Marcie, still mourning the loss of that relationship.

Still hoping for something to happen.

"What was that?" Teddy said. Every time she moved, he caught a fresh whiff of her scent—the fresh, peachy, flowery one he'd noticed this morning.

"What?"

"That sigh. It wasn't an 'I'm stuck up here, what am I going to do' sigh. It was…sad. In a different way than 'I'm stuck on the top of a lighthouse with a neurotic writer' sad. Our situation isn't sad, *per se*," she said. "It's just *really* inconvenient—I mean, at least you have an easy way to pee from up here if necessary. Not so me, so if I have to go, you're going to need to look the other way. And it's possibly dangerous being up here, but not really—unless we get a bad thunderstorm. But the situation's not really *sad*."

It took Oscar a moment to extrapolate what she was saying —did the woman ever string a sentence together with fewer than twenty words and too many clauses?—and then he wasn't certain how to respond. Had she really mentioned urinating over the side of the railing?

Finally, he ventured: "It was hopeless. Not sad so much as hopeless."

"Your sigh?"

"Right."

She shifted next to him, and her arm brushed against his. Pretty soon, he wouldn't be able to see her expression—nor she his—and that might be a good thing.

"I'm guessing you were thinking about your ex. What was her name?"

"Marcie. With an *i-e*." He suspected she'd appreciate that detail, being a writer and all. Unless she was the type of writer who couldn't spell.

"With an *i-e*." She sounded pleased with that information for some reason. "For a short time, I was Teddy with just an *i*. I never tried the *i-e* version, because I figured the singular *i* was enough to make my point. My parents had messed up my life by giving me a boy's name, so I rebelled by trying to make it more feminine. I even put a little heart for the dot of the *i* when I was in middle school—I'll bet your Marcie did that. Most girly-girls did, and I'm guessing your Marcie is a girly-girl."

Oscar blinked. He tried to keep up with her—he really did —but there was just so much there…and yet her speech was entertaining, in a strange popcorn-like way. "A girly-girl? What makes you say that?"

She made a noise that sounded like a giggle-scoff. "You seem like the type to go for a girly-girl, that's all. Not that there's anything wrong with that—I know lots of girly-girls, and some of them are my closest friends. I don't really consider myself one because…well, because I hardly ever do my hair or put on makeup because I rarely see people with my job. I live in yoga pants and tanks, with heavy sweaters in the winter. And I definitely don't get my nails done—can't type worth crap with long fingernails." She let her head tip back against the wall. He suspected the mention of typing made her think about her unfinished book.

However, Oscar had managed to pull one bit of information from that long thread. "Your real name is Teddy, not Theodora or anything like that?"

"It sure is. I considered changing my legal name to Theodora at one point, but in the end, it didn't really matter. I would always be Teddy. With a *y*." She rolled her head along the glass wall to look at him.

It was still light enough for him to see her smile, and to make out the shape of her eyes in the shadows, and the way her brows rose to emphasize her words.

"You don't need makeup or fingernails," he heard himself say. *What the hell?* "I mean, you look fine. I mean, pretty. More than just fine." *Oh, bloody hell. Shut up, Oscar.*

"Why, thank you," she said, her smile growing bigger. And warmer. He swallowed hard. "That's very sweet. So, since we're stuck up here for the foreseeable future, why don't you tell me about Marcie? Since you were giving such a hopeless sigh about her only a few minutes ago. I'm guessing a hopeless sigh means you're still in love with her and harboring the thought that something might actually happen so she doesn't get married, and instead comes running back to you."

Uh. Wow.

Oscar blinked again, but before he could figure out how to respond, she was talking again, "I'm a storyteller, Dr. London —I'm always filling in the details of backstory and subtext. Yours is pretty obvious, though."

"Right." Good Lord, was he really going to be stuck up here all night with her?

At least the sky was cloudless. If a lightning storm threatened, they'd be cooked geese.

But even with clear skies, he didn't want to stay up here. They needed to figure out a way down. And he still didn't understand how that door had blown closed—and gotten stuck. It just didn't make any sense.

He drew in a breath to say so, but then, to his shock, he began to talk. About Marcie.

"She's a fourth-grade teacher back in a little town near Princeton," he said, lifting the field glasses as he spoke. There was a white forty-footer out there, with green and blue accents. It was trundling along kind of slowly. Maybe they could get the attention of whoever was on it. He pulled to his feet. "Let's try and wave at that boat—it looks like it's stopping out there."

Teddy rose and began to wave her arms, shouting. Unfortunately, she was bellowing into the wind coming off the lake, and it just tossed the noise back onto them. Oscar kept the glasses trained on the boat, which had stopped and seemed to have thrown down an anchor.

"How far away do you think they are? Can you see anyone on it?" Teddy asked, apparently realizing that shouting wasn't going to help.

"No more than a half-mile. If they look over here, they might see us. Kind of late to be fishing, though…"

"Well, why wouldn't they look over here? It's a lighthouse! Who doesn't want to look at a lighthouse?"

"But even if they see us, they'll probably just think we're waving to them." He was just about to lower the glasses when something caught his attention. "There are two people on the deck… What's that? They're—"

"What? Did they see us?"

"No," he replied, still watching the activity on the boat. "Looks like they're tossing something overboard."

"What?" Teddy's shriek was a little too close to his ear. "What is it? Ohmigod, I bet it's a *body*!"

Before he could react, she was grabbing at the binoculars.

He didn't have the chance to disengage from the neck strap before she was holding them up to her face. In an effort to avoid being strangled, he moved closer. This placed her back against him, and for a minute he was distracted from whatever was going on out on the lake. Her hair smelled really good, and the back of her calf brushed against his. It was warm and smooth, and made the hairs on his leg prickle with awareness.

"It's not a body," he said, and snatched back the binoculars in a moment of self-defense—against strangulation, her proximity, and her crazy writer ideas. "It wasn't big enough to be a body."

"Well, how big was it? Maybe the body was cut up into pieces and they're dropping parts of it all over—"

"It's probably just a bundle of garbage," he said. "And, look, now they're going away. Driving off. And it doesn't look like they saw us."

"Damn." She gazed out over the lake, squinting at the sinking sun as it still gave off some bold rays. "Who the hell would dump garbage in the lake like that? We ought to report them. Did you get the name of the boat or anything?"

"No." He sank back down onto the floor. "We could report them, I suppose, but they might have just been throwing—I dunno—a fishing net in the water?"

"Did it look like a fishing net to you?"

"No." It had looked like a bundle wrapped in black plastic; the covering shone a little in the light. It wasn't big enough to be a body, he didn't think—and why was he even entertaining such a thought? People didn't do stuff like that except in movies or books.

Teddy sighed and sat next to him. "Well, if we ever get off this thing, we can report them. Now, where were we? Oh, right. Marcie. A fourth-grade teacher. Does she have a specialty?"

Relieved to have a different topic—even if it was Marcie—he continued.

"She specializes in math, but teaches cross-curriculum. She and my sister knew each other in college—Dina is six years younger than me—and they were in the same sorority. That's how we met—she came home for Christmas one year with Dina. I'd been out of school for several years, and just finishing my doctorate, and, well—we fell for each other.

"We dated for three years, got engaged on our third anniversary, and set the wedding date for a year ago May. And then…I don't know…things started to change. We began to argue more, and had less time to see each other. There was a new principal at her school, and he had her working on a new curriculum for the math department, and…" He shrugged. "Between my work and hers, and the wedding plans…"

"And the extra work for the curriculum?" Teddy said dryly. "Let me guess—something happened with her and the principal."

She felt him tense. "I don't…think so," he replied. "I wondered…but I don't think so. Even so, we began growing apart, and—well, she's six years younger than me, and had just graduated college when we got engaged. She finally told me she wasn't ready to get married. So…we tried to get through that. And…it just didn't work out. I was ready to get married and start a family, and she wasn't."

"Except…she is now. Barely a year later." Teddy kept her voice low and empty of the venom she felt on his behalf, but the roughness in Oscar's voice told her she wasn't saying anything he hadn't thought or felt.

"Yeah. So…" He shrugged. "The guy she's marrying—"

"It's not the principal is it?" she demanded, unable to contain her outrage.

"No, thank goodness. He—Trevor—is just a guy she met —maybe eight or nine months ago. Father of a student, I think."

"How do you know all this? You don't keep in touch with her, do you?" she asked.

"No. *Definitely* not. But Dina keeps me in the loop. She—"

"All right, wait. Can we stop there for a second?" Teddy said. "How did you get a great name like Oscar London, but your sister ended up with a very boring name about being stuck cooking?"

"Stuck cooking?"

"You know—someone's in the kitchen with Dinah," she sang, "someone's in the kitchen I knooo-ohhh-ohhh-owww—"

"Okay, okay," he said, cutting her off with a chuckle. "I got it. Her name is actually Engadine."

Teddy burst out laughing. "Oh my, that is *the best*! Engadine. Engadine London. I'm *totally* using that in a book someday. So…Oscar and Engadine."

"Yes, that's us."

"Who *were* your parents?" she said in the same tone as Sally Albright when she asked Harry Burns about his wife named Helen, who was a lawyer.

"Coming from a woman named Teddy," he said, his voice shaking with laughter, "I don't know how you can point fingers."

"I'm not pointing fingers," she said. "I'm *admiring*. I told you, I love good names. But seriously—are your parents British or something?"

"My father is. And my mother was a mechanical engineer from Boston. They met in Germany, both working for an auto supplier based there. I lived my first six years between Germany and the U.K., then we came to the U.S."

"Ah, that explains a lot." Teddy's giggles had calmed, and she closed her eyes. Even with Oscar's shirt, she was getting chilly. She couldn't imagine how cold he was getting, bare-chested and all. How chivalrous it had been of him to have offered her his shirt—and a peek of what was beneath it. A little pale, but very solid and taut.

"I'm not going to ask what you mean by that," Oscar said after a moment of silence. His voice was dry, and he, too, let his head bump gently back against the glass wall.

Then he sighed again.

But this time, it wasn't a hopeless one.

It was just a sigh.

And she smiled a little.

Oscar blinked drowsily.

What the—?

It took him a moment to realize where he was—still on the top of the damned lighthouse—with Teddy slumped next to him, her head on his shoulder and her warm body tucked next to him. Somehow, his arm had come to slide around her waist and a hand settled at her hip. He jerked it away, but didn't have the heart to move and awaken her.

Did I really fall asleep?

He must have dozed or something, and his companion as well, for the night was very dark. And still. It had gotten much cooler. Maybe it was the chill that had awakened him.

The sky was as black as it got when there was a swath of stars glittering above. There was a quarter moon, and it hung high and distant in the sky, offering sketchy light that rippled over Lake Michigan below. Based on that, he guessed it was well after midnight, but not yet close to dawn.

He thought about moving, but he was comfortable, and Teddy was warm and soft next to him. Her head with its sagging, soft bundle of hair was just beneath his shoulder, and whatever shampoo she used had been teasing him all night with its smell, mingling with that of female, and now tinged with lake and the chill air.

He smiled in the dark. An interesting woman, to say the least. Practical, unruffled—except when it came to her unfinished book—and amusing, with the way her thoughts and words bounced around. Not to mention soft and pretty.

She hadn't raged or cried or stomped around when they realized they were stuck up here. No accusations or recriminations. She'd just taken it in stride—maybe even better than he had done, he realized with a grimace.

Of course, he thought as his lips quirked into a smile, she probably didn't mind, as this was a foolproof excuse for not working on her book. He gave a short laugh, thinking he might tease her about manufacturing the whole thing—at least when it was all over and they were down from here—when suddenly he felt the air change.

All at once, it was *icy* cold. Not just chilly from the lake wind, but like bloody winter in Vermont—it was a cold like he'd never experienced. A sharp, unnatural cold.

This shocking, startling chill front had come from nowhere. The wind wasn't blowing...the frigidity was just *there*. As if a cube of dry ice had been dropped on him.

As he looked around for some sort of explanation, he saw it.

What the hell?

A phosphorous-like substance, with the consistency of smoke or a cloud, hovered there on the gallery to his left, right next to the door from which he and Teddy had come out. It was bluish-green, glowing in the darkness…curling and billowing and moving…

Oscar fought to keep his breathing steady, and his thoughts from scattering. *Some sort of alga,* he told himself. *Or moss. Growing on the side of the lantern—glows in the dark, so we didn't see it before. Or some sort of plant or moss blown up from the lake or from a tree…like a glow-in-the-dark sagebrush…*

He stared at it, his nose feeling as if it were iced over, his fingers like tiny shards of icicles, goosebumps all over his bare torso—and then Teddy bolted awake.

"So cold. It's so— What is *that*?"

But Oscar was already on his feet as the cloud—or moss or whatever it was—suddenly darted away, hovering for a moment above them. Then it swept *over* the railing and disintegrated as it tumbled down into the darkness.

"What was that?" Teddy cried, stumbling as she dragged herself upright. Oscar automatically reached out to grab her so she didn't accidentally launch herself over the railing. "That— that glowing cloud thing?"

"I don't know," he managed to say. He noticed the air temperature had suddenly gone back to normal. "Some sort of —alga or somethin—"

All at once, a horrible, night-shattering cry split the silence. Terrifying and shrill, it was as if someone was in agony.

Her eyes popped wide, Teddy grabbed Oscar's arm as the scream reverberated in his ears.

Then it was gone, just as quickly as it had come.

Everything was silent except for Teddy's panting breathing and his own heart pounding in his ears.

"What was *that*?" she said, grabbing his arm. "What in the *hell*?"

"I—I don't know," he said, mostly managing to keep his voice steady.

But *holy hell*. It was the same sound he'd heard last night—the same tortured, terrified scream. "I think it must have been an animal in heat or—or something like that," he said, ignoring the fact that it hadn't come from down below, but from *right up here.*

"Whatever it was, it was in pain," she said, still gripping him tightly. "Good grief. Did I really fall asleep?"

"We both did," he replied. "I—" He stopped speaking and gently pushed her away as he fairly leaped over to the glass door.

It glowed slightly from the residue of whatever had been *floating* there, which was how he could see that *the door was ajar.*

Wordlessly, he pulled on the handle and the door opened. Teddy gaped at him, her eyes wide and gleaming in the moonlight, but for once, she said nothing.

Instead, she walked through the door, and he followed her.

Neither of them spoke all the way down the one hundred and sixty-eight steps to the bottom.

FIVE

TEDDY WOKE the next morning with an uneasy feeling in her belly.

It took her a few minutes, lying there in the patchwork-quilt-draped bed, staring up at the plain white ceiling, to realize what it was.

The nauseating feeling was a roiling mixture of nervousness and guilt, mixed with a high level of creep factor related to whatever had happened on top of the lighthouse last night. The nervousness and guilt were, of course, related to the fact that she'd made no progress on her book. But the creep factor—

She put it out of her mind.

"I can't think about that right now," she told herself. Because if she did, she'd have a nervous breakdown.

It was after seven thirty—a reasonable time for a writer on deadline to get her butt up and to work (whereas a writer who wasn't on deadline might sleep until nine, and a writer who'd just finished her book might sleep until noon), so, feeling determined, she rolled out of bed.

Teddy showered in the clean, serviceable, but aged bathroom allotted to her suite, and decided on yoga pants and a tank top with a hoodie over it, as it was a little chilly yet this morning. Very comfortable, very get-down-to-work, she told herself.

She bundled up her damp hair with a bunch of clips and pins at the back of her head, uncaring how it looked and that a few strands straggled over her neck. She brushed her teeth (she couldn't write unless she'd done so, and couldn't understand people who claimed they immediately opened their laptop to start work, first thing in the morning, while still in bed), and padded out through the curve-topped door into the shared living space to get a cup of coffee.

Teddy was relieved when she heard the sound of the shower from down the hall where, presumably, Oscar's room was. She didn't want to see him this morning.

A different kind of walk of shame, I guess, she thought with a pained grin as she poured coffee into the filter of an ancient coffee maker.

While it hissed and burbled and went about exuding a delicious scent, she looked out the kitchen window. This side of the keeper's house faced the woods that contained the little hot spring that Dr. London (for some reason, it tickled her to think of him by his title) was using as an escape from his real life. She caught a flash of russet—a deer—as it foraged in the thick greenery, and a red hawk was sitting in a tree, watching for its own opportunity for breakfast.

At last the coffee was done, and Teddy poured a full mug, added a glop of milk (wishing for one of those mini-frothers; she should ask Harriet to send her one) and some stevia, then quickly slipped out of the kitchen and back to her suite. Just as she was closing the door separating the two spaces, she heard the bathroom door open down the hall.

Whew.

When she got back to her room, she found a text from Declan, apologizing that he wasn't going to be by this morning as planned, because he'd forgotten his sixteen-year-old daughter had a doctor appointment in Grand Rapids.

LMK when is a good time to come by. Don't want to mess up your work, he added in a closing text.

All right, then. Good. No distractions this morning.

She could get right to work, and work all the way until lunch without having to stop.

Teddy sat down at her laptop, setting the mug of coffee next to it. Then she got up and found a pillow for the chair—it was too low without one. She settled that into place and sat down.

Then she got up and made her bed. *Can't work with a messy bed.*

Then she sat back down, opened up the laptop, and was confronted by the same blank white screen she'd faced yesterday.

SIX

TEDDY POISED her fingers over the keyboard and stared at the screen.

No words came.

Then she closed her eyes, imagining the scene, and settled her fingers on the keys.

No words came.

She opened her eyes and sighed, took a drink of coffee, then set the mug down and closed her eyes again.

It'll come.

She opened her eyes and stared at the blank white screen.

Oscar was absolutely not going to think about what happened on the top of the lighthouse last night.

He took a shower—steaming hot—and carefully kept his mind blank during the whole thing by picturing the table of elements and reciting each one, in order, with its chemical symbol.

As he toweled off and dressed, he hoped he wouldn't run

into Teddy in the kitchen. She hadn't said anything last night once they left the top of the lighthouse, but knowing her, that meant she'd saved up every thought, comment, exclamation, and question overnight and would soon be bludgeoning him with them.

All he wanted to do was bury himself in his work, and now he had *two* things from which he needed to distract himself: Marcie's wedding and that—whatever it had been— on the top of the lighthouse.

The word "ghost" teased the back of his mind, but he thrust it away with the same alacrity he'd have done to the lethal *Zaire ebolavirus*.

Though when he came out to the living room he smelled fresh coffee, Teddy wasn't there. Evidence indicated she'd made the brew (enough for both of them, it appeared) but retreated to her wing of the cottage.

Good. That meant he could work in peace.

And he did. After plugging in his earbuds and today queueing up Coldplay and Kings of Leon, he set to work preparing a few slides of samples from the hot spring.

Once he had a plate ready, he placed it on the microscope dash. He turned on the lamps, made a few adjustments— magnification, light—and took a look.

Normal water molecular structure. Tardigrades, ostracods, phages, and a variety of other, harmless microbial specimens. Wait.

"Hm." Oscar frowned, squinting a little more. What the hell was that? He dialed back on the magnification to see the full image. A little jump of interest spiked inside him. *Never seen anything like that before.* He adjusted the magnification and looked closer.

Instead of the soft, organic shapes he was used to seeing, Oscar was examining something that appeared crystalline and spiky. Shiny and silvery, even under the microscope. That little jump of interest turned into something more like a leap, and he moved the slide around to see if there were other examples of this unfamiliar microbe. There were…randomly, but more than one example. He quickly pulled out samples from a different Cubitainer—maybe that first one had somehow been contaminated.

But no. There they were, the unrecognizable crystals, noticeable only at one hundred magnification. His spike of interest had blown into full-fledged curiosity.

Was it possible? Was there something unique enough about the hot spring to make this trip actually worth something? Oscar had never seen anything like that spiky crystal organism before. It didn't look like anything else.

Impossible. But…

"I should go get another sample," he said. Just to make sure what he was looking at was uncontaminated.

He'd get it himself this time. He'd climb into the pool, gather three samples himself, making sure it was done correctly…and then he'd take another look.

"Another sample of what?"

He turned, jolted out of his music and thoughts.

Teddy was there. She must have walked into the kitchen without him even noticing. She looked determined, for her hair was pulled back into a messy knot at the back of her head and she carried a slim silver laptop that looked as if it weighed hardly more than a magazine. In the other hand was a steaming mug of coffee.

Oscar pulled out his earbud, leaving Chris Martin to mutedly sing into the room. "How's your writing going?" he asked.

She made a face. "I don't want to talk about it. What are you getting another sample of?"

"The hot springs. There's a unique crystal sort of microbe—"

"Great. I'll come with you." She put down the laptop as if it were a hot potato. "Wait till I change."

Teddy knew she should stay at the cottage, sit her butt in a chair, and focus on the laptop.

What better time to work than when her housemate was away from the place, and no longer sucking up all her air?

But here she was, traipsing through the woods with Oscar —who was making no effort to hide his grumpiness. Not that he had any real right to be grumpy. *He* was the one who'd taken over her place and was distracting *her*.

People didn't understand how writers (or any artist, she supposed) could be distracted simply by another person's presence. Even if they weren't interacting with them. The truth was that they sucked up all the air just *being* there.

Teddy sighed. If only there was a quick fix for her writer's block. If only she could take something, or make a wish or something—

"Here we are," Oscar said unnecessarily. He set down his heavy pack and began to take off his hiking boots.

She sat on a large boulder and began to pull off her walking shoes. They weren't as heavy-duty as his boots, but they protected her feet. "Too bad that's not a fountain of youth or wishing well," she said, looking at the coiling steam rising from the softly bubbling pool. "Something that granted your heart's desire when you threw in a coin, or jumped in or drank it or something."

Oscar looked at her as if she'd sprouted a third ear. "What?"

"I'm just saying…don't you think that maybe the Native Americans—I think they were Chippewas around here— might have considered a place like this special, or even sacred and holy, with it being the only hot spring in the whole region? Probably the only one they'd ever seen. I mean, think about it—in the dead of winter, they're trudging through here, crossing the huge Lake Michigan on all that ice—they'd have had no idea how big the lake was to begin with—and suddenly they see steam rising from the middle of a snowbank. And there's this pool of hot water—in the middle of winter! Don't you think that'd give them something to wonder about? Like, there was some sort of mysterious or supernatural element to it?"

He was still looking at her oddly. "Sure." Then he glanced at the pool. "Maybe."

She grinned at him. "See, you *do* have an imagination."

"I never said I didn't." Now he sounded grumpy again.

"Right." Teddy walked over and slipped her fingers into the water. It was *hot*. And it would feel so good on her skin. "I wish for whatever energy is in this pool that it helps me attain my heart's desire," she said, trailing her fingers through the churning pool.

"Your heart's desire? What are you talking about?"

She shrugged, feeling a little foolish. After all, he was a fact-based *scientist* who couldn't even run with her plot idea about random bad stuff. "I don't know. What if it *is* a sacred or special or holy place, and this pool *is* special somehow? I figure I'm going to increase the chance of getting what I want by—"

"By wishing for your heart's desire over a hot spring?" He was looking at her as if she'd grown that third ear again. "You're an interesting woman, Teddy Mack."

"But," she said, "what if you only *think* you know your heart's desire? Like, mine right now is to figure out how to finish this damn book. That's all I want. But what if deep down inside, my heart's desire is really to find another career? Or to write something different? Then I wouldn't finish the book, my career would be over—or at least it would change—and then I'd move on. And that would be my heart's desire—even if I didn't actually articulate it."

He shook his head. "I'm pretty sure most people know what they really want."

"So what's your heart's desire? What do you really want?" She gave him a cheeky grin, then it faded. "Oh. You want Marcie back."

He didn't respond. But he didn't need to; sadness was written all over his face.

Suddenly sober and feeling bad for bringing it up, Teddy pulled off her sundress, under which was her bright blue one-piece bathing suit, and climbed over the rocks to slide into the pool.

"Ohhh," she groaned as she settled into the heat of the water. It felt good, but it was *hot*. She swam over to where the little trickle of a waterfall poured into the pool and let the cool spill over her. "Ohhh…my…God…"

When she opened her eyes, her hair slicked back from her face, she saw that Oscar had zipped off the bottoms of his cargo pants, turning them into shorts, and taken off his shirt. And…yes indeed, her memory from last night was dead on: he looked pretty damned good for a nerdy scientist who was mourning the loss of his fiancée.

Good enough that Teddy took her time checking him out (now that it was daylight) when he wasn't looking. He wasn't bulky or hugely muscular, but wiry and toned and well proportioned. Though he had a farmer's tan, his shoulders and upper arms were covered with freckles that gave him a lightly bronzed appearance along the top. His calves were muscular, and he didn't have knobby knees, which was a major bonus in her book.

When he came over to the pool, Teddy looked away, suddenly acutely aware of the fact that not only were they alone here and now, but they were sleeping under the same roof. And they'd been trapped up on the lighthouse together, with her slumped against his warm, solid torso last night…

All of a sudden, the pool seemed even hotter, and she smoothed a hand over her wet hair and moved under the cooler waterfall again.

Get a grip, Teddy. You have a book to focus on.

But getting laid might lube things up…so to speak.

As if! I don't even know the guy.

You could get to know him.

"Pretty warm, huh?" Oscar said as she came out from under the waterfall. He eased into the pool with his own sigh of pleasure, leaving his tools and gear untouched on a nearby rock. "Your face is really flushed."

I'll bet it is. "So is yours."

"Even though it's pretty warm already, it feels good in the water." He leaned against the side of the pool, and the water surged and bubbled against the rocky rim. The waterfall splashed down between them, sending little sprays of cool droplets against her skin.

"So you really don't like my RBS idea?" Teddy asked, pulling her attention from his freckled shoulders and the patch of blond-red hair on his chest. It was either that, or talk about what had happened up on top of the lighthouse last night, and *that* she wasn't ready for.

"No."

She sighed and sank deeper into the water, despite the heat. Rivulets of sweat and water ran down her cheeks and throat. But maybe if it was a sacred, special pool, it would take a while to do its work. So she had to soak in it for a bit. "Well, I've got to get my hero out of a difficult situation regardless."

"That's right. He's got to save the world." Oscar eased lower in the water too. His hair, now damp from the humidity, had begun to curl up into tiny, dark waves around his temples and neck. "You know what always gets me about books and movies like that is how complicated they get. Why does villainy have to be so complicated? Why can't it be a simpler situation than a plot to infect the entire city of New York with a virus—which is ridiculous anyway—or…or mechanized robots that are going to pilot a bunch of planes and crash them into the ocean with important people on them?"

Teddy sat up, and the water surged away from her. "Hey, that's not a bad idea. Mechanized pilots…they could be flying Air Force One, maybe."

"No, no, no," he said, waving his hand and sending droplets of water flying. "Too complicated. Couldn't you just write a computer hacker who sends out a false news report—sort of like *War of the Worlds*, but done purposely—that causes the stock market to crash or even the Internet to go down because of too much traffic and not enough bandwidth? Then he could take over communication and cause all sorts of chaos."

She stared at him. "*Yes.* I like it. Hmm. That might work. Let me think on that…" She settled back and stared at the waterfall, working through the details.

"So you said your hero's caught? Well, what about a trapdoor? Or what about a skylight? Put in a trapdoor or a skylight and he somehow—"

"*Yes!*" Teddy shouted, erupting from the pool with a violent splash. Her brain exploded with ideas and images and *answers*. "That's it! That's it! That's perfect!" Exhilaration and relief burst over her, and she was filled with joy. *That was it.*

Before she realized what she was doing, she surged toward Oscar and threw herself into his arms. She hugged him, then pulled back and smacked a kiss onto his warm, damp lips. "Thank you! You're amazing! You're—"

He pulled her back to him and kissed her again…this time much more thoroughly. His lips were warm and full and he tasted faintly of salt and sulfur. His torso was warm and wet against hers. And firm. When she pulled away, she saw droplets of water clinging to his eyelashes and that his pupils had widened.

But her brain…it was on fire. It was furious—unleashed, undammed, and finally, after *months*, the ideas were flowing and spilling free. The energy pulsed through her like the roar of pool churning around her.

She had to go.

She had to *write*.

SEVEN

ONE MINUTE, Oscar was easing into a long, deep, wholly unexpected and *hot* kiss…and the next, he was sitting in the pool alone. The water surged and splashed even more violently than before now that she'd sloshed out of it.

"Thanks again!" Teddy called as she shoved her feet into her shoes. She looked as if she'd just been awarded a million dollars: her eyes were bright, droplets of water sprayed from her hair, and her movements were quick and energetic. "You're absolutely *brilliant*, Dr. London! I'm going to dedicate this book to you!"

And with that, she charged off into the bushes in the direction of the lighthouse.

What did I say?

Oscar stared after her, figuring he owed himself at least a good look at her rear end. Which, as it happened, was barely covered by the blue swimsuit. And it was, as he'd noted previously, quite a fine rear end.

He let out a long breath and slid under the water to his shoulders. That had been an unexpected but extremely pleasant moment, a fact that his long-neglected hormones were still reminding him. He wasn't certain what he'd done or said to induce such a reaction from her, but he wasn't complaining.

In fact, it took him a few minutes to put his scattered brains back together.

But now that the writer and her distracting conversation were gone, Oscar had the opportunity to get back to work uninterrupted. He heaved out of the pool and got his equipment, then, methodical as always, went to work.

Ninety minutes later, he returned to the cottage with new samples. The heat and humidity of midday had nearly dried his clothes, and he was hungry for lunch.

He wondered if Teddy had, by chance, made anything to eat. Maybe she'd left something for him to nibble on. It would be the polite thing to do.

After all, he *was* brilliant and had, apparently, somehow, helped her. He grinned to himself.

But when he got inside, the place was quiet and the kitchen empty of even a crumb. The lack of dirty dishes in the drainer indicated she hadn't eaten and then run, either.

Oscar set his samples on the table and unslung his pack, then tiptoed to the connecting door and eased it open.

Teddy's bedroom door was closed and silence hung over the cottage.

He waited a minute, but when he heard nothing else— including the agonized groans from yesterday—he decided it was best to retreat.

He was just about to walk back through the connecting door when he heard a thump, like someone smacking a fist onto a table.

He tensed, but then heard, "Brilliant! My God, I am *brilliant!*" from behind the bedroom door. After that, silence reigned once more.

Oscar scratched the back of his neck, chuckled to himself, then went to the kitchen for lunch. At least now he could work uninterrupted. He ate, and within forty minutes had another fresh, uncontaminated sample on his slides.

"It's the same thing," he muttered. They were there—those microscopic, spiky crystalline shapes that had no business being in the hot springs. They didn't even resemble anything from nature. A niggle of excitement tickled his brain, and he looked again, admiring how beautiful the shapes were. Like spiky snowflakes, all shades of blue and gray.

It didn't mean the hot springs had magical powers. That would be ridiculous.

But what if they *did?*

No way. He'd been hanging around that crazy writer for too long; she was starting to get into his scientific head.

Oscar tried another sample on another slide. And took a different sample from one of the three Cubitainers he'd filled up himself. He continued to find the same results.

He pulled out his laptop, connected it to the Wi-Fi hub he'd brought, and began sending off images of what he'd found to friends and colleagues. He did some more research, looked up a few unrelated things, and then checked his email. All the while, Oscar felt a strange sort of comfort knowing that Teddy was just beyond the curve-topped door, doing her own work…and not bothering him.

Then he picked up his computer tablet and began to read an e-book by a new-to-him author named T.J. Mack.

And the next thing he knew, he had to turn on a lamp—and he was hungry again. Oscar looked at the time on his computer. Eight thirty?

In the evening?

Where had the time gone?

And where was Teddy? He eyed the connecting door. He'd been engrossed in the book, but surely he would have heard her if she came out looking for food. Maybe she was sleeping by now.

Oscar considered, but he didn't hesitate for long. He rose and again went to the connecting door. There was silence. This time, he walked all the way across the small vestibule to her bedroom door, and carefully opened it a crack. But he didn't even need to look inside, for he heard the busy clicking of a keyboard. Damn, she typed *fast*.

"You *bastard!*" she cried. At first he thought she was talking to him, but then she added, "I've got you right where I want you." Then she actually gave a maniacal chuckle, and the keyboard clacked faster.

Fighting a grin, he peered inside and saw that she was sitting at the desk, clattering away on the laptop. He wasn't certain whether to bother her, but he did take a minute to admire the way her clipped-up hair exposed the back of her neck. All at once, he had the urge to plant a kiss…right there. At the base of her slender neck.

And then he remembered the handful of warm, soft, curvy woman who'd thrown herself at him earlier today. And the sweet-peach-scented one who'd curled up next to him on the lighthouse last night and gushed over his name and his sister's.

He swallowed hard.

He had no business thinking about Teddy that way when he was in love with another woman.

And of course he was still in love with Marcie.

Oscar pulled back sharply from Teddy's bedroom door. He'd just realized he'd spent the last eight hours engrossed in his work—and then Teddy Mack's book—and he hadn't thought of Marcie once all day.

He hadn't even picked up his phone to check for a text from Dina, nor, when he'd been sending emails to his colleagues, had he considered skimming through Facebook to see…well, to see if anything had happened. After all, last night was the bachelorette party.

But it didn't matter. So what if he'd been able to put Marcie out of his mind for a few hours? Nothing had changed.

Oscar looked back at Teddy, then closed the door. *She'd* found her heart's desire today, whether the damned hot spring was sacred or special—or not.

Definitely not.

There was no such thing as magic—or ghosts.

One other thing he was grateful for: Teddy had been so engrossed in the idea of a magical wishing-well hot spring and her RBS idea that she hadn't brought up the strangeness from last night.

Thank heaven for small favors.

The next morning, Oscar boiled water for tea because it made him think of his paternal grandmother, who always said, "There's nothing can't be helped by a soothing cuppa."

He hadn't slept well at all, because, well, *hell*—he'd been half expecting to hear that horrible, terrified nocturnal cry. After all, it had occurred both nights he'd been here—one of them while he was on the top of the lighthouse.

The fact that he hadn't heard the awful scream should have been a relief. But instead, it made him want to know "why not?" on this third night—not to mention from where it had come the previous nights. And so he'd tossed and turned, waiting to be jolted from the slumber he couldn't attain—and, once he'd finally fallen asleep, he realized he'd dozed later into the morning than he'd meant to.

Animals in heat, he reminded himself. *Or maybe a peacock.*

This new idea popped into his head as he stared out the kitchen window sipping from his mug.

He liked it.

It wasn't unheard of for people to have peacock farms—and he knew the birds' cries were bloodcurdling. That thought, along with the strong cup of Tetley (his grandmother's favorite), did soothe him. He'd do a little checking to see whether there were any people who owned peacocks around here. Or maybe Wicks Hollow boasted a small zoo.

He washed out his teacup and noted that, once again, there was no evidence Teddy had been in the kitchen. Hmm. Had she really not eaten since erupting from the steaming pool yesterday?

It wasn't any of his business.

But during his shower, he considered the situation. *Let sleeping dogs—or busy writers—lie,* he told himself as he scrubbed his hair with the floral shampoo that had been stocked in the bathroom. He should buy something else so he didn't walk around smelling like a jasmine blossom. Not that anyone was going to get close enough to smell his hair anyway.

Except Teddy.

The thought, which popped into his mind with startling clarity—and was both visual and shockingly sensual—was terrifying and intriguing, and the distraction caused him to nick the corner of his jaw while shaving. Stanching the blood, which pooled and ran down into the shower drain like he'd murdered someone, Oscar managed to finish the rest of his shower without inflicting any other damage. But after vigorously brushing his teeth and dressing in cargo shorts and a soft blue cambric shirt, he found himself walking toward the connecting door to the lighthouse.

Let sleeping dogs lie, he told himself firmly. His hand reached for the knob anyway, and he turned it and walked through before he could stop himself. Everything was quiet and calm as he crossed the small vestibule.

He paused at Teddy's door and heard the mad clicking of her typing. Well, she was still alive.

He knocked.

No answer. More click-clattering.

He knocked again, a little louder.

No answer. Incessant clicking, some clattering. A muttered curse.

He opened the door and peered in. "Teddy?"

No answer. A pause in the clicking, then a louder curse—followed by an emphatic thump when she slammed her hand onto the table and growled at the computer.

Oscar hesitated again, but damn, as far as he knew, she hadn't been out of the room for more than twenty hours. Surely she needed to eat. Or…something. So he went in and said her name again, rather loudly and near her ear—which wasn't covered by headphones this time.

She jolted and shrieked, spinning in her chair as she'd done the first time he startled her. "Oh my God, you scared the hell out of me. *Again.* Don't sneak up on me like that!"

"Sorry. I thought you might be hungry. You haven't eaten since yesterday."

Teddy blinked as if trying to assimilate the meaning of his words. After a moment, she said, "I had a few granola bars and a couple of apples."

Oscar looked at the discarded wrappings on the floor. And two brown cores. Some empty water bottles. "Oh. Good. Well, I won't bother you, then."

"Okay. Thanks." She turned back to her computer and was clacking away before he even shut the door.

Well, *hell.*

Yesterday he'd been "brilliant" enough to warrant an enthusiastic hug and a sexy kiss…and now he was nothing more than a pesky gnat, buzzing around her head.

Oscar went back out to the dining/living room where all his equipment was spread out. He ignored it and went into the kitchen to scrounge for something to eat in the well-stocked refrigerator.

Apples and a couple granola bars? He shook his head and made an extra omelet. He had no idea if Teddy had any food issues, but unless she was vegan—and of course she wasn't, because she'd had chicken the other night; and clearly greenery didn't bother her, as she'd prepared the salad—the tomato and spinach dish should give her a little more boost than some honey-soaked oats.

When Oscar brought it into her makeshift office, he merely slid it onto the table next to her and left the room. The delicious smell would eventually penetrate her fog and she'd eat when she was ready.

At least, that was how it happened for him when he was in the throes of work.

Oscar busied himself cleaning up the kitchen and then took another look at his temporary lab. Maybe there was another place he could get a water sample, and compare it to the hot spring. The spiky, snowflake-like crystals could just be a unique microbe in the soil here. He hiked around the mainland area until he found a small creek that ran near the steaming pool. After carefully collecting four samples to test, he brought them back to the cottage. He had no idea why he was compelled to pick a small bouquet of wildflowers on the way, but he stuck them in the empty wine bottle from their first night and placed it on the kitchen table.

For dinner later, he made Teddy a tuna sandwich and added a handful of raw carrots, along with the bouquet-spiked wine bottle, to her tray. He smugly noticed the omelet plate was empty when he delivered them. She grunted, glanced at him with glassy eyes, and said, "Getting closer," and went back to clicking. Without even a thank you.

That night, Oscar closed his window, stuffed in earplugs, and set up his laptop to play white noise all night in an effort to make sure he wouldn't be able to hear the scream if it did occur. As a result, he slept fairly well, but his dreams were a wild mixture of Teddy Mack lecturing him about not getting his hair wet in the hot spring—what on earth was that about?—and then Teddy, Dina, and *Marcie* sitting in the hot spring, drinking cocktails with fancy pink umbrellas…while he dug a hole.

For what, the dream didn't deign to tell him.

Probably his grave after he went crazy, cohabiting with a neurotic writer.

The next morning, he did find a soggy tea bag that indicated Teddy had somehow found her way to the kitchen, along with an ajar cabinet door and an empty box that had once held granola bars. He made peanut butter toast and drizzled it with honey, then filled a small dish with blueberries. Wordlessly, he delivered them to her, then settled down with his computer and lab and, after putting on his reading glasses, began to work.

Later that evening, he grilled some chicken (his cooking repertoire was very limited). He made a salad and brought a portion of both to Teddy, who actually managed to focus her eyes enough to thank him this time.

Oscar settled on the covered porch, in the same chair he'd

used the first night he and Teddy ate together (the only night, as it happened), and worked his way through the salad and grilled chicken. He felt strangely alone—though that was something he usually preferred. That preference was one thing that had caused some tension between him and Marcie.

Her complaints had begun after they were engaged—that Oscar didn't spend enough time with her; that he was always in the lab or had his nose buried in a journal or the computer. He didn't think anything had changed since they got engaged, for he'd always been someone who preferred silence to chatter, and solitude to houses bursting at the seams with noise, people, and things.

But tonight, as he watched the sun edge closer to the distant horizon, Oscar almost wished that Teddy was sitting in the chair next to him, as she'd done three nights ago.

He twisted the top off his B-Cubed IPA (apparently it was from a local brewery) and was just lifting the bottle to drink when he heard the sound of a vehicle. Curious, he stepped off the porch and walked around to the small gravel parking area on the southeast side of the lighthouse.

It was a large capped pickup that seemed to be filled with tools—including several long pieces of some kind of metal. Iron, maybe.

A well-built man with dark auburn hair climbed out. He was about Oscar's age, and was wearing battered shorts and a close-fitting t-shirt that appeared to have seen better days. He was holding a paper bag that seemed to carry something heavy.

"Hello," Oscar said. "What can I do for you?"

"I'm Declan Zyler. Who are you?" the man replied, looking around with a frown.

His brows lifting at the unexpected and unnecessarily blunt response, Oscar replied coolly, "The name is Oscar

London." He sized up the man. More muscular than he was, but Oscar was surprisingly quick on his feet and a little taller. He could take him if he had to. Probably. "What can I do for you?"

"I'm looking for Teddy Mack. Where is she?" Suspicion fairly rolled off the newcomer—as if he expected to learn that Oscar had stuffed a comatose Teddy into a closet somewhere. Or worse.

His spine stiffened a little. "She's kind of busy. What do you want with her?"

"Look…" Declan's jaw was a little tight, and then he relaxed a bit. "I'm her cousin. She's supposed to be here, working on a project, but she didn't mention anything about a —a roommate. So…" Now he gave Oscar a narrow-eyed look. "Where is she?"

"You're her cousin. Ah. That makes sense. It's just that Teddy's been working on her book pretty much nonstop since yesterday"—*when she grabbed me in the hot spring and kissed the hell out of me*—"and I know she doesn't want to be disturbed." He shrugged, the last bit of tension easing away. "Sorry if I was a little abrupt, but, well—"

"Yeah. Same here." Declan offered a hand, and Oscar shook it. "I guess I came on a bit strong too. Didn't know what to think about— Well, I expected to find her alone, and —what *are* you doing here, anyway? She didn't mention a— uh—whatever you are when I told her I'd be bringing over some books for her to sign."

"You had it right with roommate. Just a roommate—acci-dentally, in fact. They double-booked us here, if you can believe it." Oscar explained the situation more fully, then lifted his beer bottle. "I just opened this—can I grab one for you? It's a nice view from the porch—great place to sit and have a brew."

"Thanks. I'd like that."

Moments later, they settled on the metal chairs. There was no lingering animosity or tension between Oscar and his visitor, each having understood the other's position and appreciating it as well.

"This is pretty good stuff," Oscar said, gesturing with his beer. "Made by a local guy?"

"Yeah. Baxter James is a buddy of mine. That means I get to sample all of his works in progress. Sometimes that's a good thing…sometimes, not so much," Declan added with a grin. "There was the time he was trying a maple-raspberry stout that just didn't work out."

Oscar curled his lip. "I can see that. I don't know why some of these craft brewers feel it necessary to come up with such exotic flavors and combinations. Nothing wrong with a good, thick stout or a hoppy IPA. Maybe a hint of citrus—but even that's not necessary. A good brew doesn't need any bells and whistles if it's made with quality ingredients."

"Agreed," Declan replied, and they clinked bottles. "So Teddy's working on her book, is she? Glad to hear it. She was pretty stressed about it last time I saw her. I was supposed to come over yesterday—no, two days ago—and I felt bad that my schedule got all effed up and I couldn't make it. Just wanted to check on her, see if she needed anything, since she doesn't have a car—and bring a couple books for her to sign. The bookstore has them in stock, and I guess people heard she was in town, and they bought them and wanted to get them signed. I told the bookstore owner I'd bring them over. Plus Baxter's been making noises about coming over and sneaking a peek of what she's writing—I guess he's a big fan of her books."

"Yeah, she's been typing away like mad for the last two days. Hasn't even come out to eat. I've been bringing her a tray whenever I eat—feel like a prison guard," Oscar said with a wry smile. "But I couldn't let her live on water, apples, and granola bars."

"That's real nice of you," Declan said, nodding. "She sounded pretty miserable the last time I talked to her. I'm glad things are going well."

"I don't see much of her, so I don't really know how it's going. But at least she hasn't been moaning over having writer's block like she was doing the first couple of days we were here. The first time I heard her, I thought she was being attacked or tortured," Oscar said with a laugh. "She's an interesting person, your cousin."

"I think so too." Declan tilted his head, contemplating Oscar. "You know, Baxter is having a tasting of a couple of new beers tomorrow evening, if you're interested. Seeing as you're just hanging out here while Teddy's working."

A little surprised by the invite, but definitely intrigued, Oscar replied, "I never say no to a good beer. Where is it going to be? What time?"

"Well, now, I didn't guarantee a *good* beer—there was that maple-raspberry stout I was telling you about." Declan grinned. "But more often than not, Bax hits it out of the park. He's trying out three new brews—it'll be at the Lakeside Grille. Tomorrow evening at seven thirty."

"I'll be there. Thanks for letting me know."

"Sure. Consider it an olive branch, so to speak. For us starting off on the wrong foot."

"Not necessary, but thank you for the sentiment," Oscar replied. "I probably would have reacted the same way if it had been my sister in the situation."

Declan gave him an understanding nod. "Agreed. So how do you like staying here in the lighthouse? Have you been up there?" He tipped his head back and to the side a little, but the porch overhang blocked the view of all but the bottom third of the tower.

"As a matter of fact…" Oscar said. He hesitated over how much to say, but he figured Teddy would spill the beans if she were sitting here—the woman really couldn't keep her mouth closed—and he didn't want to make more of it than had happened. "We went up there the other night and got stuck out on the railing."

"You what?" Declan, who'd been half tilted back on his chair, let the front legs thunk to the porch floor.

"Door blew shut and must've gotten stuck or something, because we couldn't get it open. We were out on the walkway around the light. Would've been a miserable night if we hadn't gotten back in."

"I'll say."

"Teddy wanted to go up there and check it out—I guess someone jumped or fell"—*or was pushed*, he added silently, then cursed her for putting that in his head—"and she wanted to check it out for some reason."

"Yeah, I wasn't living here when that happened. It was three years ago or something. Guy who was the caretaker here was found on the ground with his head split open. Maybe he got locked out like you all did, and he tried to climb down or something."

Oscar lifted his brows. "That's interesting. Maybe that's it. After all, if the guy lived here, he'd be used to walking around the top of the walkway. So, does anyone around here have a peacock farm or something like that?"

"A peacock farm?" Declan pulled the longneck bottle away from his mouth to give Oscar a look. "No. Why?"

"Heard an awful shrieking, sort of screaming sound a couple nights ago, and then again the next night. I don't think it was an animal in heat, but maybe." Oscar chose his words carefully.

"Hm. What sort of sound?"

"Well, if I had to describe it, I'd say it was like someone being tortured. Or terrified." Oscar took a pull of his beer and stared out over the lake. "It sure is beautiful here. How long did you say you've been here?"

"Used to visit a couple of summers when I was a teen, but didn't move back until a year ago August. Long story short, I found out I had a daughter I didn't know about, and her parents—mother and stepfather—were moving away. She—Stephanie—didn't want to move and change high schools, so she convinced me I could move back and do my work here. I'm not married and wasn't involved with anyone, and I'm a blacksmith—do a lot of restoration work and also some custom jobs. She was right—lots of it I can do anywhere." A smile settled over his face. "Best decision I ever made, Oscar, I gotta say."

"You had a daughter you didn't know about and she was a teenager and you willingly moved back to be a single dad to her?"

Declan gave a short laugh. "Yep. I'm not saying I didn't have a few nights I woke up in a cold sweat wondering what the hell I was doing, but here I am. Couldn't be happier—especially now that all the ugly stuff was put to rest and we all lived through it."

"All right, you've got me hooked. How about another beer—and then you can tell me about this ugly stuff?" Oscar rose from his chair.

"That's a deal."

When he came back, Declan was just slipping his phone into a pocket. "I let Leslie and Steph know I won't be back for a while." He took the longneck. "Leslie—she's the other part of why this was the best decision I ever made, in spite of—or maybe because of—all the crazy stuff that went on last fall."

Oscar took his chair and said nothing. He could see Declan was gearing up to tell the story.

"So I move here to Wicks Hollow and get called over to look at Shenstone House—that big mansion, just on the south side of town, on a big hill overlooking the town. You know the one."

"No, actually, I haven't been into town yet," Oscar said.

"Well, that's unfortunate, because it's really a nice place, even when overrun by tourists. And we'll have to get you downtown to Trib's—or if you prefer a hole-in-the-wall burger joint, over to The Roost, where they've got about twenty beers on tap—sometime soon. Anyway, I get called over to Shenstone House where this woman's working on turning it into a bed and breakfast.

"First thing I realize is she's hotter than an iron-bending fire…second thing is, she's *smart*. She's—Leslie—is the former CEO of a tech company that went public, and she made some money and got out of the business world. So I go over there, and I don't know what a ball-busting exec from Philly is going to do here in tiny Wicks Hollow, but I'm looking at the job, and she hires me to fix the iron railing for the staircase in the main vestibule of that mansion. And I'm thinking, it wouldn't be too bad hanging around this hot, smart woman every day for a while." He grinned, his eyes narrowing as if he were remembering something pleasant. "Anyway, long story short, we somehow disturb a ghost when we're tearing up the railing base."

Oscar blinked. "A ghost."

Declan glanced at him. "Yep. Honest-to-God specter. Saw her myself. Heard her, too."

"Right."

Declan shrugged. "I learned—after the fact—that Wicks Hollow is ripe with supernatural stuff like that. There was a haunting in an antiques shop up on the north side of town just a few months back, and last summer, one of the Tuesday Ladies died and was haunting her house. She had reason to because she was murdered in her own bed."

Now Oscar realized Declan was messing with him. "All right. Got it. Lots of ghosts and goblins around here." He gave a short chuckle. "So you said something about almost not living through some craziness."

"Right. Turns out there was a big secret in Shenstone House that someone wanted to make sure didn't get out during the renovations. So they started breaking in and messing with Leslie. She was almost murdered herself one night when everything hit the fan. That's when I realized—well," Declan said, his eyes going soft again, "I'm not leaving Wicks Hollow as long as she's here. We're going to be getting married someday soon."

Oscar felt a little twinge of envy. "Congratulations. But can we go back to your daughter and the whole single-dad-parenting-a-teen thing? How's that working out?"

"Steph's great. Her mother raised her well, and though we've had some testy moments—like when she wanted Mickey Mouse wallpaper in the john, for crying out loud; how the hell would I ever have the guys over to watch football with that going on?—she's absolutely the best thing that ever happened to me. Even edges out Leslie a little—but not much."

"Lucky you." Oscar realized he'd ignored his second beer, and now lifted the bottle to drink. "Well, Teddy thinks we saw a ghost here at the lighthouse—so if you tell her about Leslie's experience—or did you already?—she's going to think there really is one."

"You saw a ghost?"

Oscar shook his head. "It wasn't a ghost. It was some sort of greenish alga or moss that glows in the moonlight. But it was caught up near the top of the lighthouse, and she's convinced it's a ghost."

"So you don't believe in ghosts," Declan said.

"Of course not," Oscar replied, and pointed his longneck at Declan. "And I can tell when a guy's yanking my chain."

But the blacksmith gave a smug smile that didn't do a thing to dispel Oscar's twinge of nerves.

When it was almost time to leave for the beer tasting the next evening, Oscar closed his laptop and took a quick shower. The truth was that he was glad to have something specific to do, for he'd not seen anything of his housemate all day again, except the back of her head when he dropped off a plate with a grilled cheese on it for lunch. Her hair had been a wild mass, half in a bun and half hanging to her shoulders, as if Teddy had been pulling at it, or running her hands through it, forgetting she'd pinned it up.

Yet, feeling a little guilty about leaving her alone—even though there was no reason he should; he wasn't responsible for her at all, and she probably wouldn't even notice he was gone—he left her a note in the kitchen explaining his plans for the evening and that he'd bring her back a sandwich or something from the Lakeside Grille. Otherwise she'd probably starve.

As he navigated his way to the Lakeside Grille in his Jeep, he once again mulled over the conversation he'd had with Teddy's cousin last night.

Ghosts in Wicks Hollow. An infestation of them, if Declan Zyler was to be believed. *Riiight.*

That was probably just what they told tourists—after all, a reputation like that would certainly draw people to the village. Declan's significant other owned a B&B; it made sense he'd help to promote the town's party line, bring in more tourists and curiosity seekers.

Well, Oscar wasn't going to be fooled or punked. But he was definitely looking forward to a meal he didn't prepare himself, and the possibility of a good beer or two (he wasn't counting on all three being winners).

The Lakeside Grille was on the northwest side of Wicks Lake. It was a couple miles from the little town and tucked away from the county road—which was why it was mainly a hangout for the locals, and, he'd been told, was usually overlooked by the tourists because they couldn't find it. But since Declan had given him directions—there was no sign for the restaurant except for a large piece of sealed driftwood leaning against a tree, with *LG* painted on it—Oscar had no trouble finding it.

The place looked like a big box with a long porch on the front of it. It had a high-peaked roof of dark green corrugated metal and was sided with dark brown shingles. There were large windows on the lakeside for obvious reasons, and two huge barrel planters bursting with colorful flowers flanked the front door. Although the parking lot was full, he didn't see anyone standing around waiting for a table.

As soon as Oscar walked in, Declan saw him and called him over. He was sitting at a round table in the middle of a collection of more round tables, all in the same old-fashioned Colonial style Oscar remembered from his grandparents' house in Boston. Scarred maple tops, slender and ornate legs, wavy chair backs, and a large pedestal that balanced each tabletop. All of the tables were filled, crowded with people laughing, talking, and eating.

There were two other men with Declan, and the fourth chair was empty. He gestured to it, and Oscar took his seat after shaking his host's hand. Already his mouth was watering —whatever the Rubenesque woman was carrying out from the kitchen smelled amazing. But before he could comment, Declan made introductions.

"This is Oscar London. He's staying up at Stony Cape Lighthouse with my cousin Teddy. This is Joe Longbow, chief of police—we just call him Joe Cap," Declan said, nodding to a man in his mid-fifties. He had short, grizzled hair that might once have been jet black but was now salt and pepper. Oscar supposed his nickname either came from his title—Captain— or the Tigers ballcap he wore. "Joe's got the night off; that's why he's here to sample as well.

"And this is Baxter James," Declan went on, using his thumb to point at a slender, handsome black man about their age. "Bax, I'm thinking you owe Oscar at least a couple of beers on the house."

"Good to meet you," said the brewer, offering his hand for a shake. "I hear you've been keeping T.J. Mack fed and watered while she finishes her next book—and you've got my eternal gratitude for that. I've been waiting for it ever since *Titan Mist* came out last year."

"It's my pleasure," replied Oscar, feeling surprisingly comfortable, surrounded as he was by strangers. "And when it comes down to it, now that she's got the book going, Teddy's pretty easy to see to. I just slip a plate through the slit under the door, and when she's done, she pushes it back out. No knives allowed, though—I don't want her getting any ideas about escape before the book's done."

Baxter looked at Oscar for a second as if unsure whether to believe him, then they all laughed. "Well, I'll be honest—I wouldn't mind a sneak peek or some sort of hint as to what's coming next for Sargent Blue. Can you tell me *anything?*" As he spoke, he put a trio of juice-sized glasses down in front of Oscar, then filled one with a nut-brown beer from the pitcher next to him. "Consider this a bribe: I call this my Steel-Edge Porter. It's got a bite to it, but a smooth finish. Let me know what you think."

"There's a trapdoor," Oscar said, lifting the beer to examine it. Not cloudy, very clean, a good dark brown color. It smelled fresh and sharp. "I was helping her figure out how to get Sargent Blue out of his latest situation," he added modestly, and Baxter's eyes went wide. "And she jumped on my idea of a trapdoor." *And then she jumped on me.*

"Why the *hell* didn't *I* get double-booked with T.J. Mack at the keeper's cottage?" Baxter grumbled. "Lucky dog."

As Oscar sipped from the beer, he realized he was damned pleased he'd been stuck with Teddy at the cottage—and not because she was a famous writer. Not because she was a writer at all.

And he was also very glad it wasn't the handsome, toned Baxter James who'd been the one having plot discussions about RBSs in the pool with Teddy. No, Oscar was just fine hanging out with the sweet-smelling, talk-your-ear-off, ping-pong conversationalist and bouncy personality who gave pretty sexy kisses when someone gave her a good idea.

He couldn't wait to give her another one.

Baxter was pouring a second beer for Oscar to taste when the curvy waitress came up to the table.

"Hi there, handsome. I'm Mirabella—but just call me Bella. Welcome to the Lakeside. My husband Reggie and I own the place." Bella looked to be just on this side of fifty, but she was a well-preserved woman with a huge bust and matching curvy hips and ass, displayed by the tight dress she wore. It was pale pink with dark pink flowers splashed all over it, and a round white collar and cuffs at the end of elbow-length sleeves. The apron she wore over it was bright green. Her white-blond hair had a light purple streak in it that coiled around into a puffy style that would have fit right in on the set of *Grease*.

Oscar felt like he needed to blink, and if he did, the wild splash of colors would be burned on the inside of his eyelids. Instead he just smiled and said, "What do you recommend on the menu?"

"Everything, honey," she said, her startling red lips curving in a smile. "But tonight, special, we've got fresh lake trout Reggie's dusted up with some flour and Cajun spices, and deep fried. Fresh right from Wicks Lake out there. You can get co'slaw with it or green beans just as fresh from the backside of the restaurant. My Reggie's also known for his Monte Cristo sandwiches, and he turns a pretty good venison burger—with or without cheese. Best served with a slice of raw onion like this." She used her fingers to demonstrate a measure of no less than an inch thick.

"I like a burger with my beer," Oscar said. "And while I've had ostrich and bison, I've never tried venison, so I'll give that a shot."

"I'll get that going for you," she replied, then swished off to grab an order that had just been shoved through from the kitchen.

"So what else can you tell us about the new book?" Baxter asked. "Anything?"

"Not really. Now that Teddy's got going, she doesn't come out of her room much. I hear her typing and swearing some-times, and once she was congratulating herself on something —I don't know." Oscar spread his hands and smiled as he sampled the second beer. "Oh. That's interesting." He managed to swallow the pungent taste as he put the glass down rather quickly.

He and Declan exchanged pained glances, and Baxter explained, "I was trying for a cherry shandy, since, you know, Michigan's known for cherries. Not working for you, then?"

"Uh…I like the porter better," Oscar said, and Declan laughed.

"He's politer than I am, Bax. Forget the shandy. Let's try the third one. Did you say it was a wheat beer?"

All in all, Oscar had an enjoyable evening, trading stories —everyone wanted to know what a microbiologist was doing in Wicks Hollow for the summer. He told them about his sampling and testing of the hot spring, leaving out the details about his escape from Marcie's wedding.

"Well, there are some legends about that hot spring," Joe Cap drawled. "About it being somethin' special."

Before Oscar could pursue that topic, Bella arrived with an efficient swish and began to slide a plate in front of each of them.

She pointed out the small piece of Cajun-spiced trout she'd added to Oscar's plate. "Just wanted you to have a taste. When's the last time you had fish right out of the lake and onto your plate in less than two hours?"

Though he lived on the East Coast, Oscar couldn't say whether he'd ever had seafood that fresh. "It smells delicious, and I can't wait to try it. And speaking of fishing and fisher-men," he said, looking at Joe as Bella darted off, "I saw a boat out on Lake Michigan the other night. Just before the sun went down—seemed too late for fishing, and it wasn't going fast enough to be a sunset cruise. In fact, it was going very slowly until it came to a stop right out there. Then the guy on it dropped something over the side into the water. Looked like a big bundle. Any idea what that might've been?"

The police chief took his time finishing the trio of ketchup-laden fries he'd just stuck in his mouth before responding. "Well," he said in that easy, drawling voice that sounded as if it might catch up to the end of his thoughts by next week, "that's a good question, there, Oscar. You said they were dropping something over the side, there? On the big lake? Sure as hell hope it wasn't trash."

Oscar hoped so too. "It was a bundle about this big." He showed them, estimating about three feet square. "Seems like if you're going to throw trash over, you'd throw something bigger—it wasn't the size of a trash bag. It definitely wasn't a fishing net."

"Did it look heavy? Could you tell? How far out was it?" Declan asked, digging into his own lake trout dinner. "Can't see that far from the porch over there."

"I was on top of the lighthouse and had a pair of binoculars," Oscar said. "Maybe it was about a quarter or a half-mile away. Two guys tossed the bundle over—it didn't seem like they were struggling with it, so I'd say it wasn't very heavy."

Joe narrowed his eyes. "I'm not sure what that could be, but I'll do some checking around. Did you see a name or markings on the boat? What kind was it?"

"Say a forty-footer. I don't know much about boats…looked like a decent speedboat. I didn't see any markings, but it was white with blue and green swooshes on it near the back—the, uh, stern, I guess it is." Oscar bit into the venison burger and immediately fell in love. Bella was right—the thick slice of onion added just the perfect flavor to the brioche bun and the mountain of mustard he'd added to the sandwich. "The thing is, it looked like a package—sort of tied up or taped up or something."

Joe's expression became serious, and Oscar got the impression that despite his easy manner of speaking, the man was sharp as any city cop or detective. "All right, then. Thank you for the information. I'll check with the sheriff and the Coast Guard and see if they know anything. When was this? Date and time. And specific location." He pulled out a small pad of paper with a pen.

Oscar told him, ending, "That was the night Teddy and I got locked up on top of the lighthouse."

"You what?" Baxter asked, his face lighting up with humor. "That would have been a great story—besides being a craft brewer, I do freelance journalism for some of the local papers and a couple magazines."

"I'm not sure T.J. Mack would want her readership to know she accidentally got locked outside the top of a lighthouse and couldn't figure out how to get down," Declan said with a laugh. "Considering that she writes about a Jason Bourne kind of guy who's always getting out of sticky situations."

"But that's what would make it a great human-interest piece," Baxter said earnestly. "I really want to do a story on her anyway." He looked at Oscar. "Maybe you could ask her." He turned to Declan. "Or you could."

"I'm not willing to risk asking her anything till she finishes the book," Oscar told him. "It's just too dangerous. But when she's done…assuming I get the right sort of bribe…" He lifted his empty glass.

They laughed, and Baxter ordered another round of the porter and the wheat beer. Everyone was very grateful when he left the shandy off the list.

As had become his habit, Oscar wore earplugs and played

white noise on his laptop that night. And thanks to the beer and a good meal, he slept like a baby.

The next morning, the kitchen showed some signs of life. The to-go container he'd brought back was empty except for an unused packet of ketchup, and he found a plate in the dish drainer and the toaster out of whack from its position against the backsplash on the counter.

He futzed around in his lab and, just for the hell of it, went on a long hike to take samples from other freshwater sources in the area. Not a bad idea to compare them with the hot springs—and Lake Michigan itself. It felt good to get out and walk around, and it was hot enough that he doused himself in a small creek.

He read a book, perused a few scientific journals that had begun to stack up, and did some drafting of a new paper he wanted to submit by the fall. And tried not to think about the spiky snowflake microbes as being anything but simply unique—definitely not supernatural. He was glad, in retrospect, that he hadn't asked Joe Cap anything further about the hot-spring legends.

He'd brought Teddy a sandwich for lunch, and then shared his spaghetti (made from jarred sauce that was probably part of her food stores, but he didn't think she'd care) later that night. He studiously avoided Facebook and barely skimmed his emails. If there was any news about Marcie, he didn't want to see it.

Counting today, only four days till D-Day. Or, rather, W-Day. Wedding Day.

Once it was over, he'd be able to move on.

He even managed to stream a James Bond flick via his Wi-Fi hub later that evening.

And so it went for that day and the next. He didn't mind the solitude, but he couldn't help but wonder if Teddy was going to be locked in her room for the entire month of July. He didn't exactly *miss* her, but there were times when he could have used some conversation.

Not that anything was keeping him from driving into town or even up to Grand Rapids if he wanted human interaction…

At about four o'clock on the ninth day he'd been at Stony Cape, he was settled on the cottage's porch, watching the gulls screech over Lake Michigan—a habit he'd settled into. There was something so relaxing, sitting there watching the waves, the birds, and the boats. It got so he'd begun to recognize a few—and that one white, green, and blue forty-footer that had appeared twice since the initial sighting.

But the boat didn't stop, nor did anyone dump anything over the side, except that first time he'd seen it. He tried and failed to read the numbers on the side of the boat—just so he could tell Joe Cap—but without field glasses, he couldn't read them. He did become captivated by a beautiful boat with a bright red sail that cruised over the water with the grace of a skater.

Oscar was nursing another B-Cubed (he was becoming a loyal fan) and contemplating life—and whether he wanted to go into Wicks Hollow again, just for a change of pace—when he heard a loud shriek.

Bolting to his feet, Oscar slammed into the cottage and ran to Teddy's room. He flung open the door to find her dancing around, whooping and shrieking.

Either she'd been bitten by something or she'd finished her book. He was guessing the latter.

Teddy saw him and, with another whoop, flung her soft, curvy self into his arms. She smacked a kiss on his cheek, then pulled her face back and announced, "I'm finished! I'm finished, I'm finished, I'm *fin-iiiish-ed!*"

He was laughing by now, and he found he didn't want to let her go, even though she was still wriggling excitedly in his arms. All warm and soft, though smelling just a bit stale.

"Congratulations, T.J. Mack. I'm sure the world will be delighted to read your sixth book."

Still in his arms, she looked up at him with surprise, pulling back. "So you know who I am."

"I'm a scientist. I know how to do research. I also occasionally read. Especially thrillers that are well researched."

Teddy hadn't stopped wriggling, so he let her go. "Thank you so much for everything—for the food, for letting me alone to work, and, most of all, for the trapdoor idea."

"So that worked, did it?" Oscar thought it would be fun to tell his dad—who was a *big* T.J. Mack fan—that he'd helped the author out of her writer's block and had given her the ending of what was surely going to be her latest blockbuster.

"Well, not really. I didn't end up using a trapdoor at all. But you got me to thinking, and that's how I ended up with a remote-controlled trolley car that helps Sargent Blue save the day."

"Oh." And here he thought he was brilliant. "But at least you got your heart's desire."

"I certainly did." By now, her giddiness had eased into mere delight. "So we have to go out and celebrate!"

"Go out?" Oscar was already easing back from both the idea and Teddy, though he wasn't certain why. Hadn't he had a great time the other night? But then, that had been about free beer. And just a bunch of guys.

"Of course! That's what I always do when I type, 'The End.'" She was still beaming, which revealed three tiny dimples at the corner of her mouth that had previously been hidden—presumably by stress. "You'll come with me, won't you? My treat, as a thank you for feeding me for the last—what's it been, a week?"

"Six days. Seven if you count today."

She stilled, her eyes wide. "I wrote over fifty thousand words in *six days*? Wow." She looked down at her hands, then back up at him. "I definitely deserve a drink. Or two. Can you be ready to leave in forty minutes? I want to try Trib's, and it's hard to get a table much after five."

Though five o'clock seemed early for dinner, Oscar decided not to argue. "All right. I'll drive."

She gave him a grin, a trio of dimples dancing with enthusiasm. "Duh. Why do you think I insisted on you going? How else would I get there?"

He gaped, then realized she was teasing him. Fighting his own smile, he shook his head. "But you're buying, remember. And believe me, I'm going to make it worth all the private chef work and the chauffeuring I've taken on over the last few days."

He could still hear her laughing as he closed the door.

Well, tonight should be entertaining, if nothing else. And he was going to get a good meal out of it.

Couldn't argue with that.

EIGHT

TEDDY SANG in the shower and danced around a bit in the small space. She shaved as she laughed with glee, and managed to avoid not only cutting her knee, but also bumping her elbow on the edge of the soap dish in the tiny stall, even when she added in a little wriggle of a dance. She shampooed the hell out of her hair, and used some fragrant scrubbing salts on her skin. *Slough away, baby.*

It had been a couple days since she'd showered.

But when she remembered how she'd flung her less-than-fresh self at Oscar, her enthusiasm dampened a little.

Though he hadn't thrust her away, so maybe she hadn't smelled *that* bad.

But…yikes.

Not that it mattered—for the guy was still totally hung up on his ex. Which was a bummer, because though she'd been brain-deep in Sargent Blue's adventure, there had been a few random moments when she remembered that wet and steamy (literally) kiss in the pool.

And the way he'd kissed her back. And the feel of his

muscular arms around her, and the firm planes of his chest beneath her hands…

Mmmhmmm, she thought as she scanned the closet (of course she'd unpacked and hung up all her clothes—it was a great way to procrastinate). Definitely, she'd want to explore that a little more—if the opportunity arose.

Which was why Teddy ended up choosing a cobalt-blue maxi dress that had a deep-but-not-too-slutty vee neck in the front and the back, and wide shoulder straps that wouldn't fall down—or require her to wear a strapless bra. The color made her eyes appear wildly blue, and didn't make her light skin seem too pasty. A silver necklace with a lot of interesting charms and disks hanging from it nestled into the bodice's deep vee, and she wore matching earrings that sparkled every time she moved. She bundled her thick hair (long overdue for a trim) into a messy chignon and chose a pop of pink lipstick. No, she didn't "clean up" very often, but when she did, she was damned good at it.

And, she discovered, so was the inscrutable but fascinating Dr. London.

He was wearing off-white chinos that neither sagged nor fit too tightly, belted at just the right place around his waist. In comparison to the previous shirts he'd worn—crisp white or pale blue—the one he'd donned tonight was positively eye-popping. He'd chosen blue as well—this time, a deep navy, with a tiny white pattern on it—and from the slight sheen of the material, Teddy thought it might be either silk or some sort of costly rayon blend.

The dark blue showed off the tan on his forearms and the sun-washed hair sprinkled there. Damp, his hair burned like dull copper instead of carrot. He'd combed it back neatly on the sides and top—though it was just beginning to curl up as it dried, and there was an errant lock that appeared ready to spring free and tumble over his temple. And he'd somehow managed a quick shave, for his chin was smooth and she caught a whiff of something fresh and male that had her hormones sitting up and taking notice.

"I looked up how to get to Trib's," he told her as they climbed into his Grand Cherokee. "I wasn't sure if you knew, and I haven't been into Wicks Hollow myself."

"Oh, good. I haven't seen the downtown area for years. My first night here, Declan and Leslie—that's his girlfriend—took me to dinner at a non-touristy place outside of town." She gestured to her dress and then to his similarly colored shirt. "Apparently, you got the memo."

"The memo?"

She gave a huff of quiet laughter. "It's a joke—we're wearing the same colors, and— Well, never mind." She winced a little at her sad attempt at humor, and began to bubble up with all of the conversation she'd stoppered up inside over the last five days. "I can't believe I wrote fifty thousand words in six days. Neither can Harriet—I called her with the news."

"That's a lot of words," he agreed. "When I write articles or research papers, they might be in the range of five thousand words or so—and it takes me a lot longer than a week."

They'd crossed the bridge from the lighthouse's island, and he eased the car onto the two-lane county highway. The road traced the shore of Lake Michigan, offering glimpses of the vast, sparkling blue through pines, birches, and other trees, as well as small bluffs and a few houses tucked into the forest that edged the lake.

She beamed at him. "I'm just so glad the book's done. Well, mostly done. Now that I have a first draft, going back and fine-tuning it and tweaking things, making some edits and maybe moving some scenes around, is much easier work."

"So it's not really finished, then?" he said as they turned off Highway 31 and onto Wicks Road.

A sign said:

Welcome to Wicks Hollow
A Hidden Jewel on Lake Michigan
Population 1500

"I'm finished enough to know that I'll have a final draft for my editor within the next couple of weeks. That's what matters. The story's done, so the pressure's off," she said, resting her head back against the seat and turning to look at him.

Nice profile, Dr. London, she thought. Strong nose, good chin, *excellent* lips. Very nibble-able.

"Well, you definitely look a lot more relaxed," he said after a few moments of silence and a quick look her way. "I like your dress."

She smiled to herself. "Thank you. So, what have you been doing all week besides delivering food to me? Which, really, Oscar, I can't tell you how much I appreciate it. Back home—I live in New York City—I can call for food delivery when I'm on deadline."

"I didn't mind. It seemed like a waste for each of us to cook separately anyway, so— Oh, damn, I forgot to tell you. Your cousin came by the other evening."

"Declan stopped by? I didn't realize."

"Yes. I— Well, since it wasn't anything urgent, I didn't think you'd want to be bothered. And he agreed."

"Thank you for that. I appreciate it. Did he leave some books for me to sign?"

"Yes. I should have remembered before we left—then we could have brought them with us. And dropped them off." He glanced at her. "He was telling me a crazy story about a ghost in Leslie's B&B."

"I heard something about that—he's promised to give me details the next time— Oh, there's a parking place right there." They'd been driving through the semi-familiar village for three blocks already, and that was the first open spot she'd seen. "Wow. The town sure has changed since I was here last."

"How long ago was that?" he asked, maneuvering his Jeep expertly into the parallel parking spot.

"You're good at that," she said. "Usually it takes me a few tries to get into a spot like this."

He shrugged. "It's just geometry."

"Yeah. Math wasn't ever my strong suit. Hence the writing career." She opened the door and popped out without waiting for him to come around. "It's been, oh, at least ten or fifteen years since I was here." She laughed, gesturing at the signs for the main intersection of the compact business district. "I always found it amusing that the two main roads at the town center area are called Pamela Boulevard and Faith Avenue— when neither of them is hardly any more than a two-lane street."

"Maybe the founders were being optimistic," Oscar said, joining her on the sidewalk.

She chuckled again. "That's what I always thought. Lofty ideals. Oh, there's the yoga studio. That's new. Leslie's aunt— her name is Cherry, and she happens to be a big fan of Sargent Blue; the lady's got good taste—anyway, she owns that. See, up there on the second floor? I bet those big windows give them a great view of Lake Michigan while they're doing warrior pose and all that.

"And if you follow Pamela Ave out that way," she said,

pointing west, "and turn north onto Elizabeth Street—and it's really just a street, not an avenue—you get to what they call B&B Row, where most of the tourists stay. That's where all the painted ladies are, lined up like they're parading down the street wearing their fancy hats and so on. The old Victorian homes just dripping with curlicue trim and garrets jutting out from the rooftops. Some of them even have little porches and balconies up there on the second and third floors—I forget what they're called—but anyway, they call those old houses painted ladies because of all the bright colors they sport."

"I know what a painted lady is," Oscar said dryly. "I'm from Princeton, remember? Cape May is nearly in my backyard."

"Oh, right," she said, and just barely stopped herself from casually slipping her arm through his to walk along the side-walk. Maybe after dinner…and a drink or two to loosen them both up. "And look at all the flowers—on every single doorstep and corner. They're so beautiful—just spilling out of these pots, and so colorful. Ooh, I love this combination of silver, green, and purple." She halted in front of the trough of mixed plants near the door of a restaurant. "Oh, this is Trib's. I'm already in love with it, just from the flowers!"

"Looks pretty crowded," Oscar muttered.

"That's why I wanted to come early," she said, breezing into the restaurant. "Hmm. I guess he likes Andy Warhol—he must have a print of everything the guy ever did hanging in here—and combined with an industrial look. But it really works. Hi, table for two, please," she said to the man who greeted them at the check-in stand. On the wall above was a huge framed print of Warhol's *Campbell's Soup Cans*.

The host looked at her, a friendly smile on his face—then, in an instant, that smile bloomed into a grin and his eyes lit up. "You're T.J. Mack," he said. "Welcome—and thank you for gracing this humble establishment with your presence! I'm Trib."

Teddy put his age around the half-century mark, but his was the face and toned body of a young, vibrant fifty. He had platinum-blond hair buzzed very close to his nicely shaped scalp—he wasn't going for bald, but it was shorter than a brush cut. His goatee and mustache, neatly trimmed, were black threaded with iron gray, and his hazel eyes sparkled with pure pleasure. He wore a pink and white patterned shirt with a butter-yellow bowtie and a creamy linen jacket. The combination was fabulous.

"I certainly wouldn't use the word *humble* to describe this place," she replied, shaking his offered hand. "It's gorgeous and seems very comfortable. It's a pleasure to meet you too. This is my friend, Dr. Oscar London."

Oscar gave her a slight frown—because she used his title, she supposed—but it smoothed away when he shook Trib's hand. "Nice to meet you. The place does look nice, and I hear you make the best pizza in the county. Is there any chance you have a table for two available now? Maybe somewhere not too —uh—loud?"

"A cozy table, and not outside," Trib said with a glint in his eye. "For T.J. Mack and her guest, absolutely. I'm a big fan, you know," he continued, leaning closer to Teddy but not bothering to drop his voice. "I have the most *devastating* crush on Sargent Blue. Put me out of my misery and tell me you based him on a real person, and that he's single and you can introduce me to him."

Teddy laughed as their host led them into the depths of the restaurant. "I wish I could—and you're not the first person to ask. Unfortunately, Sargent is my own creation—let's say fantasy, sort of—and he lives only in my mind and on the pages of my books."

"I'm crushed," said Trib as he pulled out a chair for her with a flourish. "But I'll survive."

Oscar, who'd started toward the same chair, pivoted and took the second one at the four-top Trib had chosen for them. Her housemate appeared mildly aggrieved at being cheated of the opportunity to pull out her chair. Or maybe he just wanted to sit facing the interior of the restaurant.

Trib insisted on comping them their first round of drinks, so once they'd decided on that—a Pinot Noir for Oscar, despite his mention of beer, and an Albariño for Teddy—he flitted off.

"See? It's not too crowded back here, and it's pretty quiet. Though it might have been nice to sit where we could see the street and—"

"And all the crowds walking by?" Oscar settled back in his seat and eyed her speculatively. "I thought most writers were introverts."

"Oh, most of us are. I am." When he gave her a quirked eyebrow that indicated his disbelief, she added, "I've just been saving up for the last five days—locked in my dungeon, working. Even introverts like to be around people—just not very often. And not usually in big groups." She beamed at him. "And tonight's a night for celebration, so I'm practically giddy."

"Only practically?" he muttered, and she laughed. Their gazes met, and he joined her in the moment of humor, the corners of his eyes crinkling as he rumbled a laugh.

They were still chuckling when Trib himself delivered their drinks. "We've got another famous author in the house tonight," he said, his eyes dancing. "Things are really hopping here in tiny Wicks Hollow, and especially at Trib's."

"You do? Who is it?" Teddy craned her neck to look around.

"Ethan Murphy—the one who wrote that book *The Welcome Blue Light*, about near-death experiences."

"I know Ethan!" Teddy perked up even more. "He's repped by the same literary agency I am. We've met several times. He's here? I'd love for him to join us—Oscar, you don't mind, do you?"

"No, of course not," Oscar replied. But she could see he was unenthusiastic about the idea.

"Maybe just for a drink," Teddy said, suddenly realizing that having more people at the table might derail her opportunity to get to know her nerdy housemate—and supremely excellent kisser—better.

"They've just been served their appetizers," Trib said, looking across the restaurant. "But I'll mention to Ethan you're here and suggest he might come over to say hi later."

"They?" Oscar asked, and Teddy smothered a laugh. He seemed to be even more cautious around new people than she was.

"Ethan and Diana, his main squeeze," Trib replied. "They come up nearly every weekend, and spend most of July and August here in the summer. He's got a spectacular log cabin on Wicks Lake. And she's the one who inherited the old house that was haunted by her dead aunt," he added, just before flitting off to speak to another customer. He tossed the last words over his shoulder: "Last summer."

"Haunted by her *dead* aunt?" Teddy said, looking after him with a curled lip. "Well, that's kind of r—"

"I know. There seem to be a lot of ghost stories in this town," Oscar said. "Probably helps to bring in the tourists."

"I was going to say 'redundant.' Of course her aunt was dead if she was haunting the place. You ever hear of a not-dead person haunting a house?" She tasted her wine. Crisp, light, and a little fruity. Just the way she liked it—and the way she felt tonight. It was as if a huge stone yoke had been lifted from her shoulders.

No, the book wasn't officially done yet, but she hadn't been exaggerating when she told Oscar she'd have it finished in a couple weeks. Cleaning up and polishing a finished manuscript was an easy process for her.

Oscar was looking at her—from behind glasses he'd obviously put on for reading then menu. And Teddy's heart gave an extra big thump.

She loved guys with glasses. Especially scholarly-looking ones like the tortoiseshell horn-rimmed specs he was wearing.

That was why Sargent Blue wore reading glasses and was charmingly far-sighted—which also contributed to some of the plot elements in the series. After all, who ever heard of a spy-slash-adventurer who had imperfect eyesight? No one expected Jason Bourne to have to whip out a pair of glasses to read his mobile phone.

"What?" she said, realizing Oscar had been speaking while her hormones went into overdrive over the glasses.

He removed the spectacles (probably a good thing, all things considered) and looked at her closely. "I said, I've never heard of *anyone* haunting a house—except in movies or books."

"So you don't believe in ghosts."

"I… Well, I don't know. I never thought about it."

Teddy narrowed her eyes at him over the rim of her wine glass. "So I suppose that's why you haven't mentioned the elephant in the room."

"What elephant?"

"Well, there are actually *two* elephants in our room, if you want to be accurate," she said primly.

His expression popped into: *Oh boy.*

She nearly laughed again, because she practically read the

words hanging from his mouth—and his lips didn't even move.

"Right," he said—aloud this time. "So, did you look at the menu yet? Probably a good idea to do that before the server comes over and interrupts us."

"Yes, that's a good idea," she replied. "Wouldn't want our secret pachyderm discussion to be interrupted. Nicely done, Dr. London."

He made a noise that sounded like a snort or a smothered chuckle—or maybe he was choking on fear—but Teddy was already looking at the menu and missed his expression. Still, she was having a grand time teasing him. He was so cute when he had that deer-in-headlights look. And there was also the glasses aspect.

Nonetheless, she was a little nervous bringing up the topic of what had happened at the top of the lighthouse.

And that spectacular kiss in the hot spring—that being Elephant Number Two, of course.

But clearly he was nervous as well.

So... She lifted her wine in a small, private toast, and thought: *To exposing elephants in the room. Why the hell not?*

Oscar had managed to keep Teddy from veering into conversational topics he preferred to avoid—at least so far—and they were already halfway through their main courses. He found it was fairly easy to send her off on different tangents by asking a question or making a comment about anything *un*related to ghosts and whatever that other "elephant" was.

Though he had a suspicion he knew what she was talking about.

He *hoped* it wasn't what he thought it was, because the last thing he wanted to do was have a discussion—and, clearly, with Teddy Mack, it would be a *Discussion*—about how he'd turned a quick, impulsive "thank you" kiss into a full-fledged, hot-blooded, toe-curling, passionate one.

He lifted his wine to take a larger-than-normal drink and managed to keep from ogling her mouth. Much, anyway.

"So," he said as the previous topic of conversation (whether she traveled for research for her books) wound down, "I was wondering—"

"Nuh-uh-uh," she said with a cheeky grin that revealed three tiny dimples at the corner of her mouth. She waggled her fork at him. "You've avoided the topic long enough, Dr. London. And quite expertly, too. My turn to steer the conversation."

"How are your scallops?" he asked, a little desperately.

"They're gorgeous. Fresh, perfectly cooked, and smooth as silk." She grinned knowingly at him as she gently moved her nearly empty plate aside. "Nice try, but don't you think it's time we actually talked about what happened on top of the lighthouse?"

"Do we have to?"

"I think it's best. Unless you'd rather discuss the *incident* in the pool first."

He gritted his teeth, grew a pair, and dove in. It'd be better if he drove the direction of that track himself. "Given the choice…perhaps that is a better topic. Addressing the—er— incident. In the hot springs."

"Really?" She seemed surprised—and perhaps even a little bashful about the topic, if the extra pink in her cheeks was any indication. Which he didn't get at all, because *she'd* been the one to bring it up—twice.

He would never understand women.

"Because I owe you an apology," he told her. "For—er—

taking things to a—er—different level. I realize you were simply, um, exuberant in that moment, and didn't mean anything by it." He cleared his throat. "I should have said something before now, but you were busy and I didn't want… to disturb…"

Teddy's expression had his voice trailing off. It was a combination of shock and maybe a little bit of— Well, he didn't know what it was. He had no idea how to read women. Especially one like Teddy Mack.

"You're apologizing for kissing me back after I flung myself willy-nilly into your arms and kissed *you?*" Her brows had drawn together with little furrows between them.

"Yes. Yes, I am."

"I'm not certain whether to be insulted or overcome with laughter, Oscar. Did you *feel* me fighting you off? Pushing you away?"

Oh my God. His heart dropped and he broke out in a cold sweat. His ears rang. "*No!* No, I didn't. Christ, Teddy, I didn't realize—"

But she was goggling at him as she began to shake with laughter. "No," she managed to say, wagging her head vehemently as she tried to catch her breath and form words. "*No, Oscar, geez,*" she said, tears streaming from her eyes, "that's not what I meant." She wiped them away, settled herself, then looked him dead in the eye. "I was trying to say: did you feel me pushing you away or fighting you off, because—*no, I wasn't.* It was a mutually enjoyable moment," she said. Her voice had gone schoolteacher prim, and he imagined she'd capitalized the phrase in her mind. "There's no need to apologize."

With that prissy tone came a little bit of reserve, too; she eased back in her chair a little and picked up her wine as if it were a barrier.

"I see." He felt a little faint with relief. A mutually enjoyable moment. He could get on board with that.

"Good." She set her glass down, folded her hands in front of her, then leaned forward. "Now, Dr. London, why don't you grow a pair and let's talk about what happened at the top of the lighthouse."

He stifled a groan, then picked up his glass. "Fine. You first," he said, gesturing toward her.

She beamed at him, and his insides went a little mushy. Dammit, Teddy Mack was just so pretty to look at, with her gleaming blue eyes and that thick, cocoa-colored hair—and those soft lips. Her cheeks were flushed pink from the bout of giggles, and he had to keep dragging his eyes up and away from that dark, shadowy vee at the neckline of her dress.

"All right. Let's talk facts first. The door slams shut—somehow. It didn't feel windy enough for it to blow closed from being flat against the window behind it. Did it?"

"No. It wasn't. Nor was what wind there was coming— Wait." He shook his head and lifted a hand. "Let me try again. The wind was not coming in a direction that could have blown the door closed—according to physics, anyway."

"Right. So what happened?"

"Freak of nature?"

She narrowed her eyes at him again, the way she did when she was about to spear him with a question or comment. He fought back a grin as she said, "How about a ghost?"

Ugh. Why did she have to say it out loud? He marshaled his efforts. "Why would you think it was a ghost? If such a thing even exists."

"And what makes you think they don't?" she purred.

He sighed and had to concede. "I don't know."

"Well, now we're getting somewhere." Her smile turned feline, matching her tone, and her dimples winked slyly at him. "Seriously, Oscar, what other explanation for the door mysteriously blowing closed—and locking—then mysteriously becoming unlocked right after that horrible screaming sound? Not to mention the freezing air, and that glowing thing—"

"Some sort of alga blown in from the lake—"

But she shook her head and kept talking. "No. It had to be a ghost—or some sort of supernatural event."

"Are you talking about ghosts, Teddy Mack? I thought you stuck to spies and saving the world. Ghosts are *my* thing."

Teddy was already up and out of her seat to greet a tall, good-looking man whom Oscar deduced was Ethan Murphy. The newcomer was accompanied by an attractive woman who was elegant in a Jackie Kennedy sort of way—even her hair was similarly short and dark, and she wore a slim lavender dress that looked summery and cool.

"What a small world. It's *so* great to run into you here in Wicks Hollow," Teddy said as she shook Ethan's hand. "This is my friend, Oscar London. He's a professor at Princeton, so you two can commiserate about how you have to fight off all the young coeds on campus," she said with a wicked smile.

Oscar had already risen and was shaking Ethan's hand—and trying not to be mortified by her comment. Which, unfortunately, was true. He had more than a few young female students—and, twice, male students—make it very clear that they'd like some extra, private tutoring in the lab. It could make things very sticky sometimes, not to mention contaminate any lab samples.

"It's a tough job, but someone's gotta do it," Ethan said as he shook Oscar's hand. "Nice to meet you. What's your area of study?"

"It's *not* ghosts," Teddy said, and gestured to the table as Ethan laughed. "Have a seat; join us for a drink, won't you? It's

Diana, isn't it?" she added, turning to Ethan's date. "I'm Teddy."

"T.J. Mack—it's a pleasure to meet you! I *love* your books," Diana said, shaking Teddy's hand and then reaching across to do the same with Oscar. "I've just started reading for pleasure again—taking more time for myself and slowing down my crazy workload—and I just finished *Dead End*. Couldn't put it down!"

"Thank you," Teddy said. "I'm glad you enjoyed it."

As they all sat down, Oscar accepted that he was now part of a four-person group instead of an intimate dinner for two. Which, he realized, was fine with him.

So, as he didn't really want to talk about ghosts—and the fact that Ethan had already indicated his comfort with the topic—he jumped into the conversation. "We're celebrating that Teddy just finished writing her sixth book."

"Sixth? Wow. I'm just finishing up the notes on my second," Ethan said with admiration and a touch of envy. He waved at Trib, who'd been hovering nearby as the group meshed. "How about a bottle of that Prosecco we had a couple weeks ago when Fiona and Gideon were here? A finished book is always cause for celebration."

"Thank you," Teddy said. "While some people think the most wonderful words in the English language are 'I love you,' I think there are no *two* sweeter words than 'the end.'"

"Agreed on that," Ethan said.

"Do you actually *type* 'the end'?" Diana asked. "Most books don't actually end with those words, do they?"

Oscar watched as Teddy's eyes began to sparkle in that way they did when she talked about her work—at least, when she wasn't tied up in knots over writer's block. This would be nice, having the extra couple here. Then he wouldn't have to manage the conversation, or even participate in it—and he could just enjoy watching her. She was so animated, with such vitality—and it was such bullshit that she claimed she was an introvert. *He* was an introvert.

"I do, because it's a major cathartic moment to type them," Teddy said. "And a lot of authors I know still do. It came from a tradition back when writers would send their work to the publisher in hard copy—and sometimes in batches. The words 'the end' let the editor know it was the end." She shrugged. "Like I said, I do it because it feels so good to know the bloody thing's finished."

"So, tell me about Sargent Blue," Diana said, leaning across the table a little. "Is he based on someone you know?" She had to move back almost immediately, however, because Trib had arrived with four champagne flutes and the bottle of bubbly. "I'm madly in love with him, and I just *love* that he has to wear reading glasses."

"Move over, honey," Trib said as he began to work out the Prosecco's cork. "I already laid claim to the man—even though Teddy here says he's only a figment of her imagination. Her *fantasy*, I think she said."

Yes, that was what Teddy had said. Oscar remembered that because it got him to thinking about just what that fantasy was. A guy whose hands were lethal weapons, but had to put on a pair of glasses to read his dinner menu? What sort of fantasy was that?

Still, he wanted to know.

Teddy, who'd been given the first taste of sparkling wine at Ethan's request, sipped and put down the flute. "It's lovely. Thank you, Ethan. And yes, well, I confess—Sargent Blue is a sort of conglomeration of things I like in a man."

"*Tell* me about it," Trib murmured as he leaned over to fill the glasses.

"Such as?" Ethan had picked up the thread now, and he

seemed to be watching the rest of them carefully. He'd settled back in his seat, lounging comfortably in a casual shirt and shorts, with perfect dark hair and a face any woman would find attractive. He looked more like a minor celebrity than a boring college professor like Oscar.

"Well…Blue's smart. And quick on his feet. He's got a quirky sense of humor," Teddy said.

Oscar snorted. "The guy's a librarian turned agent. He spies on people and kills them if he needs to."

Teddy leveled a serious look at him. "He only kills people in self-defense—*or* if they're about to kill someone else. That's part of his code, and part of—"

"What makes him so compelling," Diana said on a breathless sigh that seemed so out of character for a woman who appeared as buttoned up and elegant as she did.

"So a moral code makes a man compelling," said Ethan, lifting a brow at his date. "Fascinating. Let's talk about that a little more.

"And here we go—the anthropologist has arrived," Diana said with an affectionate laugh.

"Of course it does," Teddy said. "And that's often the core of what writers write about—characters who have a moral code and what they do when that code is challenged. How they act or react when the easy decisions are taken away from them, and they're faced with a *Sophie's Choice* sort of thing."

"That's what makes a story compelling. And that's part of what makes your books bestsellers," Diana said earnestly. "That and the nonstop action and that well-sketched characters. But I do have to say—I loved the scene in *Blind Alley* where Blue had to put on his glasses in order to see the wires so he could defuse that bomb beneath the restaurant. It just made him so *real* to me—not this incredibly talented superhero sort of person who's so far removed from anyone normal."

Teddy smiled. "I'm glad it worked for you." Her gaze scanned the table and landed on Oscar, who'd been less vigilant about the conversation topic since it had gone off on the tangent of "fantasy men." He realized this just as she smiled at him with those cat eyes and said, "So, I think Dr. London and I have a ghost at Stony Cape Lighthouse."

Oscar nearly choked on his wine. Why did she have to keep calling him *doctor* like that? It sounded so…flirtatious.

"Really?" Trib, who'd been flitting by, halted in an exaggerated comical fashion. Resting a hand on the back of Teddy's and Diana's chairs, he leaned forward. "Another ghost in Wicks Hollow? Shocker."

"Don't you have customers to see to?" Ethan asked with a grin.

"I do, but this is much more interesting," Trib replied with a flap of his hand. "And if you don't spill, Teddy Mack, I'm going to out you to Maxine and Juanita. And then they'll tell Iva, and you'll really be in trouble. Iva *loves* her ghosts."

"Who are they?" Oscar asked as Ethan said, "Ouch. That wouldn't be good."

Ethan looked at Oscar. "You haven't had the pleasure, then. Lucky soul. And how *does* one explain Maxine and Juanita—and the rest of the Tuesday Ladies?"

"Never mind that," Teddy said. "Oscar's just trying to change the subject again because he doesn't want to talk about the weird things that have been happening at the lighthouse."

Damn. Foiled again. Oscar gave her a weak smile and lifted his champagne flute in a white-flag toast.

"Tell us. Can't be any weirder than what happened last summer when my Aunt Jean was haunting me," Diana said as blithely as if she'd been ordering a glass of water. She glanced at Oscar. "Don't worry—I didn't want to believe it at first myself."

"But then she really had no choice because ghostly Jean began throwing books around, and she messed up her kitchen once," Ethan said. "And that's when Diana called me over to rescue her from the specter."

Her eyes widened and began to shoot sapphire sparks. "That is *completely* not true. You never rescued me, you—" She began to laugh. "You did that on purpose."

"I just like to see you get all stiff and prissy so I can soften you up later."

"Oh, get a room, you two." Trib snorted. "Some of us don't want to live vicariously through your hot and heavy romance."

"Why are you complaining? Did things go south with Lionel?" Diana touched his hand. "You two seemed to be getting along so well."

"No—well, I don't know," Trib replied, his voice approaching a distraught whine. "He's just been so—*distracted* lately. I don't know. Anyway, forget about me—I want to hear about the ghost at the lighthouse, Teddy. Do you think it could be Stuart Millore?"

"You mean the man who jumped—or fell—off the top?" Teddy replied.

"Or was pushed," Oscar added, and was rewarded when his housemate gave him a warm smile. His insides, dammit, lurched.

"Or was pushed. Maybe he *was* pushed. In fact, Oscar, wait—don't you remember? That's exactly what we were talking about when the door blew shut and inexplicably locked. About whether he might have been pushed. Which would make it *murder*," she added unnecessarily.

The sparkle in her eyes should have made him wary—after

all, she was excited over someone getting killed?—but Oscar thought he was beginning to understand how her mind worked. A little strange, but logical in its own way.

"And if there's murder," Ethan said, "it makes sense for a ghost to be attached to the location."

"And for said ghost to scream bloody murder at one thirty every night in a reenactment of its dying moments as its corporeal person catapulted from the top of a lighthouse," Teddy said, her eyes still dancing.

"Every night?" Oscar repeated weakly.

"Yes. Surely you've been hearing it too." She gave him a sharp look.

Well, yes. But he didn't realize *she* had been hearing it.

"Anyway, I don't think you can deny it, Oscar. There's a ghost haunting Stony Cape Lighthouse."

NINE

"YOU HAVE SOME QUESTIONS," Teddy said, resting her head back against the seat of Oscar's Jeep. She was relaxed and happy, had been well fed and well entertained this evening, and best of all: the book was done.

She'd had just enough wine to make her a little loose, but far from sloppy or goofy. And she couldn't stop thinking about how cute Dr. Oscar London was—and what a fun dinner partner he'd turned out to be.

"Just a few," he said, his mouth a little grim as he followed the broad sweep of a curve along the wooded road. "Why didn't you mention hearing the scream every night?"

"I was too busy trying to finish a bloody book," she said. "I had other more important things on my mind than a ghostly presence. Why didn't *you* mention it?" she countered, enjoying her companion's adorable sense of unease.

"I only heard it once—besides the night we were trapped up on top of the lighthouse," he said. "The next night I didn't hear it, so I thought it stopped after that."

"It didn't. I heard it every night except the one night you didn't hear it. Always at one thirty on the dot. Hard to miss."

"You didn't say anything about it."

"Nor did I come running over to your side of the cottage to make sure you weren't being tortured to death," she replied teasingly. "Or vice versa."

Well, that shut him up. She grinned to herself.

"After the second night, I wore earplugs and played white noise," he replied as he navigated the Jeep off the main road onto the narrow, bumpy path that led to the Stony Cape island bridge. Trees arched overhead like a green tunnel, casting the road into an eerie darkness. "So I didn't hear it. In case it happened again."

"Classic avoidance," she said.

He rolled his eyes, then glanced at her. "Did you hear it the first night you were here?"

"Not the first night. I'd had a few too many B-Cubeds at dinner, and I put earplugs in and slept like a log. Which is how I'm going to sleep tonight—the sleep of the innocent… or, in this case, the sleep of the author of the finished book."

"But it's not really finished," he reminded her. "Technically."

Why did he keep mentioning that? "It's close enough for me to sleep the sleep of the author of the finished book."

"Got it." He turned the wheel, and the Jeep bounced onto the rut-filled road that led to the island. "Well, again, congratulations. Really. I'm very happy for you."

It wasn't even nine o'clock yet, so it was still very light out. The sun wouldn't set for at least another hour.

"I think we should go up to the top of the lighthouse and look around," she said impulsively.

He glanced over with a look that clearly said, *Are you crazy?* and she began to laugh.

"Don't you want to see if the ghost comes back again?

With that amorphous, phosphorescent greenish-blue glowy stuff you claim is algae?"

"Not particularly."

"But it would be your chance to take a sample—that way you could *prove* it's just algae and not some ghostly specter."

He clamped his lips shut, and Teddy continued to smirk at him.

"Well, if you don't want to do that," she said, lowering her voice to a purr, "maybe we should walk back over to the hot springs. Have an evening soak. I'm still in celebration mode. You have to understand—fifty thousand words in six days, with no human interaction…I feel as if I've been freed from solitary confinement."

She saw his Adam's apple bob sharply in his throat, and her lips curled in a satisfied smile. *Marcie Schmarcie*, she thought…and realized, suddenly, that it wasn't just a joke.

She really liked the guy. And he was pretty hot for a nerd. Plus he was smart and dry-humored. And she thought he should definitely be ready to move on from Miss Marcie the boring schoolteacher.

"Um…" He pulled into the parking place next to the cottage and stopped the Jeep with a little jolt. Turning the key, he said casually, "All right," and shocked her into speechlessness.

As she climbed out of the vehicle, she was still reeling a little, but she wasn't a writer—and good with snappy dialogue —for nothing, so she said, "Okay, I'll go change. Suits or no suits?"

Oscar tripped, stumbling as he caught himself, and sent a few rocks skittering over the parking area. But he didn't look at her as he started for the cottage. Teddy was certain he was pretending he didn't hear her, and that made her smirk even more.

"Meet you back here in a few minutes," he said before ducking into the cottage.

He was as good as his word—which were points in his favor, Teddy decided; he could have taken a lot longer or even "forgotten" about the plan, getting distracted by his lab work. Instead, he was waiting for her with a towel slung around his neck.

"I see you opted for a suit," she said, glancing at his dark gray swim trunks and a soft, slightly wrinkled button-down shirt that made him look more like a tourist than a college professor. "And then some."

"I figured protection against the mosquitos would be a good plan. What about you?" he replied, eyeing the loose, knee-length coverup she was wearing.

Teddy gave him a Cheshire grin. "You'll just have to wait and find out. Come on now—don't you want to have another MEM as part of my evening of celebration?"

"MEM?"

Her smile turned sly. "Figure it out, Dr. London." And with that, she turned and started off toward the path that led to the hot spring.

Oscar stared after her, a bemused smile playing at the corners of his mouth. MEM. Of course he knew what that meant: mutually enjoyable moment.

And damned if he wasn't remarkably interested in following up on the possibility—and so he fell in behind her.

For some reason, it seemed a shorter walk to the hot springs tonight than it had the previous times. Maybe because most of those other times he'd either been alone, or been slogging along with bags of equipment.

Which reminded him that he hadn't checked his email to see whether any of his colleagues had gotten back to him with an idea of what those spiky crystal microbes were.

He paused to fix an untied shoelace (to be honest, he'd neglected to retie it because he'd been in a hurry when changing his clothes, in hopes she wouldn't change her mind about walking all the way over to the springs), and by the time he began walking again, Teddy was far enough ahead of him that he couldn't see her any longer. But he could hear her traipsing rapidly along the trail, pushing aside branches that grew out over the rudimentary path.

When he came around the corner to the small clearing where the churning pool was, he discovered she was already in the water. A quick glance told him she'd tossed her coverup over a bush, and left her sandals (impractical for hiking, but at least they didn't come untied) next to it.

She was submerged up to her neck, and Oscar's heart leapt as his belly did a scary, excited dip. He couldn't tell whether she'd made good on her implicit threat about going suit-less— and he wasn't precisely sure how he felt about that either way.

There were parts of him—well, one part in particular— that was *very* intrigued and hopeful, and another part that was a little…not really nervous, not wary, but just *careful*. After all, it had been a while since he'd had much of an MEM with anyone since Marcie.

The thought of his former fiancée drifted into his head as he bent to untie his shoes, then poofed into nothing when he saw Teddy watching him. She had that smile she'd been wearing off and on tonight—almost a smirk, where it saucily curled the corners of her lips, and with a hint of feline to it.

A predatory feline.

"Come on in. The water's great!" she called, and inched up a little from the depths to reveal creamy white—and bare—

shoulders. Even though the pool churned around her, he could see there were no straps over her delicate shoulders. The hollows dipping behind each of her clavicles were suddenly very intriguing, and the glistening moisture scattered over her skin beckoned like Odysseus's sirens.

Oscar swallowed hard, then let himself smile with pleasure. Whatever she was—or wasn't—wearing, he was definitely going to shoot for an MEM.

Or more.

He stripped off his shirt and added it to the pile her coverup made, then slipped out of his shoes.

When he finally climbed over the barrier of rocks that made the sides of the pool, he sighed with pleasure as the hot, bubbling water enveloped him.

"I know," she said, tipping her head back against the wall behind her. "It's heaven, isn't it?"

She appeared so sensual, so feminine and at ease and so delicious, with her silky neck bare and exposed, and her eyes closed in bliss, that he couldn't look away.

Oscar didn't know what possessed him—and he'd be forever glad it did—but before he even settled in the pool, he surged gently over to her.

"Let's get this out of the way," he said, sliding a hand up her bare, water-flecked arm. And he tugged her closer as his other hand settled on her shoulder.

When she slid into his arms, her warm, wet body slick and soft against his, he smiled and covered her lips with his.

Not suit-less, but close, he noted as he slid his hands around her and discovered the scrap of a bikini top. Then his thoughts frittered away and became a whirlwind of heat and pleasure. The soft moan she gave when she met his mouth with hers sent a stab of lust into his belly, and the eagerness with which she kissed him back stoked it hotter.

Her lips—those soft, curling, smirking, always moving ones—were lush and tasty and fit perfectly to his. The water from the pool bubbled and steamed around them as he pulled her against him, then settled back against the side of the wall and went deeper. Tongues and teeth stroked and clashed, breaths and sighs mingling with the churning stew of the pool and pleasure.

He slicked his hand over her hot, damp skin and felt her silky-smooth legs twining sexily with his beneath the pool's surface. She tasted a little salty and a lot sweet, and it was a long while before he could make himself pull away.

"Mmm," she said, smiling at him. She was so close that he could see the speckles of water on her face, and one tiny drop clinging to an eyelash. A smudge of dark makeup was dashed near one eye, and her lips were full and puffy and glistening. "That was nice."

"I thought so too," he replied, and gently released her. His heart was still thudding and there were parts of him that berated him for putting space between them, but Oscar found he wanted to look at her a bit more, even though he'd spent all evening doing so. And if he kept her in his arms any longer, both of them would be suit-less in very short order.

"What a wonderful way to end a day of celebration," she said, eyeing him with that feline look again.

He crossed his arms over his middle and contemplated her from a relatively safe distance. "I don't understand how you can be so celebratory when you're not really finished with the book."

She chuckled. "That really bothers you, doesn't it?"

"Well, I mean, what if you get writer's block again? How can you relax when it's not sent off to your agent or editor or wherever you send it to? The project isn't finished." He was genuinely concerned for her.

She smoothed back a few strands of hair that were clinging to her throat and seemed to understand his worry. "Here's the thing, Oscar. I *could* send it off tomorrow to my editor if I wanted to. It's that done. But I want to tweak and polish it more before I do. That's all." She smirked at him. "I do like the idea that you're very concerned about me *finishing*."

Hoo boy. Oscar nearly swallowed his tongue. "Well," he managed, aware that his face had gone a little warmer, "it just makes for a—uh—happier situation all around."

She burst out laughing, and his heart pinged a little when her eyes crinkled charmingly. "You do surprise me, Dr. London." Again with the purr.

It was as if she knew what it did to him when her voice dropped like that and her eyes went all soft and sly.

Now it was his turn to tease. "But I have to admit, I'm a little offended that you didn't use my idea of a trapdoor."

"Well," she replied, "even though I didn't use it, you reaped the reward of giving me the idea, didn't you?"

All righty, then. He grinned back. "Excellent point."

"So, uh—what have you been doing to keep your mind occupied during these last few days without me to entertain you?"

"Oh, this and that. I've hiked around the area a lot. Drew some more samples from this pool—I found something unexpected in it—and also from some other water sources in the area. I've been testing them, and have contacted a few colleagues as well. Oh, and I cooked for a neurotic writer a few times, and went head to head with her cousin when he showed up wanting to bother her."

"Head to head with Declan?" She perused him with a long look. "I think if it came down to it, you could've taken him."

For some reason, her comment pleased him absurdly. "Fortunately for him, it didn't come to that. But he was more than mildly shocked to find that you'd shacked up with a guy he didn't know about."

"Either that or he thought you'd kidnapped me and locked me away and was having your way with me—or worse."

"Yes, I actually think that's what was on his mind the first time he saw me. Hence the nearly head-to-head bit. But I didn't know who he was, and I figured you didn't want to be bothered. After we cleared things up, we ended up having a few beers and watching the lake for a while. And the next day I joined him and a couple buddies—Baxter and the police chief—for a few beers at the Lakeside. You didn't even notice I was gone."

"True enough, but that burger was so good. Thank you for bringing it home for me. I wolfed it down cold at about two o'clock that night. After the nightly scream." She shifted in the water, easing out of it a little, obviously to give herself a break from the heat. Now he could see the hot pink strip of the bikini top covering her lovely breasts, and how her shoulders and chest were flushed red. "So you mentioned you found something unusual in this water. I'm assuming it's not some dangerous microbe or something."

"I'm not certain what it is. I've sent the image off to a few colleagues—it looks something like a spiky crystal snowflake, but not. So far, no one's given me any information about it."

"Do you have a picture of it? You could do a reverse image search online. I had to do that once when I was trying to identify a certain weapon for Blue."

"Hmm. I could try that. Speaking of Sargent Blue—and let me say that as a straight male reader, I find him nearly as compelling and well drawn as Diana and Trib seem to—but what's all this about him being your fantasy? A spy who can't read without his glasses and has a ferret for a pet pushes your buttons?"

"And a cat. He has a cat as well, named Armstrong. He adopted him in the fourth book, *Blind Alley*."

"I just finished *Traitor Square*, so I'll move on to that one next. Thanks for the warning. So. What is it about him that's your fantasy?"

"Oh, well…" For the first time, Teddy seemed a little bashful. "Well, it's partly just who he is—that moral code, you know. But there's the glasses part." She sighed, then tipped her head back against the wall again—so she didn't have to look at him? "I have a real thing for guys who wear geeky-looking glasses. Plus I thought giving him a liability would make him more realistic," she added quickly. "And, of course, add some plot difficulties. Can't make it too easy for the character, you know."

So she liked guys with glasses, did she? Well, well, well. This was becoming more interesting.

"And he's resourceful, and knows about a lot of different things—I always pictured him as a sort of assassin-like librarian. He's a little bit of a geek, I guess. He came to his spy work relatively late in life, after a lot of classes, including a library science degree." She surged completely up out of the water now. "Whew," she said, fanning herself as she perched on the side of the pool. Her legs were like white beams against the dark rocks and water in the lowering light, but they definitely had a pretty shape. "It's getting dark and the bugs will be coming out soon. And I'm about done stewing in this water. Pretty sure I'm cooked all the way through."

Oscar helped her climb out of the pool and accidentally-on-purpose bumped her up against him so they went body to body all the way from hips to knees. He saw no reason not to slide his arms around her and pull her even closer, and she appeared to agree that taking advantage of the moment was a good idea.

He found her mouth again, but only for a moment before he had to taste the warm, salty, damp skin of her neck and throat. The feel of her curves against him was delicious, and when she slid her foot up along his calf, he dragged her up closer. His hand tangled in the damp bottom of her bundle of hair, and her hands shoved up into his hair as she turned the kiss deeper and hotter.

All thought evaporated from his mind as he filled himself with the taste, scent, and feel of her there in the moonlight—damp, hot, sweet. He couldn't get enough of the way her mouth fit to his, the way she made a very soft, deep moan in the back of her throat whenever he nibbled along the side of her neck or around the myriad of earrings she wore.

At last, she pulled away, arms linked around his neck, breathing heavily. Her pink-covered breasts rested against his chest, and he knew she must be able to feel the solid erection filling out his swim trunks. "That was very nice, Oscar. *Verrry* nice."

"An exceptional MEI, I think," he said when he caught his breath and could formulate the words. Then, in order to preserve his brain function and protect them from being eaten alive by the mosquitos, he stepped away—because otherwise, things were going to get a lot more serious very quickly. It took him a few tries to get his shirt on properly—and forget about buttoning it.

He'd just slipped on his shoes when Teddy began to laugh. "I just got it. MEI."

Oscar glanced at her, and they said it together: "Mutually enjoyable interlude."

She gave him that feline gaze, now gilded by moonlight, which gave her an exotic, elfin look. "And I certainly hope it's not the last of them."

And with that cat-in-the-cream expression on her well-kissed lips, she marched off into the woods.

He followed, keeping up with her this time—and walking as quickly as possible in order to leave the mosquitos and gnats behind. That was the bad part about being in or near the woods.

It took about twenty minutes for them to make their way back. As Oscar had had the foresight to bring a flashlight, there were no casualties on the trail, even though it was past ten and very dark by the time they came out in the clearing.

"Oh my God, *Oscar.*" Teddy's hand whipped out and grabbed his arm tightly. "*Look.*"

He lifted his gaze to where she pointed—to the top of the lighthouse.

There it was: the mass of some amorphous entity, glowing bright lime green against the night sky. It was floating near the dark lighthouse cap.

TEN

"WE'VE GOT to go up there," Teddy said, even as apprehension stabbed her in the gut.

"No we don't," Oscar said in a tone that bespoke finality. But he was standing there, staring up at the glowing green thing as if part of him needed to.

Teddy wanted to go up there and check it out, but at the same time, she really didn't. So there was no reason to argue.

Instead, they both stared up at the display. She edged closer to him—partly because she was a little chilly now, standing in a wet bikini with the wind from the lake and no sun, and partly because it felt good when his arm came around her and she nestled against his solid, warm body.

The entity floated on the west-southwest side of the gallery that ran around the top of the lighthouse. It was lower than she remembered it being the last time, closer to the trees and not as near the railing.

Eerie, translucent, glowing lime green, and it billowed and shifted like a cloud as if moving with the wind. It didn't seem to want to form any particular shape, like many ghosts did—

at least, from what Teddy remembered from books and movies —but it wasn't stagnant.

Then it began to expand, growing to a larger diameter. It frothed and undulated and roiled like an angry neon storm cloud as a sharp, agonized scream filled the air.

Teddy jolted, grabbing for Oscar's arm, as the hair on the back of her neck and everywhere on her body shot straight up. The scream filled her ears, and the malevolent green cloud roiled against the dark, skeletal tree branches…and then, all at once, it was gone.

And the world was silent.

They stood there for a moment. Teddy could hear her heartbeat pounding in her ears and the rasp of her own breathing. She was aware of the tension vibrating along Oscar's arm, which had pulled her tight against him.

"Okay," she said finally. "Okay."

He released her. Continuing to look up at the dark silhouette of the lighthouse against the starry sky, he said, "It was early tonight. It came early."

Teddy blinked. "You're right. It's always been at one thirty. I wonder why."

"So do I."

His voice was quiet, and the underlying calm in his tone told her that Oscar had accepted the fact that there was a supernatural presence here.

"It looked different. Than before," she said. "So. What do we do now?"

He looked at her with surprise. "You're asking me? Aren't you usually the one with the plan?" There was a note of affectionate teasing in his words, and the way he looked at her made Teddy feel warm again. "But since you did, I think the best idea is to try and get some sleep. And tomorrow morning

—when it's light—we can go up and check out the lighthouse again."

For once, she was ready to relinquish control. It had been an exhausting week, and an emotional rollercoaster of an evening. "Yes. Let's do that. In the light. And we can try to find out more about Stuart Millore tomorrow, too."

Oscar unlocked the front door to the cottage and pushed it open. After reaching in to turn on the light, he stepped back so Teddy could enter first.

Exhaustion hit her. She just wanted to be prone. In her bed.

Not necessarily alone, however.

She turned to him as he came through the door, and, looking up into his shadowy face, she stepped into his embrace. To her relief and pleasure, his arms slipped around her right away and he dipped his head to kiss her gently on the mouth.

"Are you all right in your side of the cottage alone?" he asked, pulling back to look at her. "You're welcome to stay over here—there's room for two in my bed, or I can sleep on the floor or the couch." He smiled softly, indicating the choice was completely hers and he was fine either way.

"I think—"

"Oh my God." He shoved her aside then darted past, his attention suddenly fixed on something behind her.

Teddy spun around to see chaos. "Oh my God, *Oscar.*"

His very organized lab setup was no longer neat as a pin. His chair was upended, a computer screen was turned over, and bottles and slides and petri dishes were strewn all over the floor. Some were intact, some broken. The door to his mini fridge sagged open, and his computer was tipped over. The packet of plastic gloves had been torn open and the pieces strewn all over. The empty gloves looked like ghostly white hands.

But the thing that made her heart stop and her breathing go shallow was the angry red lettering on the wall:

GO AWAYYYYYY

"Stay here," he said. "Call the police. I'm going to check my bedroom to see if anything else—"

But Teddy had already flung open the connecting door. "*My laptop*," she cried, sprinting toward her bedroom.

Her room was in similar disarray: the bedclothes torn off, the curtains and window shade off-kilter, the desk chair on its side.

"*Nooooo.*" She sank to the floor next to her laptop. The screen was smashed and all the cords had been yanked free, including that of the full-size keyboard she used.

"*Teddy.*" Oscar's voice held shock and horror. He crouched next to her, settling a comforting hand on the back of her shoulders, rubbing gently. "I'm so sorry. Maybe the screen can be fixed. As long as the rest of the—*oh.*"

She showed him the back of the bottom of the laptop: it had been smashed on that side as well. Struggling with anger and grief, she pulled to her feet, cradling the murdered device.

"Who would do this?" she said, looking around with eyes that no longer saw clearly. Furious tears pooled, glazing her view. "Who?"

"I don't know." Oscar hugged her close as he dialed his phone one-handed. "I'd like to report a break-in and vandalism at Stony Cape Keeper's Cottage," he said.

When he hung up, he drew Teddy close into his arms. Still

hugging her laptop, she rested her head on his shoulder. "Is there anything I can do to help?" he asked.

She knew he was talking about the computer and the book she'd just finished. "I'll need a new laptop," she said with a pained laugh. "Thank God I backed up the manuscript to a jump drive."

He tensed, then relaxed and pulled away to look at her. "You did? Oh, thank God." He sounded as relieved as she felt. "I thought… I was afraid you'd have to start all over."

Her heart swelled at the absolute *truth* in his voice. "I always do. Every day. It's one of the few things I'm a little OCD about. I back it up, remove the flash drive, and put it in my purse—because what if there's a fire? Or I'm in my car with the laptop and get in an accident, and the computer is smashed? There are a million and one things that can happen. When I'm at home, I also back up to the cloud, but because of no Wi-Fi here, I had to settle for a flash drive. Which— Wait a minute."

She pulled away. "This had to have happened while we were at the pool. Just within the last couple of hours."

"I know." He took her hand, and she felt the comfort of it —for she'd just realized that it was only by chance they'd come back to the cottage and missed the vandal.

Or whoever—whatever—it had been. She shivered.

If they'd come back any earlier…

As if reading her mind, he squeezed her hand.

"Let's go back to the other side and wait for the police."

The next morning, Oscar woke to a light rain pattering on the roof of the cottage and Teddy curled up to him in his bed. She was warm and soft, and she smelled delicious. Her thick hair tumbled over the pillow like a dark cloud, and he reached out to finger a thick lock of it as he looked out at the drab morning.

Teddy slept with her mouth slightly open, emitting a delicate snore that made him smile affectionately. *Even in her sleep, the woman doesn't close her mouth.*

One arm was tucked beneath her chin, and the other draped over his waist. Their feet touched, with hers settled on top of his.

It was the mingling of their feet that struck him the most. It felt so natural. And comfortable.

Unfortunately, they were both fully clothed—and had been since they crashed onto his bed after the police (Joe Cap had answered the call) left late last night. She'd pulled a light blanket over both of them, covering up herself and the tank top and shorts she'd changed into after taking off her wet bikini, then slipped into an exhausted sleep while Oscar lay there for a while, just holding her and thinking about everything that had happened.

Now, with a pang of regret and a bark of disappointment from his hormones, Oscar eased away from his bedmate. Much as he would have liked to kiss her face, so slack and pretty in repose—and more—he decided it was best to seek a cold shower instead.

When he got out of the shower, he smelled coffee from the kitchen. Dressed and groomed, he came out to find Teddy sipping from a mug, looking at the mess his makeshift lab had become.

"I'll help you clean up," she told him. Her hair was a wild mass spilling over her shoulders, and her eyes were a little puffy from lack of sleep. She was still wearing that little black tank top and a pair of boxer shorts, and he fought with himself over whether he should suggest she change clothing. His hormones won.

She gave him a wry smile as she began to straighten up the bottles that had been tipped over. "We'll salvage what we can. Then maybe we can go get me a new laptop. That is, after we go into town to make our official report. I almost forgot about that."

He agreed, and they set to work to the tune of James Blunt (her choice) mixed with Ray LaMontagne (his). Both artists seemed about right for a dreary, rainy day of cleaning up.

"It's bad enough they—he—*it*—had to mess up the place. But to use paint?" she said, scowling at the red writing on the wall. The graffiti even spilled onto an amateurish painting of a lighthouse that hung above the sofa. "As if that would scare us away." She gestured with the spray-paint can, which had been left on the floor. Red paint had dripped from it, reminding him unpleasantly of blood.

Oscar eyed her with interest. "Knowing that someone broke in and scrawled 'Go Awayyyy' on the wall doesn't make you the least bit nervous and want to leave?"

"Well, a little. But mostly it makes me want to know *why* they want us to leave. Doesn't it you?"

He sighed as he stacked a few petri dishes. "Yes, dammit, now that you mention it. Of course it does. But I'm also concerned about safety. Yours, in particular."

"Yeah, I know. Me too. Yours, I mean." She gave him a cheeky grin, and he bit back a smile.

"And did you just say 'it' a minute ago?"

Rising from sweeping glass into a dustpan, she shrugged. "Well, it might have been the ghost. I mean, after last night, Oscar, you *can't* deny there's a ghost here."

He muttered to himself and turned back to picking up test tubes—the ones that hadn't been smashed, anyway.

"Come on, Oscar," she said. "Admit it. We *saw* the ghost."

"Fine. There might be a ghost, but I'm certain it wasn't a phantom that caused this sort of destruction and smashed your laptop."

"How do you know? Ethan told us at Trib's that when Diana's aunt was haunting them, she tossed things around in the kitchen. Same thing." Teddy spread her hands to indicate the disaster in the living room.

Oscar didn't respond. He wasn't entirely certain whether he'd prefer it to be a ghost or a mortal who'd done all of this.

Then, suddenly, he had an answer. "A ghost doesn't need to wear gloves," he said, snatching up a rubber glove that had been left slumped on the floor. "Look. It's got spray paint on it —dribbled all over it, probably leaked from the can. You can see, if he was holding the can while wearing the glove—see the paint would have spilled just like this."

Teddy came over to examine it. "I'm impressed, Dr. London. Good eyes on you. Well, we can bring that and this"—she pointed to the spray paint—"when we go in to file the report. I'll put them in a plastic bag—like a real evidence bag!" she added with a grin.

Oscar rolled his eyes, but couldn't hold back a smile. Only a writer would be excited about having to use an evidence bag.

"Speaking of which, I know Captain Longbow looked around outside last night, but he might have missed something in the dark. We should take a look." She glanced outside. "Now, before it starts raining any harder. If there's anything to see, the rain will obliterate any tracks."

"Good point. By the time he or Officer van Hest come back to look around in the light, it could be gone," Oscar replied. He couldn't resist: the idea of playing detective put an enthusiastic glint in Teddy's eyes.

Again, he thought, what a strange and interesting woman

she was, and followed her outside. Fortunately, the rain was still soft and quite pleasant.

Oscar made a quick circuit of the parking area, which was dirt sprinkled with gravel and probably wouldn't show much in the way of tire tracks. But if there were tracks, that would tell them how the invaders had arrived.

As he finished his perusal, he commented, "Joe Cap said he saw no evidence of a forced lock or door, but—"

"Footprints!" Teddy squealed. Oblivious to the little drips running down her face, she was standing near the exterior door to the lighthouse—a door that, to his knowledge, neither of them had used. "Right along the side of the building here. Because of the overhang, the rain hasn't gotten to it yet. Maybe he came from the beach!"

Crouched on the ground, she was busy snapping pictures with her flip phone. "It looks like a boot of some sort—a hiking boot, not a cowboy boot like Captain Longbow was wearing. And it's too small to be yours," she added, looking down at his large feet as he walked up next to her.

"Let's take a look at the beach," he suggested, wishing he'd brought an umbrella. His hair was dripping in his face, and he had to keep pushing back that one annoying lock that always fell forward.

Teddy agreed, and shot to her feet so quickly that she nearly clocked him on the chin with her head. He grabbed her by the arm to steady her, and they started off through the knee-high, blade-like grass that grew in the sandy ground separating the sod and dirt from the expansive beach. The hollow, circular reeds were damp and sharp, and water sprinkled all over his jeans as he pushed through them.

Again, Teddy seemed unconcerned about the dribbles of rain. She even took off her sandals once she reached the edge of the water, holding them in her hand. "I can't believe I haven't walked down to the beach more than once since I got here," she said, looking out over Lake Michigan. "I'm pitiful."

Despite the rain, the huge body of water was relatively calm today, sending little waves curling onto the beach around her toes—which, he noticed again, had bright pink toenails. But in the distance, dark clouds were gathering. More rain would be coming—and soon.

"Well, you've been a little busy," he said. "And I haven't come down here much either. It's such a nice view from the porch, and then I don't get sand in my shoes—like I am now. Plus we're getting wet."

"It's just a little bit of rain," she said, smiling at him in that way of hers that made her dimples dance. "And it's summer, so it's not even cold." A little droplet clung to her lashes, and another one drifted down her cheek. It looked like a tear.

He brushed it away, and their eyes met as his fingers curved under her chin. Oscar felt his heart give a good, hard *ka-thump*, and for a moment he couldn't breathe.

He just…fell.

"I really like you, Oscar," she said after a moment, sounding a little shaky. She reached up to tuck back that annoying curl that fell onto his forehead. Though the gentle rain muted his vision, he saw the way her blue eyes softened.

"I really like you, too, Teddy," he replied, then bent to kiss her gently. When he pulled her into his arms, the rain didn't matter at all.

A boom of thunder in the distance had them breaking apart, but she grabbed his hand when he would have pulled away. "We'd better finish looking around before the sky opens up. It looks pretty nasty out there."

She tugged him along the beach—what she was looking for, he didn't know. But he did know he liked the feel of her hand in his.

"I don't see anything— Wait. What's this?" He released her in order to crouch over the deep crease in the sand, stretching vertically from the water. There were footprints on one side of it. "Looks like they had a boat here—they look like the same footprints."

"They sure do," she agreed. "That's how they came. By boat."

Oscar looked out over the water. He couldn't help remember the blue and green forty-footer he'd seen that first night—and the men dropping something overboard.

It didn't take a genius—or the Coast Guard or Joe Cap, or even a thriller writer—to know it could be something as ugly as the part of a body…or some other package that a colleague would pick up later.

Teddy must have been reading his mind, because she said, "Remember that boat the night we were trapped up on the lighthouse? You saw them drop something over the side—right out there."

"I know. I told Joe Cap—er, Longbow—about it the other night at the beer tasting. He said he'd look into it."

"It was probably drugs," Teddy said, that enthusiasm back in her voice. "I mean, what else would it be?"

Oscar couldn't help but laugh. He caught her hand again and swung it between them as he looked at her. "It could be any number of things. Probably trash, to be honest."

"Or a body," she said, those eyes sparkling with excitement, raindrops on her lashes.

"So says the thriller writer," he replied, squeezing her hand. "Let's go back before we melt. I'll take a few pictures for Joe Cap," he added when she looked as if she were going to protest. "We can tell him about it when we go in to file the report. Let's finish cleaning up inside."

An hour later, the two of them dashed through the now-pouring rain to Oscar's Jeep to go into Wicks Hollow.

Teddy had taken a quick shower and put her hair into a thick, loose braid, then pinned it into a knot at the back of her head. It was the only way she'd be able to keep it from exploding into frizz in the damp humidity. She wore black capris with a sleeveless pink top and hot-pink sandals that almost matched her toenails, and felt she looked much more perky than she actually was after such an eventful day and night.

"I'm starving," she said as they approached the quaint town. It was still raining heavily, so the streets were empty of tourists and there were lots of parking places. "We didn't have breakfast and it's after eleven. Why don't we stop at Orbra's Tea House? Apparently she makes the world's best cinnamon scones, and it doesn't look busy."

Oscar was amenable to this, and moments later, they surged into the tea shop with soaking umbrellas.

"T.J. Mack! Come in, come in!" The sturdy, statuesque Orbra nearly squealed as she strode from the back of the shop, drying her hands on her calico apron. "And set your umbrellas right there in the stand. Nasty day to be out and about, but you came to the perfect place. Nothing like a good cup of tea to warm the bones."

"Bring 'em over here, Orbry," came a gravelly voice from across the room.

Teddy's head had been bowed against the rain and beneath her umbrella, so until she heard the peremptory voice, she hadn't realized anyone else was in the shop.

"You sit yourselves right here," continued Maxine Took, who'd dragged herself out of the chair she'd commandeered at the table near the largest window in the shop. She brandished her walking stick, reminding Teddy that she was going to use it to murder someone in one of her books someday. "And who's that with you there, Teddy?" Maxine peered at Oscar from behind thick glasses.

"*Ayiyiyi*, Maxie. Let the poor things sit down before you start badgering them," said Juanita, who hadn't gone to the trouble of hoisting her generous bottom from the chair on which it sat.

Before she could react, Teddy, along with Oscar, was ushered to the large, round table in a prime spot in the tea shop. In the center was a Scrabble board, obviously in mid-game. Along with Maxine and Juanita was another woman, probably in her sixties. She had round apple cheeks and cotton-candy-white hair in a modern style. Pleasingly plump and petite, she was dressed in a neat pale blue outfit and wore a large yellow diamond on her left ring finger.

"Sit down, sit down—mind you, now don't bump the board. I'm kicking Juanita's patootie right now, and I don't want her using any excuse to call off the game." Maxine grasped Oscar's arm and yanked him unceremoniously into the chair next to hers, narrowly missing bumping him into the table.

"Maxine, you're the only one who ever tries to cancel a game—when you aren't winning." Juanita looked up as Teddy took another empty seat at the table. Today, her nail polish was magenta, matching her bright lipstick (of which only remnants remained at the edges of her lips, likely due to the plate of half-finished scones in front of her). Her bright orange-red hair clashed furiously with the lip color and nail polish, but was offset a little by the dark blue eyeshadow she wore, which matched her paisley top.

The large leather bag with beady-eyed Bruce Banner in it

sat on the deep-set window sill next to the table, likely so the little dog could have a good view of both interior and exterior. "You should see all the crafty ways Maxie tries to forfeit a game without actually forfeiting it," Juanita explained.

"Lies," Maxine said, pointing a dark, gnarled finger at her friend. "All lies." But her eyes glinted with humor. "You missed my birthday party, Teddy Mack. *Eighty-one*, and I'm still as sharp as a tack. Worth celebrating, don't you think?" Her question was more of an accusation.

"Oh," Teddy said, genuinely confused. "I'm sorry. I've been working so hard on my book I didn't realize—I don't even think I knew about it. When was it?" She looked at Oscar for help, but he wasn't doing anything but ping-ponging his attention between them. He looked as if he were afraid to open his mouth.

"Don't worry about Maxine," said the third woman, who'd been silent until now. "She just likes to fuss—and to get presents. The prettier the wrapping, the better. Anyway, I don't think you were even in town for her birthday—which was back in June." She smiled at Teddy, reminding her of a softer, less formal Queen Elizabeth II. "I'm Iva Bergstrom. It's a pleasure to meet you—you *are* T.J. Mack, right? Declan's cousin, the famous writer?"

"Of course that's who she is. Why do you think I asked her to sit down? And her companion here." Maxine sniffed and made a show of eyeballing Oscar. "What's your name there, boy?"

"Maxine, Juanita, and Iva—I'd like you to meet my friend Dr. Oscar London," Teddy said. "He's a microbiologist who teaches and researches at Princeton."

The tips of Oscar's ears turned a little pink at her pompous announcement, but Teddy didn't mind. She figured the best way to nip in the bud any commentary from Maxine was to come out with guns blazing.

And it worked.

"Princeton, you say?" Maxine asked with genuine interest. "Microbiology?"

"Yes, ma'am," he replied.

"Oscar brought his own lab with him," Teddy added, casually tossing her housemate to the wolves. "He set it up in the keeper's cottage. He even brought his own refrigerator *and* a centrifuge. And what's the other thing? Oh, a shaker."

"You brought your own refrigerator?" Juanita exclaimed, her Hispanic accent particularly thick. "That's a man who's prepared. I *like* a man who's prepared." She gave him a very warm smile, and Teddy smothered one of her own.

"Stop flirting with the boy, Neety," Maxine said. "You've had Melvin Horner in your sights for years now. He's the town veterinarian," she explained for the newcomers. "Too bad you can't get him to put a ring on it like Iva here did."

"Now, Maxine, I told you it's only a gift, not an engagement—"

"What if I don't want a ring?" Juanita shot back, cutting off Iva's protest. "What if I just want to jump his bones whenever I want—then go back to my *own* house afterward?"

"Or better yet, do it at yours and kick him out after," Maxine said with a nod. "That's the way I always did it."

"Exactly." Juanita sniffed, and the two smiled at each other like the old friends they seemed to be. "Isn't that what Cherry's doing with that hot and sexy William Reckless?"

"He sure is ringing her bell," Maxine said, shaking her head. "That man's one long, tall, cold drink of water."

Whatever might have come next was forestalled when Orbra elbowed her way into the conversation. She towered over them, all six-foot-plus of her, and offered menus to Teddy and Oscar. "All right, you three wildcats, let them alone so they can order. I can see poor Ms. Mack is—er, is it all right if I call you T.J.?"

"Call me Teddy. All my friends do, and that's my real name," Teddy said.

"Thank you, Teddy." Orbra seemed particularly tickled by this. "Now, what can I get the two of you? It's on the house today, so get whatever you like—you've given me so many hours of enjoyment, reading and listening to Sargent Blue and his adventures. I'm just honored you're here. Maybe we could take a picture and I could frame it and hang it on the wall?"

"Of course," Teddy replied, looking up from the menu. "I'll be happy to sign it if you want."

Orbra looked as if she might float away on cloud nine. "That's very nice of you, T.J.—er, Teddy."

"The scones are good today," Maxine said—implying they weren't always, and clearly needing to reinsert herself in the conversation. "She ain't serving those lavender-blueberry ones she tried out on us one time. Thought I was gonna choke on 'em, even with the clotted cream to help 'em go down."

"You ate three of them," Juanita said, rolling her eyes. "And I thought they were *divine*, Orbry. I do wish you'd make them again."

Orbra turned a cool smile on her friend. "I happen to have a batch coming out of the oven in a few. I'll make certain not to put any of them on *your* plate, Maxie." She gave Teddy an arch smile as Maxine sputtered. "What kind of tea would you like, dearie? I've got a lovely zhen vin pearls white tea that's delicate enough for summer, but has a bit of a caffeine kick. The gunpowder green is very smooth, if a bit grassy if you like that style. Or if you want herbal, there's a cherry-mint blend I'm trying out that seems to be going well. Blended with rooibos leaves."

Teddy, who'd been looking over the extensive list of teas, was glad for a recommendation. She didn't know the difference between an oolong and a pu-erh, or what on earth rooibos was. And then there were emerald greens, and leaves, and pearls… The only words that looked familiar were *chai* and *Darjeeling*. "The zhen pearl tea sounds great—"

"As long as she don't burn it," Maxine interjected. "Orbry knows you don't brew white tea or green tea higher than one-seventy, but she brought me a jasmine pearl green once and it was *singed*. Nearly burned my tongue off, and there was a bitter aftertaste—"

"One seventy-*five*, you mean. And that was because Annie was new," Orbra snapped. "I know better than that, and you know it, Maxine, so quit your tattling. Annie was new and she poured the wrong temperature water over the tea leaves, and now Maxine won't ever let me forget it. That was *ten years* ago, for crying out loud."

Teddy glanced at Oscar, who seemed just as fascinated—if not taken aback—by the complications of tea brewing as she was. "I didn't realize you had to brew tea at certain temperatures," Teddy said, deciding she could put that in a book someday. "You really have to do that?"

"It's like serving wine at the right temperature," Juanita explained. "It's not that it *ruins* the taste—"

"It *scalds* the *leaves*," Maxine grumbled. "Boiling water's okay for herbals, but—"

"—but it just tastes better at the right temp." Juanita smiled. "I owned a few restaurants before I sold them off and retired, and we were very careful to keep the wines we offered at the right temperatures. Just makes the picky people happy," she added with a meaningful eye-roll at her friend.

"Her restaurants—they were called Nita's—were written up in *Midwest Living*," Maxine said. "So you can bet your patootie Neety did it all right. Damn it, I sure do miss that chicken mole you used to make, with the crispy fried spinach on top. And your homemade corn tortillas. It was just the right amount of spicy and peanut-y. And your rojo sauce."

Juanita smiled. "I'll make them again, just for you, Maxie. As soon as you beat me at Scrabble." Her grin turned crafty.

"All right, all right," Orbra said, slamming her hand on the table and making the Scrabble tiles jump. "Knock it off, you two. Teddy and Oscar will never come back if you don't stop talking about jumping bones and arguing. Now, what can I get for you, there, young man?"

"Don't order coffee," Juanita said in a stage whisper. "There's not one bean on the menu."

"Um…I like Tetley tea," Oscar replied.

"Tetley?" Orbra sounded as if he'd just ordered roadkill. "Tetley tea?"

Maxine's eyes went wide, and she looked at Juanita, and they both looked at Iva, and all three seemed to be holding their breaths. Under her breath, Maxine was making *uh-oh* sounds.

"You mean the stuff they sell in the *stores*…in *tea bags*?"

"Yes, ma'am," Oscar said. "My grandmother—she's from England—she used to always serve me Tetley tea when I was sick. She'd put honey and very, very thin slices of lemon in it because I didn't like milk the English way."

Orbra seemed to deflate a little. "Well, that's good and fine, young man, but I'm afraid I don't have any Tetley here. We only offer the finest *loose* tea at Orbra's Tea House, sourced directly from the growers. But I can make you a nice Darjeeling with honey and very thin lemon slices, and I venture to say it'll be just as good—or better—than what your granny used to make."

The ladies at the table released their breaths, and Teddy

winked at Oscar, who was either oblivious to the undercurrents or didn't care.

She rather suspected it was the latter. He was fun like that.

"Very well. I'll get those pots going for you, and I'll be bringing little sandwiches out shortly. Egg salad, cucumber, chicken salad, and pimiento cream cheese." Orbra, who towered over the table, arched a brow as if to challenge anyone to ask a question or decline a flavor. Then she whisked off to the kitchen.

She'd hardly left when Iva closed her hand over Teddy's arm. "So you have a *ghost* up at Stony Cape Cottage!" Her eyes were dancing with delight.

"Yes, that's right," Teddy replied, a little shocked by the sudden change of topic. "How did you hear about that?"

The three ladies burst out laughing. "Honey, there's no secrets in Wicks Hollow—especially when it comes to ghosts," Juanita said, petting Bruce Banner's tiny head so enthusiastically that it bounced a little. He didn't seem to mind. "And Iva here can sniff out a supernatural event better than a bloodhound."

"I'm very sensitive to the metaphysical," Iva said as she patted Teddy's hand. Her round cheeks were pink with pleasure, and her blue eyes danced. "I read a little bit of tarot, and I'm currently rearranging my condo using *feng shui* applications. If you ever want someone to look over your office —where you write your books—and make sure it's got good *feng shui*, you just let me know. But that's enough about me. Tell us about your ghost!"

"Well, it appears to like to hang around at the top of the lighthouse," Teddy said slowly. Oscar, she noticed, was *not* participating in the conversation. Instead, to her surprise, he and Maxine appeared to be in an intense conversation of their own—and for once, the octogenarian's voice was at a normal volume and didn't dominate the table.

"Does it manifest into a specific shape?" Iva asked. "Does it *do* anything?"

"It screams," Juanita said. "I told you that."

"Yes, yes, I know," Iva replied impatiently. "But I want to hear it from Teddy herself. Otherwise, how will we figure out what to do?"

"What to do? You mean…like how to put it to rest?" Teddy asked. Not that she hadn't had a similar thought herself—after all, that was the reason for ghosts, wasn't it? Something had to be fixed in order for them to rest in peace.

"Well, obviously something's wrong, or it wouldn't be haunting the place," Iva said. "Now, tell me all about it."

Teddy glanced at Oscar, who was still talking to Maxine. Now he was animated, using his hands to gesture and demonstrate something. She heard him say something about algal blooms and vibrio—whatever that was.

She turned back to Iva. "It's like a green phosphorescent cloud. And it just kind of hovers there—I haven't seen it form into anything substantial."

"It's green? So we have a real *Mystery of the Green Ghost*," Iva said with a smile. When Teddy looked at her funny, Iva replied, "That's the title of a book my younger patrons used to check out of the library many years ago: *The Three Investigators and the Mystery of the Green Ghost*. That was a wonderful series for youngsters—much better than that prim and perfect Nancy Drew, in my opinion—I enjoyed those too, but the original ones written in the twenties, rather than the cleaned-up versions they did in the fifties. She was a little sassier in the originals.

"Anyway, the Three Investigators was mostly written for boys, but a lot of my girls devoured them too. In that book, the green ghost took the form of an old Chinese man. And it was a sickly neon-green color—the ghost, I mean."

Teddy blinked at the very detailed non sequitur and wished desperately for tea and food. Her brain was feeling very soft and mushy. "I see. You're a librarian?"

"Yes, indeed. For over forty years. Loved every minute of it, and I have an entire noggin filled with all sorts of random information and trivia." Iva smiled, tapping the side of her head. "I understand Sargent Blue is a librarian too—or was, until he decided to get into the spy business."

"Yes, that's right."

"Smart idea, making a main character a librarian. You wouldn't believe the stuff we pack away over the years—literally and figuratively." She tapped her temple again. "And I've always thought the narrow, dark stacks tucked deep in the second basement of a university library would be the perfect place for a killer to be stalking his prey."

Just then, Orbra returned, pushing a multilevel cart. On top were two mismatched teapots, each made of lovely, hand-painted china. Next to them were two teacups and saucers made of china so delicate that they were translucent.

On the second level of the cart were two-tier trays laden with scones and sandwiches on paper-thin bread. The bottom level of the cart had small plates, cloth napkins, and an assortment of jams, jellies, clotted cream, and butter. Teddy's mouth began to water.

Even as Orbra set out the tea service, Iva continued her questions. "Does the ghost do anything besides just hang around up there at the top of the lighthouse?"

"The first time we saw it, it was right there, suspended on the gallery next to us," Teddy replied. "Right by the door. But last night, it was lower, and a little further away from the lighthouse. And the color was a little different—more neon green. It might have just been from where we were standing."

If Oscar wasn't all that interested in investigating the ghost, at least she had someone else to bounce ideas off on. "Also last night, the appearance was much earlier than usual. It was around ten o'clock instead of one thirty. I don't know what that means."

"You've seen it how many times?"

"Only the two, but the scream comes every night at one thirty. Except last night, it came at around ten," Teddy replied.

"There's a scream?"

Teddy explained, then continued, "We hear the scream every night, but I only saw the ghost two nights—because I was in bed the other nights when the scream came. And I wasn't going to look out the window to investigate." She gave a wry smile.

"Was last night's sighting before or after you discovered the cottage had been ransacked?" asked Orbra.

Teddy gaped up at her. "You know about the break-in?"

Orbra shrugged. "My granddaughter, Helga, is one of Joe Longbow's local cops. She told me you'd be coming in today to make a formal report. There's not much kept quiet here in Wicks Hollow."

"Oh—Officer van Hest. I didn't make the connection. Yes, we're going to the station after we finish here." Teddy took a bite of what appeared to be the infamous lavender-blueberry scone, and her eyes widened with delight. "This is incredible," she fairly moaned, then took another bite of the warm, crumbly scone buttered with clotted cream. "The best I've ever tasted."

"Well?" Iva said as she sneaked a pimiento sandwich off the tray. "When did the ransacking happen?"

"We noticed it after we saw the ghost. But we were just

coming back from a—a walk when the ghost appeared at the top of the lighthouse, so the ransacking could have been done at any time after we left—we were gone for maybe ninety minutes at the most. But Oscar says it's not the ghost who did the ransacking because whoever it was wore a pair of gloves. He found them."

"No, no, it wouldn't be the ghostly presence," Iva said sagely. "You've only seen it at the top of the lighthouse, and the specter falls off then disappears. There's no reason to believe it has broached the house itself."

"So the ransacking is unrelated to the ghost," Juanita said.

"Possibly," Iva said. "Or, possibly, the ghost decided to show itself to the ransackers. That could be an explanation for its early appearance." She looked at Teddy. "It was trying to scare them off, perhaps."

"Yes, I wondered the same thing," Teddy replied—which was true, but she hadn't thought it until just this moment. Still, she *had* thought of it.

"So either the ghost was protecting its house from being messed up or damaged, or the person ransacking it was known as a danger to the ghost."

"I guess that follows," Teddy said, though she was certain, given time, she could think of at least three other reasons the ghost might have appeared early last night. "But I don't know how we're going to figure out what the ghost wants until we figure out who it is. Or was."

"Exactly."

"But what's more important, at this point," Oscar said, suddenly joining the conversation, "is figuring out who broke in—and, just as importantly, why they want us to leave."

"Exactly," Iva said again.

"We found some clues," Teddy said. "Some footprints by the side of the lighthouse that's farthest from the main entrance and parking area—they're hiking boots. And it looks like a boat was dragged up onshore there on the island's beach. Probably last night, because the marks looked fresh. We got pictures of them before the rain got too hard and washed it away."

"Not many reasons someone would beach a boat on that little island," Orbra said, bending over to refill Teddy's teacup. "How's that not-Tetley tea going down there, young man?"

"Don't tell her I said this, but it's better than my grandmother used to make," Oscar replied with a smile. "And your scones? Hers aren't even close."

"All right, then," Orbra said, looking mollified. "Now you finish up your sandwiches there and head on over to the police station. Helga's been waiting for you."

"How did she know— Oh, right," Teddy said, holding up her hand. "Everyone knows everything in Wicks Hollow."

ELEVEN

OFFICER HELGA VAN HEST possessed the same calm efficiency as her grandmother, and Teddy liked and trusted her right away. Helga had strawberry-blond hair that she wore in a no-nonsense chignon, and was a taller, slenderer, and more elegant version of her grandmother. Her blue and gray police uniform was starched crisp, and her fingernails were short and painted with a clear gloss. Teddy approved of the fact that Helga, who had a pretty oval face and intelligent hazel eyes, didn't completely disdain her femininity, and wore pale pink lipstick and small gold studs in her ears.

Not that Teddy didn't like or trust Captain Longbow—she absolutely did—but when Helga insisted on taking over from her boss's hunting and pecking on the computer keyboard in order to print out the form for the incident report, Teddy cheered inside.

This was after the police chief had struggled for five minutes to find the right file to open, because for some reason, his computer had become disconnected from the network. And then to figure out how to unjam the printer's paper feed.

And all that was *after* he couldn't get the computer mouse to work for some inexplicable reason.

"He's a damned good cop and an excellent police chief," Helga confided to Teddy, "but the chief's a walking time bomb when it comes to anything electronic. All he has to do is get in the vicinity of anything computerized and it goes berserk. I think it's his aura or something—there's no other explanation for it. It's gotten to the point where I don't even let him into the break room, because that's where we keep the fax machine. Once, he stopped in the doorway and the machine just went bonkers. And no one was using it."

Oscar showed Joe and Helga the rubber glove with the paint on it, and Teddy told them about the footprints by the side of the cottage and the mark of a boat's keel on the beach. "Oscar took pictures because by now, the rain will have washed all the prints away," she said.

Joe reached for Oscar's phone, but Helga gave him an arch look and intercepted it. "Best not to let the chief touch it," she said. "He could delete the entire contents without pressing a button."

"Now, Helga," Joe said. "That's a bit of an exaggeration, don't you think?"

She lifted a perfectly arched sandy-brown brow. "Might I remind you of the time you merely cut the tape on the box with your new, fully loaded computer tablet?"

The chief pursed his lips and changed the subject. "Oscar, I wanted you to know the USCG is looking into what you saw out there—the blue and green boat with the men dropping something over the side. So far they haven't found anything, but they're still looking. I've also got Helga asking around about a boat that meets your description at any of the local marinas."

"So far, nothing, but I'm going to call the sheriff's office and put the word out there," said Helga as she slid the incident report in front of Teddy. "You can sign on the bottom here, and Dr. London, I'll have a copy of your statement printed off in just a second… Cap, how about stepping out of the room for a few? Give the machine a break from your aura?"

Joe grumbled, but rose from a tweed office chair that looked older than he was. "I'll send this off to the lab to see if they can raise any fingerprints on it," he said, holding up the plastic bag with the paint-streaked glove. "But this is little Wicks Hollow, not Chicago or New York, or even Grand Rapids. We aren't going to hear back on this for a good while."

"That's right," Helga said, grimacing a little. "I got spoiled working in Chicago, but unless there's a homicide to light a fire under their behinds, the lab doesn't see any reason to get on our stuff."

"Last fall when Baxter James found Marcus Levin—poor man got clubbed with his own five iron—the lab got on things pretty quick," Joe said in his easy voice.

"Well, I'm not really holding out for a homicide on this case," Oscar said firmly. "A break-in is plenty enough to deal with. Teddy, are you ready? We've got to get you a new computer."

They drove to Grand Rapids, which was about an hour away and the biggest city near Wicks Hollow, to get her a new laptop.

"Thank goodness I have the flash drive," she said more than once, and dug in her purse to check that it was still there at least three times. "I'm glad your laptop wasn't destroyed."

"Same here, but at least my work is easy," Oscar said dryly.

"Just throw a few things on a plate and stick it under the microscope and my work is done."

Teddy laughed. "I'm sorry—that was my neurotic-writer-on-deadline personality talking when I said that."

"I figured." He reached over and curled his grip over her hand, and they drove the rest of the way back to the cottage with their fingers entwined.

It was dark by then, and Teddy was aware of her body tensing with apprehension as they drove over the bridge to the postage-stamp island. What would they find this time?

But the cottage sat, seemingly undisturbed, with the lights they'd left on burning in the windows. As she climbed out of the Jeep, Teddy couldn't help looking up at the lighthouse, which rose over them like a forbidding dark tower.

"Tomorrow, we're going back up there. To the top of the lighthouse. We *have* to," she said, when she felt him ready to protest. "We haven't been up there since that first night."

"All right," he said, fitting the key to the lock.

They curled up on the sofa in the living room, which had been cleared of what was left of his lab equipment, and, at her insistence, streamed a few episodes of *The Big Bang Theory* via his Wi-Fi hub.

"We need something light and airy," she said.

He seemed to understand that she was apprehensive, and instead of making any seductive moves—which, she allowed, wouldn't have been rebuffed by her—he just tucked her under his arm on the sofa and stroked her hair as they watched.

Eventually, she fell into a deep sleep, slumped on the couch until the nightly scream startled them both awake.

"Back on time," she muttered, looking at the clock. "One thirty, on the nose. Bastard."

And then, knowing she was safe, and feeling cherished, she

followed him back to his bedroom to curl up on the bed next to him.

***

The next morning, Teddy woke first. Still fully clothed in the boxers and tee she'd put on for the television show, she had a moment of regret that that was the case. But last night would not have been the right time to act on her increasing attraction and affection for Oscar.

Having the ugliness and uncertainty hanging over them would have marred what she expected—anticipated—would be a delightful Mutually Enjoyable Night.

And she appreciated that Oscar seemed to sense that as well. That was, she realized, one of the reasons she was really falling for him.

Really falling for him.

Like, *falling* falling for him.

The idea made her a little queasy, but in a hot, happy, electric sort of way. She hadn't ever felt so comfortable, or so understood by anyone, ever.

He was just so cute. And smart. And kind. And very sexy, with his hair all rumpled and his face creased from sleep. The dark blue tee he wore clung to strong, square shoulders, and gapped a little to expose a bit of collarbone and the patch of hair that grew on his chest.

Looking down at the coppery stubble that had sprung up overnight along his jaw, she couldn't resist leaning over to nibble his lips. And then to fully cover his mouth carefully, softly, with hers.

She felt his breathing change, the slight shift in his body when he awoke, and then he was kissing her back as one arm lazily slid around her to pull her up close against him.

"Mmm," he said, burying his face in her hair. "You smell as good as you feel, lying here next to me."

She rolled over on top of him, one leg sliding between his as she pulled his face back to hers. A curtain of her hair fell over their faces, and he gently brushed it away as his other hand slid down to cover her butt.

"You have," he said, then kissed the corner of her mouth, "the sexiest rear end I've ever seen." He gently patted it. "I've been dying to get my hands on it ever since the first time I saw you in the hot spring pool."

"Well then, Dr. London," she said, low in her throat, "what are you waiting for? Get your hands on it."

He laughed against her mouth and slid both hands down to cover her butt as she arched down into him and his very awake erection. "Mmm," she murmured. "Someone's up."

"I'll say." With a quick movement, he flipped them over, her hair and the blanket tangling them up awkwardly and a little painfully (on her end).

Teddy began to laugh as they tried to extricate themselves without pulling out her hair or falling off the bed, and they were just getting back to business when he froze and lifted his head as if to listen.

"*No*," he said, falling back on the pillow and pulling her with him. "I refuse to hear that."

But Teddy had heard the car drive up, and, laughing again, she pulled out of his gentle grip. "It might be Declan."

"So? He'll understand. He's a guy."

"Or the police," she said, teasingly avoiding his reach. "It could be Joe Cap."

"He's a guy—he'll understand too." Oscar reached for her, but she danced away, noticing with pleasure how his eyes followed her.

But it was neither Joe Cap nor Declan—nor anyone of the male persuasion.

"Oh, shit," Teddy said when she saw who was getting out of the powder-blue Cadillac SUV. "It's Maxine. And Juanita. And Iva."

That got Oscar popping up out of the bed, his eyes wide. "No way. What time is it? What in the *hell* are they doing here?"

He was frantically looking for appropriate articles of clothing when she slipped from the bedroom and made a mad dash through the cottage to the other side—where her clothes were. She was *not* answering the door in her boxers and tee, especially after all the discussion about jumping bones from the day before.

She heard the peremptory knocking on the front door just as she yanked a sports bra into place, but ignored it. Oscar was closer, plus he'd had the proximity of clothing, and so was probably already dressed.

In fact, she took her time—pinning up her hair, brushing her teeth, and finally coming out to save Oscar after she decided on a happy yellow sundress that she knew looked particularly good on her. She even checked out her too-big butt in the mirror.

But hey, if Oscar thought it looked good, then that was fine with her. With a smile and a hope for good things to come, she left her room.

"Good morning, ladies," she said when she joined them in the living room. "To what do we owe the pleasure?"

"We brought Sunday Morning Scones," Iva said, offering a paper sack. "From Orbra's."

"It's a bribe," Maxine said in a stage whisper as Oscar took the bag. "She wants to see your ghost."

And that was how it turned out that a whole stampede of

them—Maxine, Iva, Teddy, and Oscar—began to clamber up the steps to the top of the lighthouse. Juanita and Bruce Banner elected to stay on the ground level so he could investigate the grounds—and so his mistress could sample the scones. She also offered to make coffee for everyone, and no one argued with that idea.

Maxine led the way up the one hundred and sixty-eight stairs with more speed and efficiency than Teddy had anticipated. That wasn't to say the old curmudgeon *sped* up them, but she kept her pace steady and smooth.

It was during the climb that Teddy concluded Maxine didn't actually *need* her walking stick for ambulation purposes.

When they reached the top, Oscar thoughtfully eased ahead of the troop of females and pushed open the door to the lantern room so the bats could escape before anyone set foot inside.

"What a gorgeous view," Iva said, slipping past Maxine to be the first to walk in. "Now, show me exactly where you saw the Ghostly Presence." Her cornflower eyes were lit up like stars, and Teddy couldn't help but share her enthusiasm.

It was a lot less creepy up here in the middle of the day, with the morning sun streaming and the sky cerulean and cloudless.

"All right," Teddy said, leading Iva out onto the open gallery. A breeze blew in from the lake, and Teddy paused just to inhale the fresh scent. Then she showed Iva exactly where they'd been standing when the door blew closed.

"Now," said Iva. "Do you remember what you were doing at that time? You'd already been up here for a few minutes, correct? And then suddenly the door slammed shut. I suspect it might have been a reaction to something you said or did— for there was no other warning, was there?"

"I thought the same thing," Teddy replied. "And it makes

sense, because we were talking about Stuart Millore falling or jumping from up here, and *I* said, 'maybe he was pushed,' and that was when the door slammed closed."

"Exactly what I suspected," Iva said gleefully. "It sounds to me like the Ghostly Presence was trying to get your attention —to emphasize what you'd just said. To confirm it, so to speak. Then what happened?"

As she explained how they couldn't open the door, Teddy noticed that Maxine and Oscar had not joined them on the exterior walkway. Instead, they had their heads together—one iron-gray one, one of fiery copper—and were looking down into the base of the huge, reflective prisms. They seemed to be having an intense conversation, complete with hand gestures and emphatic motions.

"So you couldn't get the door open," Iva said. "What happened after that?"

"We just…waited. Sat down and tried to figure out what to do, and to wait it out. I fell asleep, eventually," Teddy said, "and then I remember waking up suddenly because it was *so* cold. Like, I felt as if I'd been plunged into an arctic lake. It was so sudden and such a sharp change in temperature that it woke me."

Iva was nodding sagely. "Definitely the sign of a supernatural presence—that sudden change in temperature, and with it being so startlingly cold."

"Right. That's what I thought. And then I saw the thing. The bluish-green something—whatever it was."

"Where precisely did you see it? What did it do?"

Teddy surveyed the area carefully before she responded. "All right. The first time, when we were up here, the—well, for lack of a better term—manifestation was right here."

"So it was standing right next to the door that had slammed shut and inexplicably locked." Iva made a little humming sound. "Right here?" She bent to examine the area closely.

"Yes. And it just sort of floated there—Oscar said it was algae or some sort of moss that might have blown up from the lake or something, but it wasn't. I could tell. It was…amorphous. You could see it billowing and blowing like a cloud."

"Did it take any sort of shape? Or did it stay sort of permeable?"

Teddy shook her head. "It seemed like it *wanted* to take some sort of shape. Like it was fighting to become taller and slenderer, and I *thought* at one point I saw something that looked like a limb—but it was so startling, I couldn't wrap my head around it. And then it just rose a little bit, floated, then dove off the walkway here—and down. And then it was gone."

Iva was watching her with wise, excited eyes. "The ghostly presence was showing you what happened. That person—it had to be Stuart Millore. Stuart, if you're here, give us a sign," Iva called out.

Teddy waited, butterflies in her stomach, her hair blowing in the breeze, but nothing happened.

"He's probably still rather weak yet," Iva told her calmly. "If he didn't take any particular form, he may not have the strength to appear at will."

"Right. But I didn't tell you about the scream."

"Yes, yes, that's right. The scream—the one that comes every night. So that came from the Ghostly Manifestation?"

"Well, yes, of course. I mean, where else would it come from? I just know the sound filled my ears. It was awful. Just bloodcurdling. And then, once it was over, Oscar noticed that the door was ajar. The one that we'd been unable to open. It was just…ajar." Teddy grimaced a little, remembering how horribly eerie that moment had been, and how she'd put all thoughts of it away to deal with later—after she'd finished her book.

And so now here she was.

"So the scream came during the manifestation? Or after it disappeared?"

"Well, hmm. It all happened very quickly, but I *think* it was after it went over the side of the railing and disappeared."

"Interesting." Iva walked a little closer to the railing. "And the Ghostly Presence went over about here?"

"Yes, right about there."

Iva eased back and looked at Teddy. "Well, that is where they found Stuart's body. Straight down there." She pointed to the ground below.

Teddy swallowed hard. "All right."

"Now, when did you notice the temperature going back to normal? Or didn't it?"

Before Teddy could respond, the gallery door opened and Maxine poked her head out.

"You solve any of it yet, Iva?" she demanded. "Time to get down and have a scone before Neety eats them all. Had to smell them all the way here, and there's gonna be trouble if they're gone by the time we get down."

When Maxine Took spoke of trouble, people listened. And so they started down the stairs, pausing at the landing just below the lantern room where their self-appointed leader gestured at a small door. "That goes to beneath the lantern. For repairs and storage. Probably got bats in there too."

"Come on, Maxie, get a move on. Now you've got me hankering for a scone," Iva said. "Besides, I want Teddy to show me where they were standing the second time they saw the green ghost. You were on the ground, right?"

"That's right," Teddy replied, studiously avoiding looking

at Oscar, because she just *knew* he was rolling his eyes—at least internally.

Back on the ground floor, the group was relieved to discover that Juanita had not only not devoured all of the scones, but she'd set up the table with cups and plates, and had made a fresh pot of coffee. She'd also found Oscar's Tetley tea bags and had them out for Maxine, who informed Teddy that she never drank coffee.

Bruce Banner, whom Teddy had never seen outside of his carrying bag, was prancing around the table trying to get the attention of anyone who'd give it to him. He bounced around, jumping up as if his rear legs contained springs, looking so cute that Teddy couldn't keep from petting his soft furry head.

"No scones for Brucie," Juanita said. "But I've got treats in my bag if you want to give him one."

Teddy obliged the little pooch, then was ushered outside before she even finished her scone to show Iva where they'd been standing when they'd seen the apparition the second time.

"But it happened early that night," Iva said. "Earlier than usual."

"Yes, it was closer to ten thirty."

"Have you seen the apparition every time you heard the scream?"

"Uhm, no," Teddy replied with a shame-faced smile. "I never looked out the window when I heard the scream. I—I didn't really want to."

"Oscar, did you see the ghost on the other nights you heard the scream?" Iva asked.

"Well, I never looked either," he replied.

"What about the chill? Did you feel that too? No? Well, you must have been too far away if the Ghostly Presence was up on the top of the lighthouse and you were all the way down here."

"So what's the diagnosis, Iva?" Juanita said, brushing crumbs daintily from the corners of her mouth.

"Definitely haunted. There's significant supernatural activity—I can *feel* it. I suggest," Iva went on, looking at Teddy and Oscar, "that you spend the night at the top of the light-house again—as soon as possible—and see what happens."

"Yeah, no," Oscar said flatly.

Teddy looked at him. "But—"

"You can spend the night up there if you like," he said, patting Iva's hand. "We'll even block the door open so you can't get locked out."

"Well, now, Oscar, dear, you never struck me as the sort of young man who'd be—shall we say, *nervous* around a flimsy little ghost," Iva said, fluttering her eyelashes. "Just like my dear, naive Gideon. He swore there wasn't any such thing as a ghost until he met it himself, under very extraordinary circum-stances." Iva smiled at him. "You never know, I may just take you up on it, Oscar. Of course, I'd want Hollis to join me—I imagine it's very romantic up there, watching the sun go down, isn't it?"

Maxine snorted and rolled her eyes, and that was when Oscar took the bull by the horns, so to speak. "Well, the open-air gallery is available for your camping-out pleasure any time you like, Mrs. Bergstrom. But for now, I'm afraid it's time for Teddy to get back to the final touches on her book—you know, she's not really *done* yet," he added in a confiding whisper.

The ladies all gasped and gaped at Teddy accusingly.

"But we thought you were—"

"We never would have come by if we knew you—"

"Do you mean it's not *done?* That's *false advertising.*" Maxine, of course, drowned out everyone else.

Oscar's tactic had the desired effect, and after allowing Bruce Banner to lift his leg and water the climbing rosebush on the side of the cottage, the three elderly ladies piled back in to Maxine's SUV.

"Thank you, Oscar," Teddy said, slipping her arm through his. "I really do need to get a little more work done—make sure the flash drive transfers, and setting up the new laptop."

Though he looked a little disappointed, Oscar didn't argue. "Just go finish the book. Then you won't have anything on your mind except...other things." His grin was filled with promise. "Because when I get my hands back on your butt, I don't want you thinking about anything but that."

She laughed and gave him a warm, sensual, body-rubbing hug. "Sounds like a plan."

And she disappeared to her bedroom office.

While Teddy spent the rest of that day working on her laptop, Oscar had his own things to attend to.

He'd had a brilliant idea for a new research project and written up the specs for his grad students, and decided he'd open it up to some of the undergrads as well. Why not?

He also did some more research on types of alga and moss that grew on the west side of Michigan. He was determined to identify whatever the glowing entity was.

He went for a swim in Lake Michigan, which, surprisingly, was invigorating and not freezing.

He hadn't set his lab up fully since the break-in, but he did do a little hiking to collect more water samples for some basic study. None of them except the hot spring had the crystalline snowflakes in them. And that continued to niggle at him.

The next day was much the same, though Teddy wasn't cloistered away as she'd been before. She brought her laptop out to work on the porch, and they decided to grill a couple of steaks and fresh corn on the cob. So he ran into town to grab the groceries and a good bottle of red.

And that was good—to give himself that little bit of space. Because as much as he wanted to plant his hands back on that enticing ass of hers, he managed to keep them to himself. He hadn't been kidding when he said he didn't want any distractions.

He wanted her attention on *him*, and *only* him when he finally got her into bed—and undressed. Because once he got her there, he wasn't intending to let her leave for at least a day.

He grinned to himself at the thought, and talked his hormones down for the fiftieth time that day alone. It would be worth it.

Oscar hadn't looked at his phone all day, so it wasn't until he was just about to prep the steaks for the grill that he noticed the text message.

It was from Marcie.

His heart lurched when he read the notification showing part of the text: *Hey.*

As his palms went damp, he did some calculations and realized her wedding had been two days ago.

Huh. He hadn't even noticed the date had come and gone. He'd lost track of the days and time—for that purpose, anyway.

Oscar smiled to himself, pleased and relieved. All good. He was moving on.

He *had* moved on.

So he didn't respond right away—or even open the text message box. He was good. It was fine. Marcie was happily married to Trevor, and Oscar was…here in Michigan. With Teddy.

Being haunted and broken in on, helping to plot thrillers, learning about brewing tea, and generally enjoying life.

And counting the hours until she finished her book—really finished it—so he could get to the project of finishing *her*.

He chuckled and set the phone aside to get the grill fired up.

But later, after they'd eaten and cleaned up the dishes, and Teddy had gone to her room to work for a little longer, he picked up the phone and opened the message alert. He was surprised to discover that was all it said: *Hey.*

At least she hadn't sent him a picture of wherever she was —on her honeymoon, he realized—or, worse, a pic of the wedding.

Because it was rude not to respond, he texted back: *Hey.*

To his surprise, a little bubble immediately appeared on the screen, indicating she was responding.

Finally, her message came through: *I guess you heard.*

He frowned. *Heard what?*

Her response bubble popped up, then disappeared. Then it popped up again, stayed there for a long, *long* time (what was going on?), then finally her response blipped onto the screen: *I didn't do it.*

Oscar stared at the words. A cold sweat slicked over his skin, and his stomach knotted. *Didn't do what?* he replied. But his mouth was dry because he knew. And then her answer came through.

I didn't get married.

He read the words again. Stared at the phone. Blindly walked out onto the porch. He needed air.

Then, with fumbling fingers, he called Dina.

"Hi, sis," he said, casually. *Very* casually, even though his heart was pounding hard and fast enough to make him feel nauseated.

"Hey, bro. How are you doing?" Did she sound cautious? Overly hearty? Blithely innocent? He wasn't certain. "You still in Michigan?"

"Yes."

"What's the name of the town again?"

"It's called Wicks Hollow. I'm staying in the keeper's cottage of a lighthouse. It's—interesting." To say the least. "So what's new there?"

He waited, his heart still pounding—and even as he held the phone to his ear, he heard the soft ding of a text message coming in. And then another one. But he didn't pull away the phone to look.

"Keeping busy?" Dina said.

"Yes." Oscar felt his brows knit together as he began to pace the length of the porch. "What happened? Why didn't you tell me?"

"About…?"

"Come off it, Engadine! You know exactly what I'm talking about. Why didn't you tell me what happened? Marcie didn't get married. Why? What happened?"

Her sigh was audible over the phone. "No, she didn't. She called it off two days before."

"*She* called it off."

"Yes, she did."

"Why?" His question was hardly more than a breath.

"You'd have to ask her that."

"Why didn't you tell me, Dina?"

"Oscar."

"*What?*"

She sighed again. "Nothing. I suppose you're happy about it."

"Well, of course I'm— Well, I don't know. I'm still a little shocked. You don't have any idea what happened? He didn't —*do* anything to her, did he? Cheat on her? Or—or anything else?"

"Not that I know of. I think she just realized it was a mistake. Oscar…"

There was silence for a moment. Another text notification came in, but he didn't look just yet.

"What, Dina?"

"Just… I don't want to see you get hurt again, Scary."

Her use of the nickname she'd adopted when she was too little to say "Oscar" made him smile a little. "I'm a big boy, little sis. I can take care of myself." He drew in a breath, still struggling to make sense of everything, still pacing—as if that would somehow clear his mind. "How's Bethany? Everything going all right with the two of you?"

"Everything's great—though I have to admit, she was pretty disappointed she wasn't able to be my date for the wedding after all. We were sort of looking forward to making a statement, too. She said she couldn't wait to see me in a skirt, since I was going to be a bridesmaid. But thank goodness I didn't end up having to wear that awful dress Marcie picked out. *And don't you ever tell Marcie I said that!*" she added fiercely.

Oscar laughed because she made a joke, but he was surprised that Marcie had insisted Dina wear a dress. "If I had known you were going to wear a skirt, I might've come just to see that. The last time I saw you in a dress was your first communion."

"Shut up," she said, laughing. "Tell you what—if you ever get married, I'll wear a dress. And happily. As long as it's not in that horrible fuchsia Marcie picked out."

"No way, sis. You'll wear a tux if that's what you want to wear." His sister had had a rough time growing up as someone who knew she was a lesbian from the age of twelve. It wasn't until she got to college that people stopped trying to pigeon-hole the blue-eyed, strawberry-blond china doll into frilly dresses and lots of makeup. That had never been her style.

"Oscar," she said, her voice sober. "I didn't tell you because I didn't want you to get all—well, to get your hopes up. I don't know what Marcie's thinking, or how she's feeling, or anyth—"

"She texted me. Out of the blue. To tell me."

Dina muttered something he couldn't quite make out, but it didn't sound nice. "What are you going to do?"

He shrugged, even though she couldn't see him. "I don't know."

"You don't have to do anything, you know," she said quickly.

"I know. Hey, I'd better let you go. I know you have to get up early tomorrow. Give Bethany a hug for me. I'll be in touch."

"Love you, Scary."

"Love you too."

Oscar disconnected, feeling strangely unsettled. Then he looked at the text messages that had come in while he was talking to Dina.

You didn't know? Didn't Dina tell u?

Oscar, we need to talk.

Are u there?

He looked down at the messages. His hand was slick and his head felt light.

His dream had come true. His deepest hope and most secret of wishes had come to pass.

Marcie was free.

And she'd contacted him.

Maybe there was something about that hot-springs water after all…

He replied to the text messages: *Okay.*

Then he walked into the house and went to his bedroom.

TWELVE

She wasn't being nosy, but the window in her bedroom was open and he'd been pacing around on the porch just a short distance away as he talked to his sister. So she knew what had happened.

She'd wait until the next morning to find out whether he'd mention it or not…but she didn't come out of her room. She was too much of a coward.

And she didn't sleep well at all.

When the nightly shriek came—she automatically checked her clock; it was back on time at one thirty—for once, it didn't give Teddy goosebumps.

She had other things on her mind.

When she came out the next morning, she found Oscar standing in the living room, looking at what was left of his lab.

And she saw immediately that he'd begun to pack up a few things. Her heart sank and her mouth felt dry as dust.

Thank God I didn't tell him.

"Hey," she said brightly. "What's up?"

"Oh, Teddy." He looked at her, and she read exhaustion

and something else she couldn't decipher in his expression. He seemed blank and bleary. "I'm just... I have to leave. Unexpectedly. I'm starting to pack up."

"Let me give you a hand," she replied, even as her stomach turned greasily. She bit back other casual comments she might otherwise have made about him going back to campus and so on. Instead, she concentrated on helping to box up the unbroken test tubes and stack the petri dishes in slots in their own carton.

"Thanks. How's the book?" he asked as he wrapped the electrical cord around the centrifuge.

"I sent it off to Harriet and my editor first thing this morning," she lied. "I did the last bit of polishing last night. So I'm now officially finished! You can rest easy—and your timing for leaving is perfect. I won't need you to keep me fed and watered anymore."

He cast her a glance. "I didn't mind at all, Teddy. Really. It's been kind of fun, even with everything going on." He hefted the centrifuge. "So you'll be leaving too, then? I don't really want to leave you here alone with all this...stuff going on." Now he looked downright miserable.

"Oh, that's no problem. I'm going to stay with Declan and Steph for a few days. Now that the book is done, I can have some fun and relaxation." Teddy was, after all, a good storyteller. She knew what her audience wanted—but more importantly, what they *needed*.

Oscar seemed relieved. "Oh, good. I'm glad you won't be staying here alone." Teddy held the door as he lugged the awkward piece of equipment outside.

When he'd finished loading the last box, Oscar came back into the cottage. He had his hands thrust in his pockets, and Teddy, who was in the kitchen making tea and fighting back both anger and tears, ignored him. When she had her emotions under control, she looked up and gave him a bright smile. "All set? Got everything packed up?"

"Yes." He stood there, awkwardness rolling off him—and Teddy didn't give him an inch.

"Want something for the road?" she forced herself to say brightly. "A cup of coffee? A piece of toast?"

"Teddy." His voice was low and maybe a little confused. "I…uh…I'm sorry I have to take off like this. So unexpectedly."

"Oscar," she replied with a teasing lilt, and decided, *I'll be damned if I'll make this easy.* "Is that your way of asking for a kiss goodbye?"

Before he could respond, she took matters into her own hands and stepped right up to him. Her arms went around his neck and, without pressing against him—she couldn't quite make herself do that; it was too painful—she lifted up on her toes to kiss him.

It was a tender kiss, soft and sensual, and she felt him melt against her. His breath caught in a little ragged sigh against her mouth, and he kissed her back. Deeply and, she thought, a little desperately.

Good.

The jerk.

She was the one to pull away, and when she looked into his eyes, she saw that the exhaustion had fled. Instead, there was heat burning there.

Then, suddenly, it was gone. He stepped back and gave her a crooked smile. "That was one hell of a goodbye."

"Make sure to look me up if you're ever in New York." Then, just to twist the knife, she added, "You can get in contact with me through my publisher. Safe travels back to Princeton, Dr. London."

She managed to keep it together until she heard his Jeep

crunch over the gravel. Then she threw her mug across the kitchen so it shattered and sat down for a good cry.

She could sweep up later.

Oscar was three hours away from Wicks Hollow when he pulled off the highway and rested his head against the steering wheel.

What am I doing?

He'd been fighting with himself pretty much ever since he got up this morning.

But he'd made a promise to Marcie. He'd come back, and they'd talk…but try as he might to imagine it, all he could think of was Teddy.

What am I going to do?

He sat in the parking lot of a McDonald's for a good ten minutes before he pulled out his phone and called Dina.

"I don't know what to do," he said as soon as she answered.

"Oh, Oscar. *This* is why I didn't tell you about Marcie."

Damn. She knew him too well.

"I left Wicks Hollow this morning. Packed up my stuff into the Jeep, and now I'm driving back to Princeton…but I'm about to turn around and go back."

"Go back?"

He didn't immediately answer her implied question. Instead, he began to talk, just dumping it all out. "After you and I talked, Marcie and I texted for a while. She said we need to talk, and I said okay—"

"Of course you said okay, because that's you, Oscar," Dina said, her voice a little tense but still filled with affection. "I told Bethany now that you knew about it, you'd be back in Princeton by the weekend. I guess I miscalculated, because you'll be back sooner, but she still owes me fifty bucks. She said you weren't going to come back at all."

He heaved a sigh. "I don't know. Ever since we broke up, I knew I wanted to try and work things out with Marcie. And then when she got engaged to Trevor, I was— Well, I figured until she said 'I do,' there was still a chance we'd get back together. Not that I said or did anything about it—I sure as hell wasn't going to go after her or anything that radical.

"When she texted me last night to tell me, and said we needed to talk, I was surprised but…all I could think was it was a miracle." He tipped his head back against the seat. "But ever since I left Wicks Hollow, all I can think about is leaving Teddy."

"*Teddy?* Uh…I thought I was the only gay person in our family. Are you shagging a guy?"

He smiled weakly. "Teddy's a she. She's…something else. Really something else. And we've been, well, sort of living together for the last few weeks."

"Wait a minute. You're telling me you've been having an affair with this Teddy person—who I'm guessing you just met there on your sabbatical in Wicks Hollow—and you just up and left her to go back to *talk* to Marcie? What the *hell* is wrong with you, Oscar? You don't jump from one woman's bed and rush off the minute your former fiancée crooks a finger!"

"No, no, Dina, it's not like that." He went on to explain the double booking and how they'd come to terms with sharing the space. "We haven't been actually sleeping together," he ended. *Yet.* "The—uh—relationship, I guess, hasn't progressed that far."

"Okay." Dina sounded less angry and more curious now. "So you're going back—to Teddy? Or is it more accurate that you're going *away* from Marcie?"

"It's Teddy I can't stop thinking about. Marcie's just—Well, she's sort of a vague dream, I guess. I mean, I still love her…"

"*Do* you?" Dina said. "Or do you just *assume* you love her—out of habit? Sounds to me like you've got a thing for this Teddy woman. Tell me more about her."

He smiled again. "Well, she likes to talk—a lot. And I find that very strange, because she claims she's an introvert. She's a writer, so we spent some time talking about her book. I sort of helped her come up with an idea that spurred her to get past her writer's block…" He remembered how the slick and soft Teddy had lunged into his arms and planted her lips on his.

And how she'd tasted and smelled, and felt when he pulled her against him.

And how he hadn't wanted to let her go.

He shifted in his seat, his pants suddenly uncomfortably tight as he remembered waking up with her that morning after the break-in…and thinking how good it felt.

"And…?" Dina prodded. "Hello? Oscar? Did I lose you?"

"No. I'm here."

"So she talked your ear off. And you didn't banish her?"

"Well, she's interesting. And smart. Funny, too—she's certain we have a ghost haunting the lighthouse, and she always wanted to investigate it, and I would go along with it just because, well, why not? And when we were stuck on top of the lighthouse, we talked a little about Marcie—I told her about everything." He remembered how indignant Teddy had been on his behalf when she thought Marcie had been involved with the principal. And how calm she'd been once they realized they were stuck on top of the lighthouse gallery.

"You told her about Marcie?"

"That was before we—well, before things changed. We'd just met."

"But things changed. So what did you tell her this morning when you left? You *did* say goodbye, didn't you?" Her voice was tight and squeaky.

"Yes, of course I did. She even helped me pack up the car."

"Did you tell her why you were leaving? Where you were going?"

"No. I just said I had to leave unexpectedly, and that's what's bothering me—she was fine with it. She even told me to look her up if I ever came to New York. *Through her publisher.*"

He had to admit, that rankled.

Dina laughed. "She told you to look her up through her publisher? Wow. That's cold." Then she sobered. "Maybe she was just having a summer not-quite-a-fling, Oscar."

Oh God. What if she was?

His stomach felt like he was trying to digest a rock. "I don't know. It didn't seem like it. She gave me a really hot kiss right before."

"She gave you a hot kiss, then told you to look her up *through her publisher?*" Dina started to laugh. "Oh, man. She was giving you a big eff-you. You might not have told her about Marcie, or why you were leaving, but I'll bet she knew. Or suspected. She was *pissed.*"

"I don't know how she could have known… Oh. *Oh, damn.* I was talking to you on the porch of the cottage. If her window was open, she might have heard me."

Dina was still laughing. "This Teddy sounds like someone I'd get along with just fine." Then, finally, she got herself under control. "Look, Oscar, the way I see it, you've got to figure out whether you're going back *to* Teddy or you're turning away *from* Marcie. Because if you go back there to Teddy, you better know the answer to that. And then you can find out where you stand with her. Though I can take a guess." She began to giggle again, and Oscar started to get annoyed.

"I'm definitely going back." As soon as he said it, the rock evaporated from his insides. He felt liberated. "*To* Teddy."

"All right, then." He could hear Dina's smile in her voice, then it faded with her next words. "I hate to ask, but what are you going to do about Marcie?"

"I'll just tell her I'm not coming." And Oscar realized he was just fine with that. Making that statement, verbalizing that decision, lifted a veil from his eyes and mind…and heart.

He didn't have any obligation to Marcie, to their previous relationship—or even to his past hopes and dreams.

He was free to do what he wanted without having to hold on to the past. He was free to relinquish old dreams or wishes and find new ones.

"I've moved on," he said, mostly to himself, but Dina heard it.

And she cheered.

Thanks to a lot of road construction and a bad accident on Interstate 96, it was after five o'clock when Oscar got back to Wicks Hollow. Dark clouds gathering in the west greeted him as he pulled into the village.

Since he didn't have Teddy's cell phone number or email or any way to contact her (except through her publisher, which he was *not* going to do), he needed to find out where her cousin lived—for that was where she said she'd be.

He didn't much like the idea of having to tell her what was on his mind with an audience around, but he'd messed things up badly enough that he supposed it was part of his payback for being an idiot. Because the more he reflected on it, the more he realized that the lack of chattiness from Teddy that morning could very well have been hurt or confusion or both.

After all, if she'd sent off the book to her editor and agent, she should have been on cloud nine, with nonstop talking and celebration, dancing around the kitchen, and probably even planting a good one on his lips—and more.

Most of all, she definitely wouldn't have waited for him to ask about it—she'd have volunteered the information.

Despite the ugly storm clouds rolling in over Lake Michigan, the streets of Wicks Hollow were filled with tourists trying to get their vacation activities in before the rain came. It took him forever to find a parking place, then he had to decide what his best strategy would be to get in touch with Declan.

It was strange, in this modern day of mobile phones, social media, and GPS, to have to think about tracking someone down a more old-fashioned—and less efficient—way.

He decided the best option would be to go into Orbra's Tea House and see if one of the Tuesday Ladies (he still didn't know why they were called that) would tell him how to find Declan's house.

Fortunately, neither Maxine nor Juanita were at the tea shop when he went in there, and Orbra was so busy with the afternoon rush that she didn't even hesitate to tell him where Declan lived.

"Little bungalow on Bell Street. Got dark red Shaker shingles and black shutters, with a white picket fence around the whole thing. His workshop is a detached garage in the back— you can't miss it because Stephanie planted a bunch of sunflowers in the front garden and they're taller than I am. Now, if you aren't going to sit down and order something, you're gonna have to shoo, because I'm backed up here."

Oscar didn't need to be told twice.

But when he found Bell Street and located the little house,

just as Orbra described it, no one answered his knock. He even went back to the workshop, peering in the window to see whether Declan was working. Though there was a lot of heavy-duty equipment and a generous collection of iron rods and chunks, everything was dark and quiet.

Having no better idea, Oscar got back in his Jeep to wait for someone to show up.

Sometime later, a loud crack of thunder jolted him from what had been an uncomfortable sleep, slumped as he was in the half-reclined driver's seat. He sat up and looked around blearily, discovering to his surprise that it was after seven o'clock.

Now what? No one was home; the house was still unlit and there weren't any cars in the drive. The rain had begun to pelt down, and everything was dark—and from the looks of it, was going to get darker still. The clouds looked *ugly*.

Damn. For all he knew, Teddy and Declan had gone out to celebrate her *really* finishing her book and wouldn't be home for hours. They might even have gone to Grand Rapids, which meant they could be gone overnight.

Frowning sourly at the thought that he was missing Teddy at her most relaxed and happy, and that she was celebrating without him, Oscar started his Jeep.

And then he realized…if Teddy hadn't really finished her book, if she'd been lying to him that morning, that meant she might not be with Declan—and was probably still back at Stony Cape Cottage. *Duh.*

On top of that, she was *alone* in a remote place where a lot of creepy and unpleasant things had been happening.

During a terrible thunderstorm.

He fairly floored the Jeep on his way out of town.

He'd been a complete idiot.

In more ways than one.

THIRTEEN

TEDDY GOT over her mad rather quickly, all things considered, and though she still felt bruised by Oscar's abrupt departure, she focused on the work she had to do, and that helped.

She brought her laptop and notes into the main living room of the cottage and set up at the desk there to do her final bit of work on the sixth book in the Sargent Blue series. To her relief, she finished everything just after four o'clock that afternoon.

The book was done.

She danced inside herself, wriggled on her chair, and sang, "Hallelujah!" as loud as she wanted without worrying she'd disturb any neighbors.

It was really and truly done, and ready to send off. And, since she'd texted Harriet three days earlier that she'd finished the first draft, her practical agent had sent her an overnight package that arrived shortly after Oscar had left. In it was Teddy's smartphone and, thank God, a Wi-Fi hub—so she was able to email the document to both Harriet and her editor.

Then, before she got dragged into looking at all of the email she hadn't checked for two weeks—fan mail, administrative things, updates from friends and family, and, of course, spam—she closed her laptop firmly. And smiled with satisfaction.

That smile ebbed a little as she wished she had someone to share the moment with. Celebrate. *Talk.* Dance.

Since she didn't, and she didn't have a vehicle to go anywhere, Teddy found herself at loose ends. A quick text to Declan garnered a response that he was in Grand Rapids at a concert with Leslie, Stephanie, and a friend of his daughter's. They'd be gone overnight.

"So I'm stuck here," Teddy said, frowning at the ominous clouds gathering over Lake Michigan. She couldn't chance the four-mile walk into town with the weather looking like that. "At least I have a bottle of wine and a frozen pizza to celebrate with. And a Wi-Fi hub that'll let me stream *Suits*. Or *Harlot*."

Or she could do a re-watch of *Friday Night Lights* or *Poldark.*

That idea perked her up—after all, she hadn't watched anything—or read anything for pleasure—for weeks.

Plus, she thought, there was still a mystery to solve. Maybe she'd try her hand at some more Nancy Drew-ing first. See if there were any other signs of mischief down by the lake or on the grounds.

That got her out of the cottage to stretch her legs. There was nothing like putting her feet in the water of a gently surging lake.

But it wasn't until she'd walked down to the beach and back again that Teddy noticed something strange.

The huge, climbing rosebush growing up a piece of lattice on the far lakeside of the lighthouse was off-kilter. Actually, the rose wasn't off-kilter, but the lattice, which at first glance appeared to be affixed to the exterior wall of the lighthouse, wasn't attached at all. It was merely leaning against the brickwork. What had caught Teddy's attention was that it was leaning at a more acute angle than previously.

As if it had been moved.

"How did we not notice this before?" she said, watching for loose stones and snakes in the overgrown garden as she made her way toward the lattice. After all, Bruce Banner had hiked his leg over it just a few days ago.

She wished for gloves, but had no idea where to find any on site, so she had to move very gingerly as she investigated. But when she got close enough to see behind the lattice, Teddy very nearly lost her shit and fell into the prickly roses—for there, behind the climbing rose, was a *door*.

A door that led right into the base of the lighthouse.

And in the dirt below, she could see a gentle groove where the lattice had been pushed aside like a sliding door. Someone had been here. Recently. She shivered, then felt ill.

Had they come into the cottage this way?

She looked around in case whoever it was had come back, or was lurking in the woods beyond. No sign of anyone, but the light was fading due to the gathering storm clouds.

Teddy turned back to the door, carefully slipping between the lattice and the lighthouse wall, and just as she reached for the knob, a loud crack of thunder startled her.

It was so unexpected and creepy that she shrieked, jolted, and stumbled against the rosebush.

"Ouch!" she cried, extricating herself from a set of really ugly thorns—big, honking, sharp ones that left scrapes and welts as well as punctures in her arm and shoulder.

Cursing at the obnoxious thing, she glanced up at the sky —it wasn't that dark yet, and despite the thunder, it wasn't raining—and made a quick decision to run inside and put on better clothing. And, she thought as inspiration struck, she'd grab a couple of oven mitts.

Garbed in a hoodie, jeans, and athletic shoes to protect herself from the thorns, Teddy was back outside forty minutes later (she'd had to call her agent back after finding a message of congratulations on her mobile phone). This time, she brought a flashlight she'd found in a drawer in the kitchen, along with the ring of keys she'd used when accessing the lantern room of the lighthouse.

It would be a long shot if one of those keys fit the doorknob, but she had to try.

But when she inched her way behind the lattice and carefully grasped the knob, she found the door wasn't even locked. Her heart thudding with excitement and nervousness, she carefully pushed it open and beamed the flashlight inside.

Instead of the dusty, abandoned room she'd half expected to find, Teddy discovered about a half-dozen large plastic storage tubs that shone dust-free in the dim light. Assured that the room was empty of anything living (at least larger than a mouse), she slipped inside and shined the light around.

It was a small room with the exterior wall slightly rounded, and two other partitions joining at a sharp angle, making the space the shape of a pie quarter. Since it lacked windows, she concluded it was just a storage room—probably used at one time for lawn tools. But someone had been there recently, because the storage bins were obviously new.

She was about to lift the lid on a bin when the beam of her flashlight fell along one of the two interior walls, revealing an unobtrusive door near their juncture. From its position, she knew it had to lead to the inside of the lighthouse. With her heart in her throat, Teddy abandoned the unopened plastic tub and eased over to the door that was tucked into the dark shadows of the room.

She wasn't worried about stepping on mice or walking into spider webs or anything like that. She was afraid she'd discover that the door had been used.

And that it led in to where she *slept*.

Get a grip, Mack, she told herself. *There's no one around but you, and no one's going to be out on the lake with a thunderstorm coming.*

At least if she determined where the door opened into the lighthouse, she could block it off so no one could get back in.

A shivery mess, with her insides twisting unpleasantly—why did Oscar have to leave before she found this?—Teddy examined the door.

She swallowed hard when she shined the light on a new padlock that dangled from the latch keeping the door closed. Her hands went a little damp, and a sudden *ka-boom!* of thunder shook the walls around her.

Okay. She was done playing Nancy Drew.

She could come back when it wasn't dark, rainy, and creepy.

Teddy hurried back out of the pie-slice room, narrowly missing the thorny rosebush, and quickly maneuvered the lattice back into place. Whoever was using it didn't need to know she'd discovered the hiding place—for whatever was in the plastic bins.

Damn. She should probably have at least stayed to look inside one of them.

But by this time, the rain had started to pour and lightning was streaking across the sky. The clouds churned as if some angry god was stirring a black stew, and Teddy, more spooked than she wanted to admit, ran back to the cottage and slammed its door behind her. Then she locked it.

After that, she went through the entire place and turned

on lights in every room, checked in every closet, and under every bed, just to make sure she was really alone.

She went through the curve-topped connecting door to the lighthouse side and, her heart thudding painfully, her palms nervously damp, she tried to determine where the door from the secret room opened. But she was directionally challenged, and a little anxious besides, and she wasn't certain where the adjacent wall—if there was one—was. The circular building made it confusing.

So she settled for turning on all the lights on that side as well. "It's like a runway in here," she said, because she needed to hear the sound of her voice.

But in the end, Teddy didn't want to stay over there, so she brought her clothes and other stuff from that part of the cottage. She locked the connecting door and pushed the couch in front of it to block it off.

All the while, she told herself it was ridiculous to be that spooked. There could be a million different explanations for everything—she was a storyteller; she knew that was true.

She'd just managed to calm her fears (comfort-watching Taylor Kitsch and Kyle Chandler on *Friday Night Lights* helped) and settled down with a celebratory glass of wine and a piece of frozen pizza when there was a terrifying crack of nearby lightning…and the lights went out.

Everything went black.

Oscar saw the great streak of lightning as it bolted through the sky above his Jeep. The horrifying, sharp crack when it struck was like nothing he'd ever heard: deafening and malevolent, and very, very close.

In the rearview mirror, he saw the tree split and, in a

shower of sparks, tumble to the ground, taking a power line with it.

And just missing the rear bumper of his Jeep.

His heart in his throat, his eyes wide, his mouth open in a silent shout, Oscar slammed his foot on the accelerator. The vehicle surged forward on the muddy road, careening sloppily to the right. Unfortunately, one tire slipped off the edge of the road into the soft, low shoulder of the two-lane track. The Jeep shuddered as it twisted and slid deep into soft mud and sand. Then there was a soft sigh as it settled in and halted.

But Oscar hardly noticed, as his eyes were still on the rearview mirror, staring at the carnage of tree and sizzling power line only yards away.

If he'd been driving slightly slower, the tree—or the lightning—would have shattered his car.

It took him several minutes to calm his racing heart and allow himself to breathe again.

Okay. He checked himself, pinched an arm, blinked hard. *Still alive.*

Then he realized he was stuck.

But still alive.

He didn't have a four-wheel-drive Jeep Cherokee for nothing, he told himself, so he tried to extricate the vehicle from its predicament by gunning the engine and rocking the car back and forth.

But the rain was so heavy and had soaked the ground so much, and the wheel had already twisted and turned as it sank, that it was only a few minutes before he realized the tires were just spinning wildly and throwing up a lot of mud. There was no getting out without a tow truck.

Damn.

The storm lashed at the windows and a few smaller

branches tumbled from trees, skittering across the path in front of him, and once even across the roof of the Jeep.

Can't go forward, can't go backward, he thought—and was reminded of an old campfire story-song from his Scouting days. "Can't go over it, can't go under it…gotta go *riiiiight* through it."

Right through the storm.

He muttered the words to himself as he considered his options. The lighthouse and cottage were only another half-mile or so down this miserable lane, now that he'd crossed over the bridge from the mainland. Of course, having been a Scout, and still the Be Prepared type, he had not only an umbrella but a rain slicker in his Jeep.

Just hope I don't get nailed by another streak of lightning, he thought grimly as he dug around for the raincoat from the front seat. *At least I'm wearing rubber-soled shoes. Maybe I should leave the umbrella here—not liking the idea of carrying a long metal implement as I run through a storm.*

With that running mental commentary, he at last located the dark blue slicker and struggled into it while seated in the driver's seat.

The only reason he was truly considering making a break for the cottage was because if Teddy was there, he didn't want her left alone in this ugly storm.

Well, and he wanted to see her.

Badly.

Badly enough to risk dashing through a storm.

FOURTEEN

TEDDY TOLD herself it wasn't really all that bad, with the power out, here on this remote little island, miles from anyone.

Her laptop was charged, and so was her Wi-Fi hub, so at least she could still watch Tim Riggins and his tight end in the Dillon Panthers football uniform.

Plus, she had a few books tucked away that she was supposed to read—one of which she was really looking forward to, because it was the latest Marina Alexander adventure. She'd saved it as a reward for finishing her book, and now she could dive in without feeling guilty.

Teddy had the flashlight, and she was certain she'd seen some candles in the drawer in the kitchen when she'd been looking for scissors a few days ago. That would help brighten things up a little.

But the wind whipped at the cottage, and the place shook with every renewed gust of wind. With the crashes of thunder sounding like a hundred massive plates tumbling to a tile floor, and the mean streaks of lightning scarring the sky, Teddy felt frighteningly isolated and more than a little nervous.

Still, she managed not to work herself up too much. "It's good research," she told herself—aloud again, for obvious reasons. "Now I'll know exactly how someone feels when they're stranded in an unfamiliar place in the middle of nowhere with a terrible storm raging around. At least I won't have to worry about anyone breaking in in this weather— *Ah—!*"

She choked back most of the scream as her heart leapt into her throat. She darted to her feet, staring at the dark, shadowy figure running toward the cottage.

"Ohmigod, ohmigod, ohmigod," she whispered, looking around for something to use as a weapon. A broom. A tennis racket. A chair.

A knife! From the kitchen. And a frying pan, because, well, *blood.*

She bolted into the kitchen, hunkering down as she ran in a probably vain effort to keep from being seen by her soon-to-be attacker.

By now, the figure had reached the door, and she heard it rattling in its hinges.

And then, as she lifted the heavy frying pan, she heard the most terrifying noise of all: the sound of a key being fit in the lock.

Ohmigod.

Okay.

Stay calm.

But her knees were watery and her heart was pounding so hard that she thought she might faint. Images from *The Shining* tore through her fertile mind as she ducked behind the edge of the kitchen door, holding the frying pan at the ready.

Maybe, with the lights out, the intruder wouldn't know she was there. She could take him by surprise, and clock him with—

Oh, damn, her laptop was open and on…the screen was a dead giveaway.

Dead.

Don't think about that right now, Mack.

Her thoughts went in hysterical loops, and Teddy realized right then and there that she much preferred writing about dangerous, scary, suspenseful scenes than living them.

The door eased open, and the figure—tall, dripping, wearing something shiny and dark that covered him from head to knee—stepped in.

She nearly fainted when she saw him look directly at the laptop screen.

"Teddy?" the figure called. "Are you here?"

She nearly shrieked with relief. And shock. In fact, she dropped the damned frying pan from shaking fingers. It landed on her toe.

"*Ow!* Oscar?"

"Teddy! What are you doing in the dar— Oh, the power line." He pushed back his hood, then stripped off the dripping rain slicker.

She dropped the knife on the kitchen counter—no need for him to know about that; she was cool as a cucumber—and stepped over the frying pan.

"What in the *hell* do you think you're doing?" she cried, with all the vehemence of pent-up nerves mingled with wild relief.

"I…" He seemed ill at ease, but it was difficult in the dim light, cast only by her computer screen, to read his expression. "I'm sorry. I didn't have any way to reach you. I—I forgot to leave my key." He held up the offending item, the little metal object that had nearly given her a heart attack when he'd slipped it into the lock.

She managed to find her voice. "You came back because you forgot to leave your key?"

Okay, that wasn't what she was hoping for—in the twenty seconds she'd had to assimilate that Oscar had *returned*—but at least she wasn't here alone anymore. Even if he was a jerk.

"No, I came back— I came back because—well, I realized I left in a hurry, and we were sort of…in the middle—or, at least, the beginning of something." He toed off his boots and stood uncertainly in the center of the shadowy room. "I came back because I wanted to know what that something was. If anything."

Oh thank God.

Teddy thought that, but she didn't act upon it. Not right away.

Until her legs carried her across the room and she slid into his embrace.

"I'm glad you came back," she said as his arms came around her. "For a number of reasons—not the least of which being it's *really effing* nerve-racking being here by myself during this damned storm. With no power. And ghosts around. And people breaking in."

"Oh, Teddy," he murmured with a quiet chuckle. He folded her tightly against his cold, rain-scented body. "I was so bloody stupid."

The next thing she knew, he was kissing her. Really kissing her—as if he was dying, or as if he never needed to breathe again.

Her thoughts dissolved and she was only aware of Oscar: his strong, sure hands, his mouth, the solidness of his body, the taste and scent of him. Her eyes closed and she tipped her head back as he slid his mouth along the edge of her jaw, nibbling and nuzzling that sensitive spot beneath her ear. His mouth was doing insanely delicious things to her, sending hot shivers through her body, making her hair rise gently along the back of her neck.

At last, a particularly violent crack of thunder brought her back to her senses—and the realization that she did, in fact, need to breathe—and Teddy eased back.

"We should—uh—catch up on a few things," she said, reaching up to brush that stubborn lock of hair back from his forehead.

"Probably a good idea. Um…do I smell pizza? I was in a hurry to get back, so I didn't stop to eat."

He'd been in a hurry to get back? Teddy smiled to herself as she replied, "It was frozen, but tasted pretty good—and fortunately, I finished heating it before the power went out."

"Speaking of which, I'm pretty sure I saw the lightning hit the tree that took down the power line," Oscar said. He went on to explain how his Jeep had nearly been fried, and why he'd been walking to the cottage and not driving.

"I'm not ashamed to say it freaked the hell out of me when I saw you running up to the house, all shadowy and dark," she said, pulling down a plate and glass for him with help from the light he was shining from the flashlight.

"Yes, I can imagine. I saw candles in the drawer over here," Oscar said, and took the flashlight over to search. "And tomorrow I can get the generator running."

"There's a generator? How did you know that?"

He gave her a pitying look over the flames of the four pillar candles he was lighting. "I wasn't going to stay in a place with all of my lab equipment if there was a chance the power would go out for any length of time. I couldn't chance my samples getting ruined."

She shook her head. "Why am I surprised? You brought your own refrigerator, after all."

"I would have brought my own generator if necessary," he

replied, setting the candles up on the kitchen table. "Fortunately, it wasn't, or I'd have had to leave the centrifuge at home because it all wouldn't have fit in my Jeep."

"Of course you would have." Teddy shook her head as another boom of thunder rattled the dishes in the cupboards.

"Well, since we're on a well out here in the sticks, without power, there's no water—or toilet," he said.

Teddy froze. "*What?*" She was standing by the sink and twisted the spigot sharply to prove him wrong. Nothing came out but a small blurp of water, then a gurgle. "No water?"

Now she had another reason to be thankful Oscar had come back. She'd have had no idea about the water (or toilet) and certainly no idea about setting up the generator. She lived in Manhattan, for pity's sake.

"We can use a bucket of water to flush the toilet if necessary," he said around the piece of pizza he was devouring. "So don't panic too much. There's a lake right out there, don't forget. Oh, I forgot—there's a hand pump in the garden. That would be much more convenient."

Right. Like she wanted to discuss bathroom procedures with the guy whose bones she wanted to jump…

"So, you came back." She decided to take charge of the conversation, and to forget how she suddenly had to pee.

No toilet? Really?

There went her idea of a romantic, candlelit interlude while a storm raged outside.

"First, before I explain all of that… Teddy, how's the book going? I realized after the fact that you were—um—exaggerating or maybe even—um—lying when you told me you'd finished it this morning."

"It's done now. I sent it off at precisely four twenty-five today. For real. My agent even called to say she received it."

He smiled, and to her amazement, he seemed genuinely

relieved as he gave her arm a gentle squeeze. "I'm so glad. Now you can really relax."

"Yes. I'm definitely looking forward to *all* the benefits of *finishing*." She gave him a very warm, very deliberate smile, and his eyes widened. Then they narrowed, and when he gave her the same hot smile full of promise, Teddy's knees nearly gave out.

She'd better sit down.

"Happy to oblige," he murmured, still looking at her in the candlelight. "Anytime. That is part of the reason I came back."

"Only part?" she teased.

"Well, I had to return the key."

Her gaze shot to his in indignation before she realized he was teasing her. "Right."

"Teddy," he said a moment later, "why do you have the sofa in front of the connecting door over there?"

She explained about the door hidden behind the rosebush and how she couldn't figure out where it connected to the rest of the cottage. "And I didn't even look in the plastic bins," she added with distaste. "I was a big old scaredy-cat."

"Anyone would have been. Especially being here alone, with all the stuff that's been going on." He looked as if he wanted to say something, then thought better of it. "We can look tomorrow. I don't think we have to worry about anyone getting there in the meantime. No one's going to be out in this storm, breaking in *or* coming from the lake. It would be impossible."

She was silent for a moment, considering a whole lot of things. Mostly that he was right, but...

"You're thinking about how Sargent Blue could get somewhere underwater during a thunderstorm, aren't you?" Oscar said after a moment.

She grinned. "How did you know?"

He merely looked at her, and the soft expression in his eyes made her heart go very mushy.

He understands me. How did he get to know me so well in only a few days?

"There's no safe way," he said, and sipped the wine, then looked approvingly at the glass. "Hm. Not bad."

"Well, scuba divers are underwater," Teddy said, pointing at him with a crust of pizza. "They're protected from the storm while they're way down there, aren't they? And they wear rubber flippers. They'd be grounded if they came onto the sand."

"And what about their big metal oxygen tanks when they're walking across the sand?" he replied with a quirked eyebrow.

"I'm *sure* Sargent Blue—or anyone who might be doing nefarious things—can get rubber-wrapped oxygen tanks," she retorted. "And everything else."

"Hmm. I don't know. I think it'd be pretty risky. Even for Blue."

"Risky is Blue's middle name," she replied, then got up. "I'm still hungry—that pizza was barely enough for one, and you ate half of it."

"We can still use the gas stove even though the power's out —by lighting it with a match."

"S'mores!" she exclaimed. "I deserve Celebration S'mores for finishing my book. We can toast the marshmallows right over the gas flame. And of course I have the ingredients. I'm on summer vacation, aren't I? S'mores are a requirement for summer vacation."

Oscar looked as if he were about to say something—probably a reminder that until today she technically *hadn't* been on summer vacation—but he didn't. She gave him a smug smile as she rummaged through the kitchen drawers.

It didn't take long to get everything together. She found a long, two-pronged meat fork that worked perfectly for toasting the marshmallows, and Oscar laid out the graham crackers and chocolate bars in a little assembly line.

"You have peanut butter cups here, too," he said, looking at her with adorable confusion.

"Yes, of course. I like them better than just plain chocolate. Smoosh it between the graham crackers and the hot marshmallow—see how the peanut butter and chocolate gets all soft and gooey?" She demonstrated, then offered him the first s'more.

"I'm sold," he said, after devouring it in one bite.

While the storm raged around them, rattling the windows and sending tree branches tumbling to the ground, they sat in companionable silence, eating s'mores and drinking wine in the candlelight.

"I've gotta say, this is pretty damned perfect," Oscar said after finishing his fourth s'more. "And much as I'd like to *finish* out the evening in a more comfortable place as soon as possible—like, right *now*"—the look in his eyes made her insides go as hot and gooey as the marshmallows—"I should do something more difficult first."

Her gooey insides solidified into stone. "What's that?"

He drew in a breath, then exhaled. "I need to give you an explanation, and then I need to—um—answer a few text messages." He set his phone on the table, and she saw that he had *a lot* of unread notifications on it. "And after that, if you're still speaking to me, I want…*you*."

FIFTEEN

THE LOOK in Teddy's eyes made Oscar's stomach do a slow flip, and he immediately regretted even suggesting that he do the difficult things first.

Why had he even brought it up? He should have just pulled her in his arms and finished where that hello-I'm-back kiss had been going...

Finished.

Oh, he couldn't *wait* to finish her off. To hear her soft sighs and moans, to see her eyes glaze with passion, to feel her writhe and shudder beneath him...

"Uh," he said, mainly to jolt himself from the very delicious fantasy into which he'd slid. Dammit. *Why* was he so damned anal retentive?

"Because that's who you are," Teddy said.

"What?" Had he said that aloud? *Christ.*

"I could see you regretting that you were going to get the difficult things out of the way first, and wondering why you'd said so out loud—it's because of who you are. And that's one of the things I really like about you, Oscar. You're a *good person.* Nice. Thoughtful. Empathetic. I'm guessing—I might be wrong—that you changed your plans, and so you feel it necessary to let other people who might be affected by that change know about the change, so they don't worry. Or whatever. Am I right?"

Somehow he followed her long, convoluted string of words. "Yes. You're right. But—"

"I think it's always better to clear the air first. Besides, then you won't have *any* distractions," she teased. "Because, Oscar, the last thing I want is for you to be distracted when you have your hands on my very sexy butt."

Now his belly dropped to his knees and his hearing went dead. The look in her eyes made him want to toss his phone out into the storm and forget about everything else.

But that wasn't the kind of guy he was. And she knew it. And, apparently, she accepted it. Maybe even found it attractive—though that might be going a little too far. Who'd find anal retentiveness attractive?

"So, lay it on me," she said, her pretty mouth quirking in that curling smile. "And I don't mean your lips—at least, right now."

He gave a pained laugh. "You know, you're quite a package, Teddy Mack."

"Well, to be honest, part of it is the wild exuberance of sending off my book. But only part of it," she added firmly.

"Right. All right. So. I'm guessing, based on the way you —uh—sent me off this morning, that you might possibly have heard my phone conversation last night." He gave her a grim smile.

"Oh. Well, I couldn't exactly help it—you were pretty much outside my window." She shrugged, looking abashed. "I didn't mean to listen—really."

He shook his head. "It doesn't matter. I don't care. So, yeah —you must have gotten that Marcie didn't get married after all. She contacted me out of the blue and wanted to talk, and that's when I found out she'd called off the wedding. Before I realized it, I told her I'd come back to Princeton so we could talk.

"It was a stupid thing to do—for a lot of reasons. I realized it the minute I agreed to do it. But I guess I was being too… what did you call me? Empathetic? *Nice?*"

"In this case, I'd say you were just being an idiot male, but that's just me," she said with a mischievous grin.

"Right. An idiot male." He rolled his eyes a little, and to his delight, she laughed. "Anyway, because I always follow through"—he gave her a meaningful look, and was even more delighted when she blushed—"on my commitments"— another meaningful look—"I felt obligated to drive to Princeton, even though I regretted saying I would. I figured I owed it to her—well, and to me—to at least, I don't know, review the situation? So I went.

"But about five minutes outside of Wicks Hollow, I realized that was bullshit. But I kept going because…well, you'd told me to look you up through your publisher, and maybe I'd misread everything—" He stopped because she snorted and rolled her eyes.

"Damned straight," Teddy said, stabbing the table with her finger. "You run off like that, you were going to have to hunt me down via my publisher if you ever wanted to see me again."

"Yeah, that's kind of what Dina said. That you were giving me a big eff-you."

She seemed surprised when he mentioned talking to Dina, but, uncharacteristically, she didn't comment.

"It was three hours of misery in the car, driving east, Teddy. I just want you to know that. It would have been less than fifteen minutes before I turned around if you hadn't mentioned looking you up through your publisher. That was one hell of a kiss you planted on me."

She preened a little. "That was my intention. I'm glad it worked."

"Oh, it worked."

"So. What about that phone call or text you have to return?" She glanced at his phone, which he'd turned on silent for his drive (since he was a conscientious driver). He hadn't even done more than glance at the display since he hung up with Dina.

"I—uh—sort of left things hanging with Marcie. Told her I'd be there later today."

"I think you're going to be late," Teddy said, stifling a giggle.

"No, I don't think I'm going to get there at all," he said, looking at her seriously. "Hell, Teddy, I hadn't thought about Marcie in *days*—I'd even forgotten the day she was supposed to get married. That should have told me something right away."

He picked up the phone and finally looked. Eight texts. Two missed calls. Plus two texts from Dina. Ugh.

"I've got to do this."

"I'll clean up in here. You can go in the other room."

He appreciated that she offered privacy, but he saw no reason to take it. He looked down at the phone, read the increasingly hysterical texts from Marcie, and decided it was best to ignore the voicemails that had accompanied her calls.

Oscar considered texting her back. It would be easier. But cowardly.

Instead, he girded his loins and called his former fiancée.

"Oh my God, where have you been? Are you all right, Oscar? I've been worried *sick*!"

"I'm fine. I'm sorry I haven't been in touch—you know I turn off my ringer when I'm driving—"

"I know, I know. You haven't changed a bit!" Her voice became warmer, but it was still a little tense. "I shouldn't have worried. Are you almost home?"

He swallowed, refusing to look at Teddy, who could surely hear Marcie's voice through the phone as she wiped off the few dishes they'd used with some paper towels. "No, actually, I'm not. That's why I'm calling. I'm not coming back to Princeton right now."

"You're not? But you said— *Oscar*, we need to talk."

"Right. Well, we can definitely do that"—he'd already decided some sort of conversation was going to have to happen—"but not till I get back. Which probably won't be for a week"—he paused when Teddy wagged her fingers in front of him—"I mean two weeks. At least two weeks." Teddy gave him a grin and a thumbs-up.

And that was when he realized he was a goner. He was one hundred percent nuts about thriller writer and über-chatterer T.J. Mack.

He didn't pay much attention to the rest of what Marcie was going on about; he just kept saying variations of "I'm not coming back right now. I'll let you know when I'm back in town." Finally, he cut her off mid-sentence (because she was starting to get a little mean) and said, "Gotta go, Marcie. Talk to you later."

Teddy began to applaud, but he held up a hand. "One more," he said. "Then…I'm turning the phone *off*. Because I've got other things to attend to."

"To which I must attend," she muttered. He flipped her off for ostensibly correcting his grammar, then used the same extended finger to text Dina.

The message to her was short and simple: *Back in Wicks Hollow. No need to go through publisher.*

Nosy Teddy was reading over his shoulder, and she burst out laughing. "Nice," she said. Then she removed the phone from his hands. "With your permission, Professor?"

"Turn it off," he said as he pulled her down into his lap.

The candles flickered on the table, the flames low and guttering in their puddles of wax, but he didn't need any light to find her mouth and settle his hands at her waist.

She dropped the dark phone onto the table and turned to straddle him on the chair, shoving her hands into his hair as she settled herself right over his hips. Pressing down *hard* with a soft little grunt.

Oh God, he thought, and closed his eyes as she kissed the hell out of him.

He couldn't keep his hands still; they slid up beneath the loose tee she was wearing, feeling her soft, warm skin as she nibbled her way along his neck while pressing down into where she straddled him. Stifling a soft moan, he unhooked her bra and slid his hands around to fill them with her breasts —the gloriously full, soft ones that had taunted him from the first morning she'd bent over in a tank top.

Teddy arched back when he found her nipples, giving a little sigh of pleasure as he teased and stroked them with the pads of his fingers. She shivered as those sexy points tightened beneath his touch, making him need more. *Now.*

"Mmm," she said, grinding herself down harder against him as she grabbed his shirt to pull him close for a deep kiss. "Dr. London, all buttoned up as usual," she purred as she swiftly unfastened each button, then pushed the shirt up and off his shoulders as his hands slid to her hips.

She bit his shoulder gently, settling her hands over the planes of his chest, then eased in for a long, slow, sensual kiss where her tongue stroked the inside of his mouth like he wanted to do inside of her. He felt the soft swell of her breasts pushing against his bare chest and thought, *That's not enough.*

With firm hands, he eased her away and pulled her shirt off. After tossing it to the floor, he took a moment to feast his eyes on the way the candlelight played over her bare torso as she leaned back against the edge of the table.

"Beautiful," he said, cupping her rosy-tipped breasts. They were splashed with golden light from the little flames, and looked like honey—so of course he had to taste.

Teddy gave a soft squeak of pleasure when he closed his mouth over one of her breasts, and she gripped his shoulders as he took his time tasting and teasing until she was shivering and gasping with pleasure. He could see her pulse throbbing in her throat, and in one delicate vein in a breast he was enjoying.

"That's right," he muttered, loving her responsiveness as he sucked and licked more deliberately while using his fingers to play with her other breast.

When she arched suddenly with a shot of pleasure and breathed a short, "Oh, *crap*, Oscar!" he smiled to himself. *Surprised you, did I?* And then he turned his attention to the other breast.

"You taste so good," he murmured after she came a second time just from his teasing her nipples. She sounded just as surprised this time around. "Teddy, love, I could do this all night, but my jeans are getting a little tight."

"Then I guess we'd better change location," she said with that husky laugh he loved. "Soon."

"How about *now*," he said, and scooped her up into his arms as he stood.

"Why, Rhett, whatevah are you doing?" she said in a falsetto Southern accent as she plunged her hand down the front of his jeans. And closed her hand around him.

Holy shit.

He nearly lost his balance—and his wad—right then, but managed to save himself. "I'm going to carry you up that sweep of stairs and have my way with you," he managed to say, thankful there weren't actually any stairs to climb.

"I sure as hell hope you don't trip," she said in his ear as he strode out of the kitchen. He stumbled a little when she stroked the head of his erection down behind the close quarters of his zipper, but was able to stay upright until he fumbled his way into the bedroom he'd used.

Then he tumbled them both onto the mattress and fresh sheets he'd left behind that morning, pulling her warm, sexy torso up against his as he slid on top of her. That meant her hand slipped out from his very tight jeans—which was a good thing, considering the situation—and also gave him the opportunity to slide *his* hand down the front of her stretchy pants.

"Very convenient," he murmured as he found her hot and wet and very ready. She shivered and arched a little against him, and he found he loved those soft moans she made as he took his time playing with her while nuzzling that warm, damp place where neck met shoulder.

By the time he coaxed her into two more climaxes, he was nearly blind with need himself. The smell of Teddy, the taste, the sounds she made were driving him wild. He couldn't get enough of her.

She must have felt the same way, for she snapped open the top of his jeans and yanked down the zipper. He groaned with relief as she freed him from the confines, curling her hand around him as he realized—

"No, wait." Oh God, hardest thing he ever had to do. He grabbed her hand and pulled it away then eased from the bed. "Condom," he managed, trying desperately to remember where he'd put them…

In his Jeep. Packed away.

Half a mile distant. In a raging thunderstorm.

He wanted to weep.

But Teddy, his Teddy, his smart, quick-thinking, and fast-talking—and wildly sexy—Teddy, was on the move. He gritted his teeth when he saw the enticing bounce of her breasts as she bounded from the bed.

"Wait here," she said, and, praise God, she was back in seconds—with a string of familiar, flat plastic packets flapping from her hand.

He didn't know whether to laugh or to cry, because there were at least five of them.

Then he didn't pay attention to anything at all but the way her fingers were teasing as she rolled on the condom, and that he was skimming her conveniently stretchy pants down over her hips, and finally, they were skin to skin.

"Oh, God," he murmured as they slid together, her curves fitting sweetly against him. She was warm and soft and smelled like perfection.

"Oscar," she said a little desperately when he reached down between them to touch her again, "I want you…now, please. *Now.*"

She didn't have to ask twice, and it was only another instant of shifting and fumbling, and then… Oh. Yes.

The sweet slide. Heaven.

Home.

They moved together, with him trying to keep it slow and

easy and Teddy urging him on, demanding more and faster and all of him.

And then the finish.

Heaven.

Home.

SIXTEEN

MMMMM.

Teddy was already smiling before she opened her eyes. But when she saw the smooth, solid corner of Oscar's shoulder, and the stretch of his half-tanned arm angling from the bedclothes right next to her, she closed her eyes again in blissful memory.

What a glorious way to wake up.

What a glorious way to spend the night, with a thunderstorm thrashing about around them. Of course, they'd done quite a bit of thrashing on their own.

Smiling again at the memory, she snuggled a little closer to Oscar. The morning was chilly, though the rain had stopped sometime around dawn, and the sun shone happily through the window.

A minute later, she realized she had to pee. And then she remembered there was no power—no water, no toilet. But he'd shown her how to use a bucket to flush the loo, as he'd called it—making her hoot at the random Britishism—so she knew it wasn't impossible.

Except that she'd need to fill the bucket first.

With a disgusted groan over her body's basic morning needs, she slithered reluctantly out of bed and pulled on the first item of clothing she found—Oscar's shirt.

Mmm. Soft. And it smelled good. Like him.

When she passed the bathroom on the way outside to get water, she saw a pail and two large pots sitting on the floor. All were filled with water. She grinned, and her heart melted even more. Because obviously Oscar had set that up last night while she was sleeping.

He had to have left their cozy bed and gone out into the pouring rain to fill all three vessels from the water pump. What a guy.

And she was definitely, positively over the moon about him. She was *toast*.

When she slipped back into bed, he woke enough to draw her into a snug embrace against his warm body.

"We've still got two left," she murmured, licking his ear then nibbling on its lobe.

His eyes popped open. "Two?" He grinned, for she knew he was remembering the strip of condoms she'd retrieved last night. "I guess we'd better get to finishing them off," he said, and she giggled against his cheek.

"I like the way you think."

And then all thoughts of humor fled when he rolled on top of her.

Sometime later—much, *much* later—they found it necessary to forage for something to eat.

And to refill the water buckets.

"I'll get them refilled, then the generator hooked up and started," Oscar said while Teddy did her best to toast bread over the gas flame.

It turned out pretty well, and she spread four pieces with peanut butter, then drizzled them with honey. She was just cutting up an apple when Oscar came in on his second trip with water pails.

"Eat first, then the generator. You probably need to replenish after all that activity last night," she added with a sly smile. "I even made tea by boiling water in a pan—though I didn't check the temperature. Don't tell Maxine or Orbra."

"Your secret's safe with me." He sat down and began to dunk the teabag up and down in his mug. "There are quite a few branches down outside, and some debris too, probably blown in from the lake."

After their breakfast, Teddy went with him to survey the damage. While he messed with the generator, she walked around the cottage. This was the first time she'd been outside since being startled away from the room behind the rosebush last night.

As she came around the side of the lighthouse toward the lake, she saw several branches on the ground. And something else that had her hurrying over to investigate.

It was a small electronic device in a zippered plastic bag. Just sitting in the middle of the ground between the lighthouse and a maple sapling.

The hair on the back of her neck prickled because she knew it wasn't hers, and why would Oscar have something like this outside (though he would for certain have wrapped it in plastic)? It couldn't have been blown in from the lake—it was too far from the beach and too heavy to have come that far.

Could someone have dropped it last night? It had to have been last night, because she'd been standing over here and walking all around the area yesterday before the storm and would have seen it then.

She picked up the bag and began to examine its contents, then realized the device was a sort of recorder. She pushed "play" then fumbled and nearly dropped the thing when a horrific, bloodcurdling scream—a very familiar one—filled the air.

"Oh my God," she said, frantically pushing the "stop" button as Oscar came bolting around the cottage.

"Teddy! What— Are you all right?"

She stared at the recorder, then looked up. Because the sound had come from slightly above her.

Oscar took the recorder from her grip as, mouth set in an unhappy line, she scanned the nearby tree and the lines of the cottage and lighthouse. He pushed the button, and she jumped when the scream once more filled the air.

They looked at each other.

"Well, what the *hell*," he said. "This puts a whole new spin on the situation."

Understatement.

"I think the speaker is up there," she said, pointing to a small black square sitting beneath a shadowy eave. "*Wow*."

She could hardly comprehend the situation.

"Someone definitely doesn't want us around here," Oscar said, still examining the recorder. "They've gone to a lot of trouble to scare us off. There's nothing on this device that gives any indication who it belongs to—except maybe it could be traced by the serial number. This is a pretty solid piece of equipment. Small and light, and good quality. Not cheap. Must've gotten blown down from wherever it was hidden." He looked at her. "Come to think of it, I didn't hear the scream last night. Did you?"

She gave him a wan smile. "No. I was pretty distracted. But I'll bet it didn't go off because it got blown to the ground."

He slid an arm around her and tugged her close. "I'm sorry, Teddy."

"What are you sorry about?" she asked, resting her head on his shoulder and curving her arm around his taut waist. She needed his solidness right at the moment. "Sorry that I was distracted last night?" She gave him a cheeky grin that she didn't really feel.

It had been bad enough that someone broke into the cottage and destroyed their stuff, but to know that whoever it was—because they *had* to be the same people who'd planted the recording, didn't they?—had had a long-term plan was disconcerting.

He gave a short laugh and squeezed her tight. "Definitely not sorry about that. I'm sorry that it wasn't a ghost—and that it's definitely mortal beings who have been fucking around with us. I mean, you were pretty excited about the ghost." He planted a kiss on the top of her head.

She grimaced. "Well, all things considered, I'd much rather deal with a supernatural element than a villainous mortal. I think they're more dangerous. After all, I write about them."

When Oscar didn't respond, she knew he agreed and was probably trying not to worry her.

"But what about the green thing?" she said a few minutes later, when they sat down on the front porch to sort things out. Her mind was finally beginning to work again.

"A projection of some sort, of course," Oscar replied. He'd pulled out his phone to call Joe Cap, but set it aside. "If we keep looking, I'm sure we'll find the projector."

Teddy frowned, then as he picked up the phone, she put her hand out to stop him. "But we saw the green thing at two different places. And it looked different each time. One time it was bluish-green—the first time—and the second time it was puke green."

Oscar shrugged, but left the phone next to him. "They obviously made adjustments. Think about it, Teddy—the scream was every night at one thirty, like clockwork. The recorder must have been on a timer. It was always at the same time, except the night they broke in.

"That night, the scream was early—*and* the green thing was projected so we could see it from the ground as we returned from the hot springs. They planned it that way so the break-in would be connected and seem like it was part of the supernatural element. They must have seen us in town, maybe, or heard that we were there—as we've learned, everyone knows everything in Wicks Hollow—and they came out here to stage the break-in and then the ghostly apparition. Maybe we got back too soon, or maybe they just intended to do it after we went to sleep—but when we left to go to the hot spring, they took advantage of the fact."

Teddy pursed her lips and thought some more. "Yes, that makes sense. They upped their game that night." Then she shivered and looked around. "They must have seen us leave to go to the pool. They must have been watching from somewhere."

"Unfortunately, yes."

"But…that first night. When we were on top of the lighthouse. There was no way anyone could have expected us to go up there. How would they have known to project the image up there? And besides, it—well, it seemed really *real*. It got so cold."

Oscar was shaking his head. "I hate to say it, but it's possible the place could be bugged—or, at least, maybe they were just lurking around here somewhere and heard us talking on the porch."

Teddy did not like the thought of being spied on all the time. It made her insides horribly queasy. But it also felt a little far-fetched to think that someone was just hanging around —where?

"Where would they have been hiding that we didn't see them while we were sitting on the porch?" She spread her hands to show the empty area around the cottage and light-house. "There's really nowhere for someone to hide close enough to listen. Unless… Ugh—I hate the idea—unless—"

"The place is or was bugged." Oscar didn't seem any more thrilled about it than she did.

"We need to look inside that hidden room," she said in a low voice in case someone was listening, and bolted to her feet. "Maybe whatever's in there will tell us who the hell is doing this, and why. And boy, Iva's going to be really disap-pointed that there isn't a ghost after all."

"Well, Iva's tender feelings are the least of my worries right now," Oscar muttered as he stood up. "Let's go take a look at this room."

She retrieved the oven mitts from the kitchen and they went out to the trellis. To Teddy's relief, there didn't appear to be any fresh markings that indicated it had been moved since she was there yesterday. Even with the heavy rain, this side of the lighthouse was on the opposite side from where the wind had come, and the rosebush was thick enough to have blocked much of it as well, so the tracks wouldn't have been obliterated.

"Very clever way to hide a door." Oscar slid it away, sustaining much less thorn damage than she had yesterday. "I forgot my phone on the porch, for its light. We'll have to share the flash." He turned it on and shined it into the room.

"Nothing looks different from yesterday," Teddy said.

"I don't see how anyone could have come here during the storm last night," he replied. "It was too dangerous to come by boat, and my Jeep and that downed tree and power line are blocking the road. No one can get through."

For some reason, an eerie shiver gripped her, and Teddy looked over her shoulder. There was no one around, there couldn't be…but she felt exposed and nervous.

They were effectively trapped here on the island.

But that was silly. All they had to do was call Declan or the police station—or even the Tuesday Ladies—and any one of them would come and get them. And soon Oscar would have the generator working. And she'd have running water again.

Teddy smiled, but she still felt uneasy.

"Well, look at this." Oscar shined the small flashlight down into one of the plastic tubs he'd opened. "Wetsuits. Face masks. Flippers. Someone's been scuba diving."

"See! I told you," Teddy said, partly joking, partly intrigued, and partly nervous. "They *could* have come here during the storm last night, deep under the water—"

"Still too dangerous with the lightning, because, look here —no rubber-covered oxygen tanks. Just plain old metal ones." He'd moved on to open a different tub and was shining his flashlight into it. "And three BCs—mouthpieces—too. That means probably at least three divers."

"I wonder what they're doing. I mean, obviously they're diving in the lake, and it seems like they're—whoever they are —using the lighthouse as a base, or at least a place to store their equipment. But why bother? What's the big secret?"

Before Oscar could reply, she heard something behind them that made her blood run cold.

Spinning around so quickly she bumped into her companion, Teddy saw a man and a woman standing in the doorway.

They were outlined by the sun, but she was certain she didn't know them.

"What's the big secret? I could tell you," said the man. "But then I'd have to kill you."

Teddy's heart plummeted and her knees nearly gave out.

Because he sounded dead serious.

SEVENTEEN

NO.

That was the only thought that lodged itself in Oscar's mind: *No.*

There was no bloody way these people—whoever they were—were going to do anything to take Teddy from him.

Somehow, he managed to keep his head clear and his thoughts smooth as he faced what was surely the most dangerous moment of his life. Without looking, he reached for and took Teddy's hand. It was freezing.

"Who are you?" he said, even as he measured the situation.

The man looked vaguely familiar, but Oscar was certain he'd never seen the woman before. Both of them appeared solid and fit, but that didn't bother him.

It was the gun the female was holding that made his blood turn to ice.

"We tried to get you out of here," she said, stepping into the room. "You had your chance. But just like stubborn, nosy Stuart Millore, you just wouldn't leave."

"Stuart Millore?" Teddy's voice sounded a little creaky to

Oscar, but as she spoke more, it gained strength. "So what did you do about him? Did you push him off the lighthouse?"

The man shrugged as the woman laughed. "Like I said, he got too nosy. And he started asking questions. He'd see us when we came to do the yard work—you think the lawn mows itself? Or those flowers just sprang up from out of nowhere?"

"That must be how you rigged up the recording of the scream," Teddy said. "Because you were here working on the yard, and if anyone saw you, you had the perfect excuse."

"That's right. Been doing the landscape work for this place and others managed by the rental agency for years now. That kept us free for our nighttime work."

"You're talking too much, Misty," interrupted her companion. "Let's get this done."

Oscar felt Teddy tense against him, and his heart skipped a beat. Whatever they were here to do, he suspected it didn't bode well for him and Teddy.

"I say we shoot 'em and lock 'em in here," the man said. "No one will find 'em for weeks—if then."

Misty frowned. "I don't want to see the mess every time we come in here to get our things. Plus—*duh*—obvious murder." Her eyes narrowed. "I liked the way we did it with the other guy. Looked like an accident."

"Three people falling from the top of a lighthouse? That might raise a little suspicion," Teddy said, and Oscar squeezed her hand.

Did she *want* to get shot, for crying out loud?

"She's got a point, Rob," Misty said. "Still, I don't want a big fucking mess in here. We've got stuff to store."

"But there's a big storm coming," Rob said. "Another one. A nasty lightning strike would be—what do they call it? An act of

God?" He laughed, and it made the hair on Oscar's neck stand on end. "The lovebirds climbed up to the top of the lighthouse to watch the storm roll in—sooooo romantic—and *oopsie*, they get struck by lightning. There's a lot of metal up there." He looked at Oscar with cold eyes. "And that lighthouse is a big old beacon in the middle of nowhere, just waiting to attract a bolt of lightning."

"Good plan. What'll we do with them till then?" Misty asked, apparently in agreement with the idea and having no qualms talking about Oscar and Teddy as if they were inanimate objects.

"Just leave 'em here." Rob glanced toward the interior of the room.

Oscar liked that idea. Not getting shot yet meant a chance to figure out an escape, so he tried not to look too enthusiastic.

"They're not going to go anywhere with these." Rob reached into one of the plastic tubs and produced a handful of zip ties. "Storm's a couple hours away. We'll have time to do a little diving before then—and this time, it won't matter if they see us walking to and from the beach." He gave Oscar and Teddy a cold smile.

"What are you diving for?" Teddy asked as Rob maneuvered over toward them.

"Buried treasure," Misty said with a laugh. She kept the gun trained on Oscar as her partner zip-tied Teddy's ankles then wrists together. And then she transferred her aim to Teddy when it was Oscar's turn.

The plastic bit into Oscar's wrists as Rob yanked the thick strip tight, restraining them behind his back. When Rob shoved him roughly to the floor, Oscar's head bounced off one of the plastic tubs and he landed awkwardly, twisting one of his wrists. The zip ties on his ankles were just as tight.

"Buried treasure? Like what—a shipwreck?" Teddy, of course, had to ask the question.

Even though Oscar's mind was filled with options for escape, he appreciated the fact that the more they knew about who these people were and what they wanted, the more it could help he and Teddy know what they faced. And potentially assist with an escape.

Still, he wasn't all that optimistic at the moment. Especially since he thought he might have just sprained his wrist.

"The granddaddy of all Great Lakes shipwrecks, in fact," Misty said as she stripped off her shorts and shirt to reveal a swimsuit. She pulled a wetsuit out of one of the tubs and began to shimmy into it, all the while talking. "Everyone else thought the *Catherine* went down closer to Chicago, but we were the ones who really found her."

When Rob tried to hush her up, she turned on him. "Who the hell are they going to tell? We already know where she is. We've already got plenty of the cargo up—and there's more to come. No one can stop us now."

Oscar felt Teddy bristling next to him, and he almost smiled. But his wrist was screaming with pain, and his head pounded from where he'd hit the edge of a plastic tub. Those things were harder than they looked.

"You're talking about the *Catherine Teal*?" Teddy asked. "The ship that went down in the late 1890s."

"That's right," Misty said.

By now, their captors had donned diving gear. Rob helped Misty hoist the heavy oxygen tank onto her back, then, with face mask in one hand and gun in the other, he tucked a pair of flippers under his arm. Giving Oscar and Teddy a salute, he said, "See ya in a bit. Enjoy."

And with that, Rob closed the door, leaving them in darkness.

EIGHTEEN

"OSCAR," Teddy said the moment the door was closed. "Are you all right? You took a hell of a fall."

"My wrist is pretty effed up, but other than that, I'm fine."

"Okay, good. Just give me a minute."

In the pitch dark, Oscar couldn't see what she was doing, but he could hear what sounded like a sharp slap, followed by a soft grunt of pain. "Damn," she whispered. "That freaking *hurt*."

"What are you doing?"

But she didn't reply, and he heard the same sound again—a swish through the air, then a slap—sharper, harder, and more violent. But this time, there was another sound, too, a faint little snap. She gave a cry of pain, followed by a gush of, "Oh, thank *God*."

"What the hell are you doing? Teddy? Are you all right?"

"Just give me a sec," she said, her voice tense. "That hurt *so* bad. I've got to get my ankles free, then I can help you…"

"What?" He heard more moving around, and by now realized she'd somehow freed herself from the zip ties. "How did you do that?"

"Do you know where the flashlight is?"

"I slipped it into my pocket. Right side, upper… Yes. There." Her hand digging around next to his thigh made him think of other, more pleasant things than being zip-tied and left in the dark, or shot, or otherwise killed, and that renewed his anger and determination not to let those assholes take Teddy from him.

Suddenly, the flashlight was on. "Oh my God, Oscar, you must be in *agony*. Your wrist is purple and so swollen. The plastic is cutting into your skin." She sounded like she was going to cry.

"I'm aware of that," he said, gritting his teeth as her movements trying to free him made the pain even worse. "How the hell did you get yourself free?"

"Hold on," she said. "There's probably something in here I can use to cut you loose. You won't be able to do what I did without really hurting yourself—"

"Teddy. If you don't tell me how you got yourself free—"

"All right, all right. Geez. It's really easy, but it hurts." By now she was back behind him with the flashlight and something she'd found in one of the tubs; Oscar realized he preferred not to know what sort of sharp implement she was going to be using to cut the plastic away from where it dug deeply into his swollen wrist. "You lift your arms up as high as they'll go, then you bring them down and to your sides in a really fast and hard motion. It snaps the plastic. Did I mention it *hurts*?"

Oh my God. Talk about hurting… He ground his teeth and closed his eyes, breathing deeply against the pain, as the plastic she was working on moved against his tender wrist. Then, suddenly, the restraints were gone.

"Thank you," he said, bringing his arms back around to

the front and gingerly feeling around his swelling hand. Yep. If not broken, then it was badly sprained.

"Now your ankles," she said. "How bad is your wrist?"

"It's not great. But it could be worse." It felt like his wrist had been placed on an anvil and someone had pounded on it. "I'm guessing you've done some research on how to escape zip ties."

"Yes." He heard the smile in her voice. "I was so happy he had zip ties and decided to use them instead of rope."

"Or shooting us," Oscar said as the tie around his ankles fell away.

"Right. Well, Misty had a point. It would have been a mess."

"Let's not talk about that right now, hmm?" He pushed himself gingerly to his feet, taking care not to put any weight on his wrist. "We need to get out of here while they're out on their dive."

"Okay, but I want to see what else is in these tubs," Teddy said, waving the flashlight around.

"No," he replied firmly, starting for the trellis-hidden door. "That's how the good guys always get caught—they spend too much time messing around looking at things when they should make an immediate beeline for freedom and safety. We're getting out of here now and calling Joe Cap, and then—Dammit to *hell*." His voice dropped to a whisper. "I can hear them out there, Teddy."

"What are they doing?"

"I don't know. Sounds like they're arguing—yes. He wants to dive now, but she wants to wait because of the storm coming. Well, maybe it'll keep them busy for a while. But we can't go out there now."

"There's that other door that leads somewhere inside the

lighthouse," she said. "We can go that way. If we can get it open."

She brought the flashlight over and shined it on the padlock.

"If we had a screwdriver, we could just unscrew the lock plate from the wall, there," he said. "Did you happen to see anything like that over in their stuff?"

"Philips or flathead?" She walked away with the light.

"Flathead."

He heard her rummaging around and went to join her. "Look at this, Oscar!" she said in a low voice. "They really hit the jackpot."

Inside one of the larger tubs was an array of gold and silver objects: plates, cups, flatware, candlesticks. Much of it was covered with algae and seaweed.

"If this is from the Astors' ship, it's going to be solid gold or silver," Teddy said. "I wonder what else they've found. There's got to be jewels and all sorts of other treasure down there. No wonder they're willing to kill for it."

Oscar dug out a silver butter knife. "This'll work. Bring the light, Teddy—but let's listen at the door first. Maybe they're gone."

They didn't hear the sounds of voices until Oscar cracked the door and listened at the trellis. "They're still out there—but now it sounds like they might be on the porch."

"They're probably drinking our wine!" Teddy said, sounding outraged about the least of their problems. "But damn, that means we can't go back to the cottage. Unless we go from the inside. All right, let's get to work on that padlock."

A butter knife wasn't the best tool, but it eventually got the job done. There were three screws that held the latch to the wall, and by the time he finished with the third one, Oscar's fingers were cramped from working in the small location and maneuvering the makeshift screwdriver with his left hand.

But at last the latch fell away. Teddy carefully pulled the door open, and they slipped through into a small hallway that didn't look familiar to Oscar.

"Oh, this is the way to my bedroom," she whispered, gesturing to the left. "And straight ahead is the door to the staircase that leads to the lantern room at the top." She pointed up.

"Can we get out without them seeing us if they're on the porch?" he asked, for he could hear their voices very close by. Apparently, Misty had won the argument and they were delaying the dive.

Teddy shook her head. "My room is right next to the porch—remember? And we'd have to pass through the connecting door, and you can see that from the porch too."

Damn. And they couldn't go back around through the trellis door, because there was nowhere to go from there but down to the lake without being seen.

"All right. Let's just wait here for a while until they—uh—go somewhere else."

Until they come for us.

His suggestion was punctuated by a distant roll of thunder, and that reminded him of the plans Misty and Rob had made for them. Oscar reached for Teddy's hand with his good one and squeezed tight. "Is there a closet or somewhere we can hide in case they start looking for us?"

She shook her head, her eyes narrowing in the dim light. "I don't think so. There isn't one in my room, and the one in the bathroom is much too small for even one of us."

"All right. We're safe here for now. Let's just…wait."

They sat next to each other, leaning against the wall in the small, dim, and dingy hall. Oscar turned off the flashlight, for it seemed to be a little dimmer than it had been.

"Oscar," she said, tilting her head onto his shoulder. "I just want you to know, there's no one else I'd rather be stuck in this situation with."

He caught himself before he laughed. "I'd rather not be stuck in this situation at all," he said. "But thank you for the sentiment."

Then he drew in a breath, because there were things that needed to be said, and in case he didn't have the chance to ever say them, he knew he'd better now. Before whatever happened happened.

"Teddy, I…realize that you were in a particularly festive mood last night. When I got back here. And you were probably a little bit—um—relieved not to be alone—or having to learn the hard way there wasn't any water after the power went out." She gave a soft, muffled laugh, and he smiled. "Anyway, look…I…"

How did he say this?

"I—uh—well, I guess what I'm trying to say is, if you were so—um—"

"Oscar?"

"Yes?"

"I have no idea what you're trying to say."

"Neither do I." He sighed. He wasn't good at this sort of thing—putting his emotions into coherent words. "Look, I guess I just want you to know that I came back last night because I was—am—really falling for you. But I don't know whether you were so, well, *exuberant* and, um, not so very mad at me for leaving and coming back because you were just glad not to be alone and you were celebrating your book being turned in, or…or not."

"Is that your way of asking if last night was just me being celebratory and not really about you and me?"

"Well, yeah." For once, she'd been remarkably succinct—and he'd been the one floundering around with random phrases and clauses.

"Well, you're right about one thing. I should have been more annoyed with you for leaving and then just coming back like—like some prodigal son," she said. "You really were a jerk."

"Right." He wasn't certain whether this was going well or not.

"I mean, I didn't make you grovel or anything," she said contemplatively, "and you really probably should have been made to do so, considering that you *left* me to go back to your former fiancée after *sleeping* with me for the previous two nights."

"Well, we didn't technically *sleep* together—"

"And if it hadn't been for nosy old Maxine and Iva and her love for ghosts, we probably *would* have actually *slept* slept together before you found out that Marcie wanted you back—"

"She never said she wanted me back—"

"Oh, *phffft*. Of course she wanted you back, Oscar."

He swore he actually heard her roll her eyes. "Well, we'll never know because I… Well, the simple fact is, Teddy, I'm falling in love with you, and I don't give a damn what Marcie wants or thinks. I only care what you want or think." *And I hope it's me.*

"Oh, Oscar." Now he heard her smile, and the knots in his belly loosened. "The reason I was so mad at you—and I was, and I really did give you a break by not making you sweat it a lot more—was because I'm feeling the same way. And you *left* me in the middle of it. But mostly I was glad I hadn't *told* you how I felt before you left, because that would have been even more awful."

"Right." He *thought* he understood what she was saying. But even if he missed some of the subtler nuances, he got the gist of it.

And now he was *damned* certain he was going to get them both out of this mess, alive and safely.

Teddy lost track of time—it was impossible to know whether an hour or only minutes had passed, sitting as they were in a dark room with no windows and no way to tell time. They held hands and she rested her head on his shoulder.

They didn't need any more words.

She could hear the storm as it drew near, and she knew that meant Rob and Misty would be coming back for them any time, regardless of how long it had been. And that was when things were going to get hairy again.

Still, she felt optimistic about their chances of coming out unscathed. After all, she and Oscar were both extremely resourceful and intelligent, and Rob and Misty…well, they probably weren't the sharpest tacks in the box.

At least, that was what she told herself.

And then it happened—Oscar stiffened at the moment she heard the sound of someone in the storage room. Whoever it was, they were on the other side of the door with the padlock. She and Oscar had closed that door behind them, but there was no way to block it, and it would only be a moment before Rob and Misty realized where they'd gone.

She and Oscar had already pushed to their feet, but to her surprise, there was no shout of surprise announcing they'd disappeared. Still, he had her by the hand and was pulling her toward the door that led to her bedroom—and the rest of the cottage.

If they could just keep one step ahead of Misty and Rob, who'd surely be coming in behind them, they'd be out the front door of the cottage and running down the road where Oscar had left his Jeep.

He opened the door to her bedroom, and they slipped through into familiar surroundings. That was when they at last heard the shout of alarm in the storage room.

Teddy led the way out through her bedroom to the foyer with the connecting door, pausing to peek out at the porch to make sure no one was there.

Let's go, she said with her hands, and Oscar pushed ahead of her to crack open the curve-topped door. He peered around the opening, and was just about to step through when an ugly noise met their ears.

And stopped them in their tracks.

It was the sound of a gun cocking. Right on the other side of the curve-topped door.

NINETEEN

"THOUGHT YOU WERE PRETTY SMART, did you?" Misty sounded annoyed. "Rob! Here! I've got them!" She gestured with her firearm (Teddy couldn't see it well enough to tell what kind of weapon it was) as she pushed through the connecting door, forcing them back toward Teddy's bedroom. "I oughta just go ahead and put a bullet in each of you right now."

"Kind of messy," Teddy said before she could stop herself. "I vote for lightning strikes on top of the lighthouse."

Oscar had grabbed her hand again and squeezed hard enough that she gasped. When she chanced a look at him, she saw he was furious—and worried. She squeezed back, still feeling optimistic—quite a bit less than a few minutes earlier, but still. They weren't dead yet.

After all, a bullet might be a sure thing, but a lightning strike wasn't.

"Get 'em up top," Rob snarled when he appeared from Teddy's bedroom. "Storm's getting nasty—it'll be the perfect way to take care of 'em, then no one can nail anything on us. They won't even be suspicious enough to check things out."

As if to punctuate his words, a wild flash of lightning lit the room, followed too closely by a loud crash of thunder.

Teddy's optimism flagged slightly. As if he understood, Oscar tightened his grip on her fingers.

"Up we go," Misty said, gesturing with her gun as she prodded them back the way they'd come, through the room in which they'd waited, and to the base of the hundred and sixty-eight stairs. "No, wait. You go first," she said, pointing at Oscar. "I'll keep your girlfriend nice and close to me. Rob, you come up behind."

And with that, Teddy had her arm gripped tightly by the taller, far-fitter-than-she Misty, and a gun pointed at her as they began to climb.

Please don't trip, she thought, imagining what would happen if she or the gun-toting Misty did so. A bullet in this small, cylindrical space, and so close to her body… She shivered.

All right, just concentrate on getting up there in one piece.

"So, you decided to try and haunt us out of here," Teddy said. "The scream, the ghostly green projection, and so on. But you only did it outside—why not ever inside? That probably would have been more effective, to be honest. And how did you get the door up top to lock and then unlock? And the freaky *chill*?" Teddy slowed her pace a little to catch her breath and so she could talk.

"One of you was *always* here," Misty said. "You never left the damned cottage, so we couldn't set up anything in here. It wasn't hard to break in when we finally had the chance. But we'd have gotten more serious if the other stuff didn't work to get rid of you—but this here is a much better solution. Keep moving.".

"So." Teddy puffed. "The first night we were here—well, technically the second night, but it was the first night we were up on the lighthouse—how did you even know we were going to be up—"

"Shut up," growled Rob from behind them. "Just stop talking and keep moving. This isn't a goddam book club." He shoved at Teddy, and she barely caught herself from taking a header into the steps in front of her.

After that, she kept her mouth shut because, one, she was getting out of breath, and two, there was the nerve-racking element of the gun near her side. She probably should be more terrified, to be honest, but Teddy had done enough research for her books to know that oftentimes in the most trying and desperate of situations, one's mind became cool and calm. It was only later that it fell to pieces.

Still. She felt clammy under her arms and her stomach was in knots. She could only see Oscar from behind, so could only imagine what he was going through.

The storm battered the exterior of the lighthouse. Lightning flared, sending shocks of illumination through the random windows in the tower, and rain—no, *hail*—pelted the glass. Thunder rumbled angrily, and Teddy fancied she could feel the circular stairs swaying a little beneath her feet from the force of the wind.

There were only another dozen or so steps to go. Her legs were trembling—not so much from the exertion of climbing, but from sudden nerves.

"All right. You and me first, mister," said Misty as they reached the door to the lantern room. "You stay here," she added, giving Teddy a little shove toward Rob, who was two steps below her. Misty turned back to Oscar, aiming the gun at him. "Keep it slow and easy—no funny stuff—or you get a bullet in your side. I hear that's a long, painful death."

Oscar cast Teddy a quick look behind him—a meaningful one, as if he was trying to tell her something—and her heart swelled with emotion as she watched him take the last step up, cradling his hand as Misty followed right behind him.

Then, just as he opened the door, she realized what he'd wanted to tell her—to remind her.

The bats.

He opened the door and ducked quickly into the lantern room as the bats erupted.

Misty screamed and jolted backward, but Teddy had already slipped up next to her by the door. She pushed past Misty, pulling her out of the way and using her frightened momentum to shove her off the top of the steps. Teddy ducked into the lantern room, keeping low beneath the flurry of bat wings. Oscar slammed the door behind her as she heard the shouts from Misty tumbling into Rob as they fell down the stairs.

"Great," Teddy said as she heard the sound of a gun firing followed by the ugly sounds of people falling. "Now what?"

"We get the lantern working, Teddy, and send an SOS. Lock the door. They'll be back." Oscar was already moving toward the massive pod of lenses in the center of the room.

"There's no *lock*," Teddy shrieked in a whisper, wriggling the knob as if she might manifest one.

Oscar swore and spun, looking around for something to blockade the door—but there was nothing up there but a broom.

They both saw it at the same time. "I'll wedge the handle under the door. It'll help keep it from swinging open," Teddy said, conscious of Oscar's injured hand. She heard the sounds of angry footsteps pounding back up the stairs. "Now would be a really damned good time for Stuart Millore to show up and have his revenge," she muttered as a huge, horrible flash of lightning lit the sky as if it was noon.

"After all, they did murder you, didn't they, Stuart?" she said.

The violence of the storm raging about the lighthouse was a sight she'd never seen, and it set the hair on her head standing straight up. Being this high, inside a room completely sided by glass—it was both awe-inspiring and terrifying to see the power of the storm.

And Rob and Misty wanted to put them outside, up here, in that maelstrom.

Oh God, we might actually die.

The door heaved a little as one of their attackers crashed into it, and Teddy swallowed back a scream. She had to find something else to stave them off. Misty and Rob had only a small space to work with on the other side; just a tiny landing and the very dangerous steps—but there were two of them, and they were much stronger than she was.

Even with his bad wrist, Oscar had somehow climbed down inside the center of the lenses, and she could barely make out his figure behind the beehive-shaped, rippled glass. In a moment of wild incongruity, it struck her that he looked like a caterpillar inside a beautiful glass cocoon.

Suddenly, light flared from behind one of the lenses. It filled the darkness, blinding Teddy because she was near that side. She stumbled away, moving to the opposite side of the lantern room as the door heaved again. This time, it was accompanied by the sounds of splintering.

Come on, she thought. *I know it's not that easy to break through a damned door!*

But she saw nothing that would help her strengthen the door any further.

"Now would be a good time for a miracle," she said, putting her weight against the door as it heaved again.

It occurred to her, randomly and hilariously, that Misty

and Rob hadn't even *tried* to open the door by turning the knob—they'd gone directly to breaking the door down, and thus the broomstick wasn't doing much good at the moment.

Oscar had the light flashing from behind the Fresnel lens —shockingly fast work!—and Teddy counted the dot-dot-dot, dash-dash-dash, dot-dot-dots he was somehow making with the lantern. But the door was weakening, and even the SOS might not help them—the Coast Guard, even if they saw it, wouldn't be able to get to the lighthouse in time, would they?

When the door gave way, Teddy stumbled back and fell to the ground as Rob barged in.

Scrambling to her feet, Teddy ran around to the side of the lantern room where the light was the brightest, facing away— out into the dark storm—and hoping Rob would be blinded if he came after her.

But before she got far, strong hands grabbed her and threw her to the ground. Teddy hit her head on the glass wall, and saw stars along with the lightning blossoming in the night sky.

"Get out of there now or I'll shoot her," Misty ordered Oscar, brandishing her weapon. "Turn that damned light off."

"All right, all right, don't shoot," Oscar said. "Small quarters in here—the bullet could ricochet and hit any of us," he added, climbing out from behind or beneath—Teddy wasn't certain—the lenses.

"Outside," Rob said, yanking Teddy to her feet by a hank of her hair. "*Now.*" She cried out in pain and moved along as quickly as possible.

Rob reached for the glass door. Just before he touched it, it burst open with a gust of rain and chill.

But it wasn't just rain. It was *ice*.

And Teddy's breath immediately frosted, hanging in the air like a dense cloud.

The world turned eerily frigid.

And that was when she saw it: the amorphous blue-green shape, billowing just outside the doorway.

TWENTY

OSCAR FROZE at the sight of the shape glowing against the thrashing night sky.

It was bluish-green, and as he watched, it stretched, lengthening into a tall figure that loomed over them. It had the vague, undulating shape of a human, but not a normal human: an elongated, horrible, furious creature with a cavernous black mouth and fiery yellow eyes.

Oscar's breath—what he managed to exhale, for his lungs had frozen (as had the rest of his body)—hung in the air, and what should have been rain were sharp, frigid needles that pounded him and everyone around him.

"What the *hell*..." whispered Misty, stepping backward, goggling at the apparition. "Is that...?"

In spite of himself, Oscar already knew the answer to that, and somehow, he had the wherewithal to grab the fascinated Teddy's hand and yank her back from the tableau in front of them.

A horrible scream—more of a cry of anger and fury rather than one of terror and fear—filled the air. It came from the apparition, he *thought*, and it rattled the glass windows, swelling in the lantern room as if attempting to combust the enclosure.

Rob and Misty fell back, petrified, their faces frozen as the apparition swelled, engulfing them, while its livid cry battled with the roll of thunder and the howl of the wind. Rain and sleet whipped up, spinning into the lantern room like raging icicles pummeling them through the fog of their cloudy, icy breaths.

"Watch out," Teddy cried over the ferocity as Misty screamed and turned to run, eyes blind with terror.

She bolted from the apparition—past Oscar and Teddy— and spun out of the lantern room door. Over the tornado around them, Oscar heard another cry, a more shocked and terrified one that was suddenly, horribly cut off. He heard the ugly, unpleasant noise of someone falling.

But that wasn't the worst of it.

As Teddy and Oscar stood there, holding hands, watching in horror, Rob seemed unable to move for a long moment. He placed his hands over his ears as the ghost's scream continued to fill the night, malevolent and bloodcurdling, and then suddenly, somehow, he was airborne…into the night, over the edge of the railing.

If he screamed, the sound was drowned out by the wild storm and the fury of the specter.

Oscar squeezed Teddy's hand, yanking her behind him when the blue-green entity roared wider and louder in front of them. His fingers were so cold that they hardly moved, and his wrist, which had been hot with angry pain, felt slightly better. His eyelashes and nose felt tipped with ice. The arctic blast of the furious ghost roared around them, and for a moment, he thought they were to be the next victims.

But from behind him, Teddy shouted, "Thank you, Stuart! Now you can rest in peace! Be off with you!"

Oscar would have rolled his eyes if the moment hadn't been so desperate, and when the ghost shivered violently, he tensed, prepared to defend them—how he would do so, he had no idea—

Then suddenly, it eased.

The noise, the storm, the energy in front of them. It softened—if one could use that term to describe an amorphous object—and then, all at once, it was just *gone.*

The freeze in the air also disappeared instantly, the rain and normal storm wind returned, and even the lightning and thunder seemed to lessen.

The only sound was the drum of rain on the roof and glass walls and the unsteady breathing of Teddy next to him.

His hands still shaky, his wrist now a mottled purple and blue balloon with no mobility to speak of, Oscar nevertheless managed to pull Teddy into his arms.

"That was…" Words failed him.

But, of course, Teddy had plenty to spare: "A real ghost, Oscar! A *real* ghost. Even you can't deny it."

He laughed and buried his face in her sweet hair. No. Even he couldn't deny it now.

"So there was a real ghost after all," Iva said, preening a little as she looked at Oscar.

They were gathered at Orbra's, of course—but after hours this time, so no one would interrupt—because the Tuesday Ladies insisted on hearing all of the details. It was three days after the shattering events at Stony Cape Lighthouse. Oscar's

Jeep had been extricated from the mud, and the power had been restored. And Teddy and Oscar had had two days of uninterrupted time to heat up the sheets, walk the beach, and otherwise enjoy being together without the specter of Marcie, the Sargent Blue book, *or* a ghost.

"There was a real ghost *and* a fake ghost," Teddy said, settling back with a cup of something called a matcha latte that Orbra had insisted she try. It was *very* green, but it was frothy and sweet, and though there was an underlying taste of grass, it was going down pretty well. "And that was what confused me at first. And what caused some of us to question the idea of a supernatural element."

She looked at Oscar, who was watching her as she held court—as, for once, Maxine was actually listening. His wrist was wrapped up (according to the emergency room personnel, it was badly sprained, but not broken), and he had a mug of tea in front of him that smelled floral and sweet. When their eyes met, he had the grace to appear a little abashed. He was *so* adorable.

"I told you I could sense the ghostly presence," Iva said firmly. "I have an uncanny ability for these sorts of things."

Maxine opened her mouth to say something, but she was interrupted as Declan and Leslie came through the door in a blur of activity.

"Wait, wait, don't say anything else. I want to hear," Leslie said. As she took a seat next to Iva, she murmured, "Did you bring it?"

"Yes," Iva replied, glancing at Teddy. "But first let's hear about what actually happened that night."

"I thought you left Wicks Hollow," said Declan, looking at Oscar with a quirked eyebrow.

"I came back," Oscar replied.

"And just in time," Teddy said. "Although if you hadn't

gotten stuck in the mud, I would have probably left before Misty and Rob showed up the next day, and then none of this would have happened."

"Which is a good thing," Oscar reminded her with a small smile. "Otherwise, Misty and Rob would still be doing what they were doing." His smile faded, and Teddy knew he was remembering the fact that Rob wouldn't ever be doing anything again. He had, of course, died after his fall off the top of the lighthouse. Poetic justice, maybe, but it was still an awful thing to happen, and a terrible memory to live with.

Misty, on the other hand, had survived her fall down the lighthouse stairs. She'd broken an arm and had a serious concussion, and would probably spend the rest of her life in prison. But she'd been able to fill in some of the details Teddy and Oscar hadn't known.

"All right, back to business," Maxine said, slamming her hand on the table. "Did you get the lantern working or not?"

"That's jumping ahead a little," Teddy said.

"Well, not really, as, chronologically speaking, the SOS happened before the real ghost," Oscar reminded her.

"Oh. Right." Teddy spread her hands and gave a little laugh. "Ha. I usually *write* the denouements, not *speak* them —so give me a little break, everyone."

They all laughed, and she continued. "So, even though we realized there had been some monkey business in causing us to believe there was a ghost—the nightly scream, and the greenish cloud thing—there were still a few things I couldn't explain.

"Like, *how* did Misty and Rob know Oscar and I were going to go up to the top of the lighthouse that first night? There was no way they could have known—and even if they did, they couldn't have blocked the door to keep us up there."

"Did you say *block* the door? Not lock it?" Maxine demanded.

"Yes, because the door doesn't have a lock or a latch on it. None of them up there do. So *somehow*, that door—and the others—wouldn't open…and then suddenly it did. And then there was the all-of-a-sudden arctic chill that came and went inexplicably. How could they have done that? Plus, that chill was just *creepy*." She looked at Oscar. "That was why I wasn't completely convinced, ever, that what we'd experienced that first night *wasn't* a ghost."

"Those thoughts occurred to me too—as we were climbing up those steps. Plus," Oscar said, "the greenish supposed ghost we saw the night of the break-in was different from what we'd seen the first night."

"*Exactly*." Teddy beamed at him, wishing they were sitting next to each other so she could smack a kiss on his cheek. "And once Misty confirmed that they actually had murdered Stuart Millore, and I remembered that we'd been talking about someone being pushed off the top of the lighthouse right when the door slammed shut…I was certain there had to be a real supernatural presence. It just made sense."

"After all, this *is* Wicks Hollow," Juanita said, petting Bruce Banner enthusiastically as he tried to lick up some of the crumbs on the table in front of her.

"That's right," Maxine said, spraying a new set of crumbs from her cinnamon scone. "It's like that Hell Mountain on the Tiffany show. But no demons."

"Hell*mouth*," Juanita snapped. "And it's *Buffy*, not Tiffany or Taffy. And it's the *Hulk,* not the Hunk. How many times do we have to tell you?"

Maxine flapped a gnarled hand at her friend and said, "No respect. No respect at all. Now, young man, if you don't tell me about the lantern, I'm going to get very annoyed."

Teddy stifled a giggle, unable to imagine how "very annoyed" could be different from regular Maxine.

"Well, I didn't have time to actually try and figure out how to get the real light working—even if it was still possible," Oscar replied. "Plus, one hand was pretty much out of commission. But I had the flashlight in my pocket, and I knew that even a small light would be reflected eighty times its actual illumination behind those Fresnel lenses, so I used that. It was easy to flip it on and off to do the SOS." He shrugged nonchalantly, but Teddy noticed his cheeks were a little ruddy.

"It was *brilliant*," she said. "That's what ultimately brought help. By the time we got off the lighthouse and came down to find Misty out cold on one of the landings, the Coast Guard had already called Joe Cap because they recognized the signal was coming from the lighthouse. He'd just reached Oscar's stuck Jeep when we called in ourselves."

"So what was the deal with the green and blue boat? Did that have anything to do with this whole mess?" Declan asked.

"Yes," Oscar said. "But only that first day. Misty and Rob had figured out the basic location of the shipwreck, and they were dropping off some supplies to mark off the location underwater. Tape and stakes and some other tools that would help them in their dive. Apparently it was too heavy and bulky to try to bring down there from a shore dive."

"What I don't understand," said Orbra, refilling their pots with hot water, "is why it took them so long. Didn't Stuart Millore die three years ago? Why did they just get started now?"

"Well, once they realized the diary entry was a good indication of the basic area where the ship went down, they still had to *find* it," Teddy said. "And in order to find it, they had to have money for equipment. So it took them a while to gather up the funds, and then even longer for them to dive.

And you can't really dive in Lake Michigan from October through April, even with a wetsuit."

"Well, that's one hell of a story," Maxine said. "Good thing I told you how to make the lantern light work, there, young man. Or you'd probably not be sitting here."

"Right," Oscar replied with a grin twitching his mouth. "I appreciated your instructions when we were up there that day."

Maxine whipped a sharp look at him. "You aren't patronizing me are you, there, young man?" Her dark eyes were sharp and eagle-like.

"No, of course not. If you hadn't given me a lecture—I mean, all the information—about how to make the light go on, I probably wouldn't have thought to try," Oscar said quickly. His face was a little ruddier now.

Teddy chuckled. "Between Oscar's quick thinking and Stuart Millore's ghost, I'd say everything worked out as well as it could."

Conversation went on to other things, and just as Teddy was about to rise to leave, Iva said, "Wait a minute there, dear. I have a book I'd like you to sign."

"Me too," said Leslie eagerly, sliding her chair over next to Iva and Teddy. She dug in her bag and produced an old, well-read paperback novel.

Iva did the same with a different paperback not quite as worn and creased. Both covers, though different, were decorated with lurid golds, pinks, and shiny metallic foil.

Now it was time for Teddy's face to turn a little warm. "Oh." She didn't look at Oscar.

"What's this going on here?" Maxine snatched up Leslie's book and read, "*Love's Forbidden Caress*? By Theodora Mackenzie." She swept those eagle eyes up to Teddy as Juanita snatched up Iva's book. "You write this, missy?" Before Teddy could reply, Maxine said, "Looks damned good. Nice and sexy. You got any more of them?"

"That one's about a blacksmith," Iva said. "It's one of Leslie's favorite books—and I'm certain part of the reason she fell head over heels for Declan here. This one here—mine— that one's about a grumpy duke who falls for a sassy governess. They're both *very* sexy, but also funny and suspenseful. And romantic." Her eyes turned a little misty. "It reminds me of when my dear Hollis and I— Well, never mind." She looked at Teddy. "You'll sign them, won't you?"

"Of course," Teddy said, using the opportunity to dig in her bag for a Sharpie instead of looking at Oscar. Not that she really cared what he thought about the fact that she'd written some romance novels, but he was, after all, a scholar. A PhD at Princeton. And…well, he'd just have to deal with it. She glanced up at him once she had the Sharpie, and to her surprise, he didn't seem the least bit shocked or otherwise put off by the knowledge.

"How did you—uh—figure it out?" she asked Iva as she signed her pen name.

"I'm a librarian, dear. I know everything."

The next day, Teddy and Oscar made their final trip to the hot springs.

"It's only fitting that we end our little sojourn here the way we began it, don't you think?" Teddy asked as she slipped into the pool. "Mmmmm."

"Definitely." He climbed in next to her, his bandaged wrist wrapped in plastic to protect it from the water. "So," he said, lounging back against the rocky wall, "you write romance novels too?"

"I knew this was coming." She sighed, tipping her head back so the cool water from the small falls dampened her hair.

"What was coming? I think it's interesting and laudable that you can write in two different genres."

Teddy's eyes popped open and she sat up abruptly. "You do?"

"Well, yes. They're very different styles of writing."

She narrowed her eyes at him. "Yes. And…?"

"And…nothing." He tried to look innocent, but she saw through it.

Teddy eyed him for a minute. "Come on, Oscar, spill."

"All right." He slouched down in the pool a little more. "My grandmother and her friends used to read Harlequin Romances, and when I went to stay with her one summer, I read a few of them."

"A *few*?"

He shrugged. "Well, it was either that and Agatha Christie, or *War and Peace*, Dickens, and Shakespeare. And I'd had enough of that in school. So, I'm just saying, I think it's admirable that you can write in two different genres."

"Thank you." She watched him for a minute longer. "That must be why you didn't get all embarrassed when the Tuesday Ladies were talking about jumping bones and getting laid."

He laughed. "Well, let's just say, my granny was a feisty, hotblooded woman. Maxine Took reminds me a lot of her, actually. I like her." He slipped further into the water and surged over to her in the small pool. "I'm guessing you need to do a lot of research for those books." He waggled his eyebrows as he took her by the shoulders, the plastic on his right hand crinkling softly. "I mean, where else do you get your ideas?"

Teddy rolled her eyes and pushed him away playfully. "Oh, I've never heard *that* one before."

"Oh." He seemed genuinely crestfallen.

She laughed heartily at his sadness. "Oscar, I get my ideas for sex scenes—as you so delicately refused to specify—the same way I get my ideas for how to murder someone, or how to hijack a plane, or how to poison an entire city: from my imagination. Not by actually *doing* it."

"Oh," he said again, easing back to his side of the pool. Still with the puppy-dog face.

She took pity on him. "But, you know, I was just thinking…when I do write another historical romance, maybe I should write one about a man who seduces a woman in a hot-springs pool in the middle of a forest. And in that case…inspiration always helps." She gave him a sly look.

He surged back closer. "I think that's a great idea."

Teddy laughed and pulled him up to her for a hot, damp kiss. "I adore you, Dr. London."

"I adore you too, Theodora MacKenzie."

She laughed against his mouth, then settled back, putting space between them again. "You never did find out about those crystalline microbes in this pool, did you?"

"No. They seem to have been an anomaly to this particular ecosystem. And in my most recent samples—yesterday—they were nonexistent." He began to nibble along her jaw, and she closed her eyes to enjoy. Then they popped open.

"You know, Oscar, maybe that's why this pool has sacred or magical or special abilities—those crystalline microbes might be the cause of it."

"What?" he pulled away, giving her a strange look. "That's ridiculous."

"That," she said, sitting up straight, "is what you said about the ghost."

"Mmmph."

"After all," she said, "I got in this pool and I ended up with my heart's desire—exactly what I wanted: getting my book done and then getting you."

"Plus a real ghost."

He surprised a laugh out of her, and she kissed him on the cheek in appreciation. "Yes, that too. Plus, I guess I should consider it research to know what it's like to be in a life-and-death, harrowing, and violent situation. Not that I ever thought that was my heart's desire." Then she looked at him speculatively. "And, actually, if you think about it, you got your heart's desire too. When you got in the pool, your heart's desire was to get Marcie back. Don't deny it," she said quickly when he opened his mouth. "You know it's true."

He shook his head. "No. Remember what you were saying before—about only *thinking* you knew what your true heart's desire was? That was true for me when I got into this pool—sacred or magical or not—the first time. But, in the end, I really did get my heart's desire."

He was looking at her so tenderly that she didn't even need for him to say the words that were coming next.

But it would be nice to hear.

And then he said, "I got to run a light at the top of a light-house. That's always been my—"

She dunked him.

Oscar came up sputtering, but grinning, and he dove toward her. He pulled her into his arms, careful of his plastic-wrapped hand. His eyes softened. "Teddy, I had no idea until I met you, but you—only you—are my heart's desire."

After a very long, loving kiss, Teddy pulled back. She was smiling. "Then I guess I was right about two things."

"Two things?"

"First, there was a real ghost. And secondly—this hot-springs pool *is* special. Because we both got our heart's desire.

And maybe—just maybe—that's why the crystalline microbes are gone now!"

Oscar shook his head, giving her an affectionate smile even as he rolled his eyes in exasperation. "Teddy, that's not how science works."

"That's because it's not science, Oscar. It's something else. After all, this *is* Wicks Hollow."

Colleen Gleason is an award-winning, New York Times and USA Today best-selling author. She's written more than forty novels in a variety of genres—truly, something for everyone!

She loves to hear from readers, so feel free to find her online and say hi!

Get SMS/Text alerts for any
New Releases or **Promotions!**

Text: **COLLEEN** to **38470**

(You will only receive a single message when Colleen has a new release or title on sale. *We promise.*)

If you would like SMS/Text alerts for any **Events** or book signings Colleen is attending,
Text: **MEET** to **38470**

Subscribe to Colleen's non-spam newsletter for other updates,
news, sneak peeks, and special offers!
http://cgbks.com/news

Connect with Colleen online:
www.colleengleason.com
books@colleengleason.com

<u>The Gardella Vampire Hunters</u>

Victoria

The Rest Falls Away

Rises the Night

The Bleeding Dusk

When Twilight Burns

As Shadows Fade

Macey/Max Denton

Roaring Midnight

Raging Dawn

Roaring Shadows

Raging Winter

Roaring Dawn

<u>The Draculia Vampire Trilogy</u>

The Vampire Voss: Dark Rogue

The Vampire Dimitri: Dark Saint

The Vampire Narcise: Dark Vixen

Writing as Alex Mandon

The Belle-Époque Mystery series

Murder on the Champs-Élysées